HIDDEN AGENDA

A secret from the past lies sealed
like a fly trapped in amber

YVONNE JENKINS

Hidden Agenda
A secret motive or plan.

Enigma
A thing or person that is mysterious or difficult
to understand. From the Greek 'riddle.'

Agenda
A list of matters to be dealt with. From
the Latin, 'things to be done.'

PROLOGUE

The bullet left the silenced rifle at 2,306 feet per second, hitting its target 2,200 feet away and an inch below the heart. It takes a steady hand and a determined will to kill, so precisely at this range. The elderly woman was killed by the first shot, but he fired his trademark, two shots in very quick succession, just to make a statement. Her body slumped immediately and thudded to the ground. Her two Welsh collies started howling and pawing at their mistress. The woman was found three minutes later by a couple walking a section of the Wales Coastal path, between Mumbles and Southgate. Amidst the glorious display of golden gorse on the cliffs above Crag cove, death had come swiftly to the elderly grandmother of two...

In this age of celebrities and sound bites, the memory of the general public is very short. Of course, celebrity is a completely farcical measure of a person's significance. Evelyn Jones was never a celebrity. Far from it, she was happy to take a quiet back seat to the extraordinary events that peppered her life. A mother and grandmother of two she combined gentle empathy with extraordinary acuity. The manner of her death made news headlines in the 'South Wales Echo' and 'The Western Mail', but already the local interest provoked by the murder of Evelyn Jones, is waning. More scandalous sensations have taken its place!

PART 1

My name is Nia Farriday. I am a Detective Chief Inspector in The Metropolitan Police Service known informally as The Met or Scotland Yard. Just last year, I achieved my goal of becoming an accredited homicide Senior Investigation Officer - an SIO. My recent promotion was accompanied by a wage rise to £58,250. As a relatively frugal person, I can live quite well on my salary and even manage to save a good chunk each month.

The Met is the force responsible for law enforcement in the Metropolitan Police District, which consists of the 32 London boroughs. Not a lot of people know that The Met has significant national responsibilities too, such as co-ordinating and leading on UK-wide counter-terrorism matters, protecting the Royal Family and certain members of Her Majesty's Government. We also protect 164 foreign embassies and High Commissions, Heathrow Airport and the Palace of Westminster. The Met is almost always called in on complex murder enquiries. And this was the reason I was on my way to South Wales. A perplexing murder case had been called in by the South Wales Police and they had requested our help. I got the call at 8.45am that morning from my boss, Chief Superintendent Brian Smythe. He believed that my previous jobs and the skill sets that I had would prove invaluable to solving a case such as this. As I am a 'Taffy' born in South Wales, he reckoned I would fit in well with the locals! I only hoped I could live up to his expectations. In his wisdom, he had seen fit to appoint me as the Met representative on this case. I was to be working with Inspector John Samson, who I had worked with before. John had been on the fast-track program and was advancing up the ranks swiftly. But I didn't hold that against him. I'd had three other professions before joining the police. He had come straight from college. I would meet him in Bridgend which is the headquarters for South Wales Police or Heddlu De Cymru, if you are a Welsh speaker, like John!

•••

It was early June in 2013. Things had been slow at the office for a few months. No exciting cases had come my way for a while. London, felt grubby, overcrowded, airless and lack lustre. Lawns, leaves and hedgerows were still green, but it was shaping up to be a hot, dry summer according to the weather forecasters. I had to admit, London no longer held the allure it had when I'd first arrived from South Wales, so many years ago to take up my place at University College London to study archaeology. To become an archaeologist had been my ambition ever since I was a child and had visited The British museum to see the Tutankhamun exhibition. I will never forget the moment that I looked upon that mask of solid gold. The golden vulture on his brow with the cobra by its side. The combination of gold, lapis lazuli, translucent quartz, obsidian and carnelian used to such artistic excellence in the poignant depiction of the young pharaoh, held me spellbound. I was in awe and from that very moment it was my ambition to become an archaeologist - me and every other child at that exhibition, I suspect! Today, nearly a quarter of a century has passed since I gained my Archaeology degree!

I was glad of a case that would get me out of the Capital while the summery weather lasted. I could see in my mind's eye the golden sweep of the beaches, the bucolic coastal landscape of the Gower Peninsular, lying waiting for me in the sun. It would be great to banish the pungent smell of air pollution for a while. I have such happy associations with that part of South Wales - most weekends during my childhood summers, my family would head out from Cardiff to the Gower. Oxwich bay or Rhossili bay were our preferred camping sites. They were happy days spent surfing on the old-style wooden longboards and sunbathing behind striped canvas windbreaks. Mum would make sure Dad stopped en route at Swansea market to pick up warm bread rolls and cheese and vine ripened tomatoes for our picnic on the beach. A moment of happy nostalgia swept over me as I grabbed my battered Gladstone bag and headed out the door.

•••

I was driving an unmarked Land Rover Discovery. I negotiated heavy traffic around Hammersmith, before joining the M4, travelling directly West towards Wales. Once past the Reading turnoff the traffic eased considerably, and I could daydream a little as I listened to some Mozart on the excellent Harmon Kardon sound system. As I passed the Calne exit in Wiltshire, I remembered my old friend David Winters who used to live in the village. I met him in South Shields after we had been recruited from school by a British shipping company.

In the late 1970's many of the big British companies sent scouts out to find the best academic students and to lure them into working for them. As an immature teenager I was tempted by one of these companies with their offer of what I thought at the time were "film star" wages and all expenses paid living. They sent me to the North of England to be trained as a radio telegraphist. My romantic ideas of sailing around the world sending and receiving Morse code and being a pioneer in the fledgling electronics field were short lived. The job turned out to be a real bore and I was at sea for months on end on a massive oil tanker with a crew of alcohol-soaked misogynists! To be fair, there were some nice guys on board too, like David Winters. But clearly this was not the life for me. So, having had a few "gap" years working on the ships, I finally succumbed to university to fulfil the passion I had for archaeology. I had great fun and met some fascinating people at university and attained a first-class honours degree from University College London. I actually worked as an archaeologist for about five years. I adored the job and the truly romantic places I visited. I had specialized in "The Levant" which now encompasses modern day Israel and occupied Palestine, Lebanon, Syria, Iraq and Jordan. The only country I hadn't excavated in was Iraq because the geo-political situation at the time was too fragile.

The disciplines needed to be a good archaeologist are attention to detail, no matter how small, patience, a yearning for discovery and the ability to piece together all the disparate artefacts and contexts to re-assemble the ancient scene. Good people management also comes in handy, especially if you have a large workforce of volunteers involved in the dig. I also had a rudimentary knowledge of computers which at that time was unusual. I was in demand as it really helped with the recording of the artefacts. Although archaeology was my dream job, the pay was atrocious. The trouble with archaeology as a profession is that it is one of those jobs that people will do just for the love of it. Many of my peers at university had families that provided them with trust funds that paid them a good income. One of my best friends going through university inherited a row of houses in London and she lived off the rents! Subsequently, between the rich and the volunteers that digs could attract, they could get away with paying abysmal wages! As a long-term career, it is hard to sustain if that is your only source of income. After five years living hand to mouth, I decided I would have to do something that paid better for a few years and build up some capital. But what else was I to do? There were countless other professions that had no appeal to me whatsoever. Oddly enough it was a fellow archaeologist from one of these rich families that got me the introduction to my next exciting job!

His daddy was 'someone big in the city'. I needed a challenge and I wanted to see just how far my street smarts could take me. His daddy's pucker financial brokerage was looking to recruit graduates as trainee brokers. I had no idea what to expect. By some miracle I got through their rigorous selection process and survived one of the most nerve wracking interviews ever - a series of quick-fire questions asked by the three directors of the company in an environment of high stress. Nothing like the questions I had been expecting. I'd spent the previous weekend reading the 'Financial Times' and 'The Economist' from cover to cover and getting up to speed on the exchange rates and the top traders in the gilt and equity markets. I was offered the job, on the condition that I had to "tone down" my punkie Viking blond hair and get kitted out with smart skirt suits from Saville Row. The brokerage paid for it all, so it was no skin off my nose! It was worth the makeover. I spent a year in training and sitting various exams to get my official qualifications. It was tougher than anything I had ever done, but I took to it like a duck to water. At the time, it was the right combination of freedom, flexibility and daring that I needed.

If at eighteen I'd thought I was going to earn film star wages at the shipping company, well this was in a different league altogether! Even as a trainee, I started on a wage triple what I'd been earning as an archaeologist, plus a company car, expense account and the potential to earn huge bonuses on top! I couldn't believe my luck. This seemed just the type of job that would allow me to accumulate capital rapidly and enable me to get back to archaeology with a big stash of cash behind me. But as we know, life doesn't always pan out the way we think it will...

When the 1987 stock market crash came, accompanied by huge winds that flattened all the trees in my London suburb, I was ill prepared for the recriminations from the corporate clients that followed. They lost millions overnight- at least on paper and they wanted someone to blame. I was the easy target. A young woman working in a man's world. I became the firm's scapegoat. I couldn't hack it and resigned soon afterwards. I had been living frugally and saving like crazy for a couple of years, so I did have a nest egg to fall back on. Why I didn't go back to archaeology right then, I don't know. At the time, the Metropolitan police wanted to increase their quota of women and were on a recruiting drive. I thought I had some skill sets that might prove useful, so did they, apparently! I was duly recruited by the Met. Obviously, my boss Brian Smythe now thought that my previous job experiences might come in handy on this particular case. By the time I'd finished this flashback down memory lane, I'd arrived at the Severn Bridge toll booth. As I was born in Cardiff to Welsh parents, it always peeves me to have to pay over six pounds to cross the River Severn from England into my homeland! I grudgingly paid the tariff and roared out of the toll booth enclosure hard on the tail of a flash Harry in a silver Porsche Boxster. As I passed the sign declaring "Croeso y Cymru" "Welcome to Wales" I was admiring the green, green grass of home!

The tunnels at Newport were a bottle neck and slowed me down to 30 miles per hour, but once through them I gathered speed again and was soon passing Castell Coch, the enchanting Victorian folly resembling a Rhine castle, on the outskirts of Cardiff. Bridgend was just twenty minutes' drive along the westbound carriageway.

• • •

As I pulled into the car park at Bridgend police headquarters, John Samson was waiting on the steps to meet me. John and I had worked successfully together a few times in the past. Most recently, we had both been instrumental in investigating a high-profile phone-hacking scandal which caused all sorts of controversy involving a number of British newspapers. We had unearthed the most abominable range of phone hacking and police bribery that the press had used in the pursuit of their sordid stories. John and I had spent hundreds of hours sifting through data and audio files to get the evidence we needed. The resulting public outcry against the papers and their owners led to several high-profile resignations. I was proud of the result we'd achieved and considered all our hard slog well worth it. We'd put a stop to some really detestable practices. So, I was happy enough to be paired up with him again. John is reliable, methodical, honest and reasonably intelligent. Stolid and dependable was how I thought of him. I know he thinks I'm a smart Alec on occasion, but I think he grudgingly accepts me.

John is thirty-one years of age and six foot tall. I noticed since I had last seen him that what had once been solid muscle is now turning into ripples of fat that are trying hard to push over his waist band. The proverbial, "muffin top". Not that I'm surprised. I remembered his love of Brains beer and his penchant for fast foods and pot noodle. No wonder he's got a battle with the bulge going on. How could people like those noodles! The very smell of them turns my stomach. I knew that by the end of the day his face would resemble a magnet for iron filings - a mass of dark stubble would appear around his upper and lower lips. He still sports a thick head of dark curly hair with just a few grey threads starting to appear around the crown and sideburns. Not an unattractive looking man, if you like the dark mysterious type. At times he could display a surly manner that I suspected masked some self-esteem issues. John was still working his way up through the ranks. He was on the fast track, so he'd probably make DCI before he was thirty-five. Not someone I would choose to regularly socialise with, but I could work with him with no qualms. Born in Carmarthen, Pembrokeshire, he has the chip on the shoulder of many Welsh speakers when they are dealing with the English. He has the whiff of the Welsh nationalist about him. A Plaid Cymru supporter, maybe? Still, I have to admit that in the last couple of years Plaid Cymru has come up with some really good policies. It isn't the extreme nationalist party it had been in the 70's when they happily looked on as Welsh nationalist extremists burnt the rural holiday cottages of the English.

During a long, boring surveillance on our last case together we'd had a heart-to-heart talk during which we'd shared some personal secrets. John had admitted that he felt he couldn't compete with real scholars like, me. I took that as a compliment. He had always felt intimidated by intellectuals and very wealthy people - people who used long words and kept making literary references that he didn't understand. He'd conceded that he'd been very wary of me when we'd first met - threatened by my supposed self-confidence and uncertain of my unconventional ways. I put that down to parochialism - he hadn't seen a lot of the world, tucked away in West Wales.

He'd told me he'd had a string of girlfriends over the years. Self-induced misery as he put it. He didn't ever pay them adequate attention and he soon got bored, so his relationships never lasted long. Truth be told, I think he fears rejection. I reckon most people underestimate him and this plays into his strengths. In this neck of the woods, he would probably be the one that got witnesses and suspects to open up to him, because they would see him as 'one of them'. All the more reason I would value his input.

Samson got on well with my boss Brian Smythe, in the uncomplicated way that is reserved for men who don't seek to know too much about each other. I was aware that he looked to me and the boss for our approval. He needed our praise when he'd got a result on a case. For all the swagger and surliness, he was just like a schoolboy who has completed his homework and needs a pat on the back, wanting acknowledgement and praise. Oh, well we've all got our little foibles!

He'd got decent GCSE results and had done two 'A' levels but hadn't gone on to university. His reason being, he couldn't stomach the academic grind and he didn't want to rack up student debts that would hang over his head for years. His choice of career boiled down to the army or the police. He suspected all the shouting of orders in the army would get on his nerves before long, so he'd decided on the police. So far, he was satisfied with his choice of work. He is a complex character although he makes every effort to appear just "one of the boys". I suspect that he makes a practice of concealing his enthusiasm as he does his imagination. He believes "a good murder is what police work is all about. The combination of a puzzle and a manhunt". Well, here was a murder case that he could get stuck into, and I had no doubt he would prove his worth, yet again.

• • •

This was the first time I had taken over a murder enquiry after the preliminary, inevitably dramatic procedures were done with: the discovery of the body, the initial scene of crime investigation, the removal of the body, the unwanted media attention. All these procedures had already been completed. We would have to work closely with the officers who had done all the preliminaries and SOCO, the forensic pathologist and the ballistics expert that the local police had brought in on this case. When South Wales Police had initially asked for assistance, the stuffed shirts in the Met had doubted the ballistics. They thought the country bumpkins had got it all wrong! A ballistics expert who specialised in historic weapons had been brought in from Bangor. He was amazed and dumbfounded when he examined the bullets. He confirmed that they had been fired from a very old rifle. The sort that had been used by snipers in World War Two. Not the sort of ammunition you see very often nowadays. Certainly not a farmer's rifle. The precision of the shots were also indicative of a skilled marksman, not an amateur. Curiouser and curiouser!

Samson and I knew the importance of finding the murder weapon, which so far had not been retrieved. Few murder prosecutions are likely to progress without finding the weapon. The local police promised that they had copious amounts of scene of crime photos and had documented everything down to the smallest detail. The actual site was still cordoned off and a tent had been erected to preserve the crime scene. Once we'd been thoroughly briefed over a late lunch, we would head over to the coast to take a look around the crime scene and the victim's house.

The textbooks say there are three cornerstones to any case: Means, Motive and Opportunity. According to Samson, none of these were evident as of yet! What the motive was, who on earth could fathom. After all, who would want to kill an elderly grandmother of two in rural South Wales? I knew from past cases that motives for murder could be ridiculously flimsy - road rage, hurtful laughter, a grudge held over years, humiliation after a failed love affair. I knew that some killers are truly crazy and there is no motive and it's just a random act of violence. The victim simply being at the wrong place at the wrong time. But I didn't think that Evelyn Jones's demise had played out like that. I've never liked the idea of total randomness when it comes to murder. Apparently, the means was an old-World War Two sniper rifle, according to the ballistics man brought in from Bangor! The opportunity had been taken by a person as yet unknown, to take two precision shots at her whilst she was out walking her dogs on a quiet coastal path.

● ● ●

Samson and I were taken up to the office of Laura Charles, the local DCI who had attended the crime scene initially. She was a small framed woman with dark shoulder length hair. She could have been any age between forty and sixty. It was very hard to tell. The only notable thing about her was her twinkling green eyes and long dark eye lashes. You would have to say her eyes were her best feature. We shook hands and did the introductions, as you do. Laura asked us if we had eaten lunch yet.

"No, I'm starving as it happens, and Samson will never say no to a meal!"

"Come on then, I'll brief you over lunch."

She spoke with a delightful Welsh accent. I liked her immediately. The canteen was light and bright and there was an impressive choice of traditional and healthier options on the menu. I was ravenous, so selected fish pie with a rocket salad. Samson went for traditional bangers and mash and Laura opted for a Caesar salad. We sat at a table near a massive window. This was all very civilised! As we tucked into our food Laura gave us a quick rundown of the case.

The fateful day, the police had been called at 9.55 am by two hikers, Mr & Mrs Jackson and shortly afterwards another 999 call had come in from Emily Evans, the dead woman's housekeeper. A bird watcher had also witnessed Evelyn's fall to the ground on the coastal path. He had run to her aid as well. Two constables from the local police station had attended initially and had got to the scene - on the cliffs above Fox Cove about nine minutes later. The ambulances arrived shortly afterwards. Three witnesses were milling around the dead woman when they arrived plus Emily Evans was on the scene with two dogs who were howling like a wolf pack and creating an almighty din. Within seconds it was evident that this was no accident, and the victim hadn't had a heart attack or just a fall. Constables Tobias Lloyd and Simone Pollard had acted quickly to calm everyone down, secure the scene and to call in back up. The ambulance crew could do nothing for Evelyn Jones, but they did attend to Mrs Jackson and Emily Evans who were suffering from severe shock.

Laura Charles said Evelyn was survived by a daughter and two grandchildren. I always find 'survived by' such a final statement - she's gone. They're left. How sad! By the time we were attacking our puddings DCI Charles had brought us up to speed with the case as it stood.

"Obviously you will also talk to both the constables from the local station and have a chat with the forensic pathologist and the ballistics expert. Now that's where it gets really interesting" Laura said. "The ballistics chap reckons the gun used is a World War Two sniper's rifle. A very specific Russian model, can you believe? We haven't found the weapon yet. But he's adamant about it. The two shots were very precise too. Delivered in quick succession to a point just below her heart. There was no mistake that they were meant to kill. Who owns a gun like that? The ballistics guy is here at Headquarters. We brought him down from Bangor yesterday. He's an odd sort of chap but he does know his stuff. I'll take you up to him once you've finished your coffees."

•••

We were introduced to Tristram Davies on the top floor of the building. He was indeed an odd-looking guy - very thin with irregular facial features and a receding hairline that he had tried to hide by combing the few remaining strands of grey greasy hair over the top of his head. He spoke, with a strong North Wales accent. I had to listen very closely to understand what he was saying. Samson seemed to have no trouble understanding him. He was from Anglesey, he told us, and he worked for the National Ballistic Intelligence Service. He explained that as part of his job he examines ballistic material and firearms recovered by police across the country, he tracks the weapons in use and can link offences where the same firearm has been used. NABIS maintains a national database of firearms, rounds of ammunition, shell cases and projectiles that have been recovered from crime scenes over the years. He told us he had known the pathologist working the case, Jeremy Highgate since university. Jeremy had brought him in as a consultant ballistics expert on quite a few cases in the past. This one interested him as he believed the bullets were fired from one of his favourite Russian sniper guns - the Mosin rifle.

He started off by asking us, "Did you see the film, 'Enemy at the Gates' with Jude Law?" He didn't wait for our reply.

"Well, he played the role of the famous Russian sniper Vasily Zaitsev during the battle of Stalingrad. The rifle he used was a Mosin. After the release of that film the Mosin rifle and the 7.62x54R cartridge became very sought after by gun enthusiasts. Did you know that Russia utilised more snipers than any other nation during the Second World War? Furthermore, a great many Russian snipers were women. The youngest female sniper in the Red Army was Klavdiya Kalugina who was just 17 when she signed up in 1943."

He was talking nineteen to the dozen and this was obviously his pet topic. I'm sure he could have rambled on about it for hours, left to his own devices. But we had pressing appointments and I had to re-focus him and keep him from going off on a tangent. I had to stop him in his tracks.

"So, Tristram you think that the bullets used to kill Evelyn Jones were fired from one of these Mosin rifles?"

"Yes, I'm positive that the bullets were fired from a M1891/30 Mosin-Nagant 7.62 mm rifle. The Mosin rifle and the 7.62x54R cartridge have a very long history and a nostalgic appeal for collectors and enthusiasts. They are currently immensely popular worldwide. "

I broke in again "Sadly, the weapon hasn't been found yet, so how can you be 100% certain of the make?"

"I'd obviously love to have the rifle to prove it. Let's hope it can be found. But I'd stake my reputation on this, just by examining the bullet casings. One was found amongst the rocks at the crime scene. They are made by a company called Barnaul based in Altai, Russia. They have been producing ammunition since the Second World War. One of Barnaul's specialties is a sporting load for a 7.62mm rifle. It's a 203-bullet grain utilizing a copper washed steel jacket and soft lead core. Muzzle velocities average 2200 and 2300 fps respectively. In Russia, this bullet is used on brown bears.

"How disgusting that they are still hunting bears" I blurted out.

"Oh, that's down to Putin and his macho man image. He encourages hunting in Russia" interjected Samson before Tristram was off again...

"The rifling of the Mosin barrel is right turning. That's clockwise looking down the rifle. 4-groove with a twist of 1:9.5. The 5-round fixed metallic magazine can either be loaded by inserting the cartridges singly, or more often in military service, by the use of a 5-round stripper clip. In this case they would have been manually loaded." he stressed.

"The 'R' identifies the cartridge as being rimmed."

This information was all delivered at a mind-boggling speed and with a very strong Welsh accent. My head was spinning with all these technicalities, and I could see Samson was struggling to follow the monologue.

I cut in, "So, to cut to the chase, you are certain that these bullets were produced by a Russian company and were fired from an old Second World War Russian rifle?"

"Yes, that's the gist of it" he said with a big smile. "But"

Oh, no there had to be a but...

He went on "Having said that its Russian, virtually every country that received military aid from the Soviet Union, during the Cold War used Mosins at various times. Middle Eastern countries within the sphere of Soviet influence, like Egypt, Syria and Iraq had them. Finland was still producing the M39 Mosin in small numbers as late as 1973! And of course, Mosin rifles were used by both Soviet and Mujahadeen forces in Afghanistan during the Soviet Union's occupation of the country and they are still used in Afghanistan to this day."

When he smiled, his face was absolutely transformed, and I warmed to him in that moment. Whatever his quirks this guy was an absolute expert in his field, I realised.

Samson took all this in and said "Right, so the actual rifle used could have come from any one of those countries."

"Yes, it most probably was produced in Russia, but it could have been sent on to any of those countries."

Samson mused "British troops returning from service in Iraq or Afghanistan could have brought one back as a souvenir, do you think?"

"It's possible, I guess. Soldiers do smuggle in mementos or souvenirs from countries they've been serving in. Unless the actual weapon is found and I can consider the internal and external ballistics thoroughly, I won't be able to confirm that, but place of manufacture is almost certainly Russia."

"We'll be speaking with the forensic pathologist later but in your opinion, do you think there is any chance that this could have been an accident of some sort. A farmer's kid trying to shoot a rabbit and hitting Evelyn?"

"Absolutely no way. A snipper's bullet is NOT random. It is deliberate and very personal. The marksman that did this will remember the detail of her eyes, the texture of her skin and so on as the trigger was pulled."

A shiver went through me...

Tristram rammed home the point "These were two precision shots delivered with measured intent."

"Wow! That is chilling!" blurted Samson.

"Yes, I'd say you are looking for someone with a major grudge of some sort against this woman. A vengeance killing would be my guess. It could have been mistaken identity of course. But whoever the intended target was, this was a professional marksman delivering a message. The use of a World War Two weapon may also have significance in this case. Behind every weapon is someone who is prepared to pull the trigger. That's who you've got to find."

He wasn't wrong and that wasn't going to be an easy task.

To stop him launching into another epic monologue, I indicated that we had to dash off to our next appointment.

"Thanks so much for all the technical information. Very enlightening. I look forward to reading your official report." I thought, good grief - that report would send any insomniac off to the land of nod!

•••

Samson and I had been assigned a temporary office for the duration of our stay in South Wales. It was light and bright and came fully equipped with all the gadgets and electronic accessories that are demanded of modern-day police procedures. We spent the next two hours working our way methodically through all the paperwork and evidence that had so far been compiled on Evelyn Jones's murder. After the long drive from London this morning and the intense meeting with the ballistics guy, my concentration was slipping by late afternoon.

"My brain is turning to custard, John. Let's postpone the visit to the crime scene until tomorrow. I want to be fully on my game when we look at it."

"Okay, no worries."

I asked Samson if he wanted to have an early dinner in the pub close to my B&B accommodation. He indicated he wanted to get home to Carmarthen for dinner, but he'd have a quick drink with me to compare notes and our initial thoughts. I'd just made a phone call to book in an appointment with the forensic pathologist as we put together our itinerary for the following day. We'd start off visiting the forensics lab then go to the crime scene and from there to interview Emily Evans at Evelyn's house followed by an interview with Evelyn's daughter Sian. It would be a full day but if I got an early night, I'd be up to it.

Samson had already done some digging into Emily's past. He read from his abbreviated notes: She had a juvenile police record - a troubled home life. No real abuse as such just a lack of attention. Neglect. Four other siblings and money was always tight. Mother did the best she could. Father had run off with a younger woman when Emily was just twelve. Three years ago, her flat in Swansea had been repossessed by the bank. According to the banks mortgage adviser, she had apparently bought at the top of the market and when the global financial crash came at the end of 2008 her job and the housing market collapsed and she was left with negative equity. Which meant that even after the bank took back the flat, she was still left with a debt to them, which she needed to pay off, even though she had no asset to show for it. Samson pondered – "maybe she harboured resentment? Did she envy Evelyn's wealth and beautiful home?"

I was quick to put a stop to any speculation at this stage. "Even if she did what possible motive could she have to harm her? It's not as if she would inherit the house. Surely Evelyn's daughter Sian will. We'll check out exactly what the terms of Evelyn's will are but let's keep a totally open mind regarding Emily."

Emily's previous employer had told Samson that when she lost her job at his art gallery and could no longer keep up her mortgage payments, she had spiralled into a depression. She had numbed the pain with a steadily increasing amount of alcohol and weed. Things had gone from bad to worse, resulting in her getting a conviction for possession of a significant quantity of marijuana. He said she wasn't a bad person; she'd just had a bit of a bad patch. When he bumped into her recently, she was like a different woman - confident and happy. She'd turned her life around. Good for her!

"How did she get the job as Evelyn's housekeeper/carer?" I asked

"Evelyn's daughter, Sian suggested she go to work for her mother."

"How did they know each other?"

"Sian is a GP who previously treated Emily for depression. She knew she was looking for work and her mother needed local help."

"Oh, I see."

It had been a long day and by now my brain really couldn't process any more information.

"Let's call it a day, John. I'm toast."

"No worries. I've had enough for one day, too."

I walked back to my temporary digs and Samson drove off, like the Devil's own chauffeur.

•••

I met Samson back at police headquarters the next morning. They had brought in a forensic pathologist from the Wales Institute of Forensic Medicine in Cardiff. Dr Jeremy Highgate was very experienced, I'd been informed. I'd never met him, but Samson had worked with him on many occasions. He said "he's a bit deadpan excuse the pun. Probably been at the job too long, so he's no longer emotionally affected by continual exposure to violent deaths. He comes over as very cold, but he does know his job and he's very thorough and well respected."

"I've met a lot of forensic pathologists that come across as uncaring. I think it's a side effect of their profession. I would imagine doing that job you have to be able to switch off your emotions to a great degree. Otherwise, it would just overwhelm you."

Whenever I visited the forensic labs, I always got a sense of deja vue. Here were the forensic scientists picking over the clues just like archaeologists would do to piece together the past - labelling and bagging evidence. As we would read the stratigraphy to make sense of the past, they would read the evidence collected to help solve the crime. We walked down two flights of stairs into an air-conditioned subterranean room with white tiles on all the walls. The universal laboratory smells of formaldehyde, unnamed acids and alkalis permeated the space.

Jeremy Highgate looked like a military man. He was tall and immaculately presented. He had a moustache and grey hair cut in a short back and sides style reminiscent of the 1950's. This man was no-nonsense! I glanced down at his shoes which were black and polished to an impossible shine. He struck me as one of the old-style gents who would never wear brown shoes except with tweed jacket and corduroy trousers. I could see what Samson was getting at regarding his deadpan manner. He welcomed us formally but pleasantly enough. Personally, I don't mind this type of personality. They just get straight down to business, they talk directly, with no ambiguity and you know exactly what you are dealing with.

"I have my report ready to go, but I'll summarise things for you now if you think it will be helpful'."

"Oh, yes please."

"As you know I attended the crime scene to make a preliminary examination of the body and an initial determination of the post-mortem interval. I carried out the autopsy this morning. It's a shame, she had to die like this because the woman was in terrific shape for her age. All her organs were in good order. Apart from slight osteoarthritis in her knee joints and hands, she was a healthy woman. She could probably have lived another ten years if she hadn't been shot!"

Jeremy passed me a small plastic bag. "These items were on the body at the scene." He pointed to an old-fashioned charm bracelet and said that she had been wearing it on her right wrist. I inspected it and amongst the charms of an owl, a horseshoe, a pixie, a Land Rover and a heart, was a little key threaded onto the bracelet with a piece of plaited red leather. Samson reckoned "it looks like the key to a wall safe."

"Two dogs leads had been wrapped around her left hand," said Jeremy.

The leads were both identical and of good quality leather with brass clips where they fitted onto the dog's collars. She had been wearing a 9K Gold Rolex watch on her left wrist. Samson held it up to the light to admire it. It had a silvered dial with black Arabic numerals and a subsidiary second's dial. The leather strap looked original. It was a high-quality time piece. The 9K gold case bore hallmarks for 'Glasgow 1938' and a personalised inscription bearing Evelyn's name and announcing 'First Prize' was engraved on the back. I wondered what contest she had won, back then. There was a five-pound note and eighty pence in change, which had been in the pocket of her coat, together with a green linen bag which when unfolded revealed the name 'Waitrose.' In the other pocket was an old-style linen handkerchief with an 'E' embroidered on it within a heart, picked out in yellow embroidered daffodils. This looked like it had been handmade. The back door key to the house and the Land Rover keys, Jeremy informed us were on a red key fob with an 'E' embossed on one side. There was no mobile phone. A miniature pair of Zeiss binoculars had been slung around her neck.

It always struck me as very poignant when I looked at the items of the dead. I'm sure all the charms on her bracelet had significance and sentimental value to Evelyn, but their significance was lost on us. Her clothes were in a separate plastic container, and they told the story of a bloody and violent death. The only item that wasn't bloodied was a floppy navy-blue sunhat.

After inspecting them thoroughly, Samson said. "I don't see anything of significance here or out of the ordinary, do you?"

"No. We'll check out the little key, but that's about it."

Jeremy wandered over to us. "You've met Tristram, haven't you? In consultation with him, I've put together a full report, which includes the terminal ballistics. It will be emailed to you today. I'll give you a print off to take away with you. You've seen the photos from the crime scene, I take it?"

"Yes, we have. They are pretty gruesome."

"A rifle bullet can cause a lot of tissue damage and haemorrhaging, as was the case here."

He went on to explain, "The severity of a bullet wound depends on the characteristics of the bullet mass, velocity and orientation of the bullet, and the tissue that is impacted. As you probably know, ballistics is broadly classified into three categories: internal ballistics, external ballistics and terminal ballistics. Tristram will have talked to you about the Internal and external, I can give you an overview of the terminal ballistics.

"It was certainly terminal in this case!" joked Samson.

Jeremy Highgate gave him a sour look and carried on.

"Overall, the effect of tissue injury depends not only on the muzzle kinetic energy, the distance from the muzzle to the victim and whether the bullet is retained or passes through the tissue, but also on the type of tissue encountered by the bullet. As the bullet hits the target object, the kinetic energy of the bullet is transferred to the target tissue. Skin and lung tissue has low density but is elastic and therefore is injured less compared with muscle, which has higher density and only some elasticity. Fluid-filled organs such as the bladder, heart and bowel can transmit kinetic energy more because they are not compressible and can result in bursting the organ."

I was starting to feel queasy now.

"As Tristram may have already told you, bullets do not typically follow a perfect straight line to the target. After examination of trajectory and yaw we have pinpointed the place where the marksman stood to fire the shots. As you will see when you visit the crime scene there is a rocky outcrop just off the coastal path about 2000ft away from where the body was found. This was where your man stood to fire the shots that killed Evelyn Jones. This all ties in with the ballistics and the eyewitnesses' statements. According to the deceased's medical history, she had no underlying medical conditions.

Obviously, the cause of death was due to the impact of the bullets, which caused the heart to explode and massive haemorrhaging. She would have been dead almost immediately. I'm available to give evidence in court, if you require it. Let's hope we can bring the perpetrator to justice. If there's anything else you need from me, just give me a call. I'm off home. I've just worked ten hours straight and my head's throbbing."

Not the subtlest of hints to bring an end to our meeting. We shook hands and made a quick exit.

After grabbing a couple of tuna and salad rolls from the canteen, we headed out to the M4 westbound towards Swansea and the Gower. We visited the crime scene on our way to Evelyn's house. It was still being guarded by two local constables who couldn't have made up my age between the pair of them! Tape marked out the area located just off to the side of the coastal path. We both surveyed the surrounding landscape and located the rocky outcrop that Jeremy Highgate had mentioned. There was still some evidence of dried blood on the grass within the taped off area. Judging from the photos we'd seen and all the witness statements, there had been a lot of it. The front of Mr Jackson's shirt had been caked in it. It all confirmed the haemorrhaging that the pathologist had explained to us.

From the rocks where one of the bullet casings had been found, we could see that the shooter would have had an unimpeded line of sight to the spot where Evelyn fell. It would have provided the perfect cover. Judging by the distance involved, the marksman would have had to be a crack shot. We paced out the intervening ground. Nothing came to light, although we didn't expect it to as this had been combed over by the local police shortly after Evelyn's body had been found. A couple of coke cans, half a dozen cigarette butts and the packaging off a Mars bar and an empty packet of salt and vinegar crisps was all that had been found. Apart from the crime scene tape that was still in evidence, it was hard to imagine that this tranquil place had been a place of carnage a few days ago. Once we had finished our inspection of the crime scene, we headed southeast along the coastal road towards Evelyn's house.

•••

Valland House is located in glorious seclusion in Crag Bay on the Gower Peninsular, between Oxwich Bay and Mumbles. This stretch of coastline is considered by many locals as Gower's best kept secret. The area is stunningly beautiful and was nominated as Britain's very first Area of Outstanding Natural Beauty. Evelyn's impressive house was nestled on the side of a gorse covered hill above a secluded bay. Quite an idyllic setting - the shallow valley adjoining the property is even complete with its very own babbling stream, flowing down to the beach. A winding four-wheel drive track led down to the house, where the track ended, thus making it accessible only to its few residents.

As we approached the house, Samson got excited when he saw Evelyn's original 1948 Series 1 Land Rover parked on the drive. He loved the old Land Rovers. "Wow that's very rare nowadays. You don't see many of these in working order. This one is in great nick." He jumped out and walked all around it. "The design for the original vehicle was started in 1947 by Maurice Wilks, chief designer at the Rover Company. He sketched the silhouette of the vehicle in the sand on the beach near his farm in Anglesey. The Series I was field-tested at Long Bennington and the early ones were painted with military surplus supplies of aircraft cockpit paint, so they came in a choice of green, green or green! These are highly sought after by Land Rover enthusiasts."

"You'd be one of the enthusiasts I take it" I replied

"Definitely. I'd love to own one but on my wages it's not possible," he grumbled

"Come on tear yourself away, we've got to talk to Emily Evans, then look around the main house."

I imagined this wonderful seclusion afforded by the property meant that when she was younger Evelyn would have been able to enjoy fires on the beach, midnight swims, the sound of the sea at night, the hooting of owls, bats sweeping low over the barn, unimpeded views of the stars and many leisurely walks through the woods, past bucolic ruined castles and ancient earth works... My reverie of this coastal idyll was cut short by Samson thumping hard on the front door of an outbuilding close to the main house. Emily was Evelyn's housekeeper and cook/companion who was currently staying in her work studio, as she had nowhere else to go. Samson was smartly and formally dressed in a dark navy suit with a silver and navy striped tie - as you would expect a detective to look. I reflected on my own outfit as I clambered out of the car - black cargo pants, red designer trainers and a loose linen shirt in bright red. I have always liked bold primary colours and comfort would always win out with me. Informality at times wasn't a bad idea when interviewing people in their homes. I think it helps put them at ease, at least that's my excuse for my less than formal attire.

•••

Samson's vigorous knocking was answered by a slim woman with slightly pallid cheeks, a shapely nose with a gold stud drilled into the right nostril. I never did understand the need for facial piercings, but each to their own, as they say. She had amateurishly applied pink dye streaked through her strawberry blond hair that was a mass of corkscrew curls. She had beautiful unblemished skin.

Samson said " Sorry to disturb you, but we need to ask you a few more questions. May we come in?"

"Oh, you must be the police." She spoke with an attractive Welsh lilt. She opened the door to admit us, and two dogs shambled towards us and barked, but with little enthusiasm. The dogs sniffed around our feet and lower legs, then seemed resigned to letting us enter. They took up their places on their respective doggy beds in front of the window, where shafts of sunlight shone through and glinted on their matching collars. The light picked up the blueish hues in their merle coats.

"Don't mind these two they won't hurt you. They are Evelyn's dogs, and they are missing her something chronic. They keep looking for her everywhere. They've been back and forth to the door whining all morning I don't know what to do to comfort them. She's had them since they were puppies."

"What a lovely looking pair. Are they border collies?" asked Samson

"No, they're Welsh sheepdogs. Similar to border collies but they are stronger and taller than collies."

We glanced over and she was right, they were bigger dogs - well muscled and alert with merle-coloured coats and soulful dark eyes set in expressive faces. They looked mournful. These dogs knew their mistress wasn't coming back.

She went on "Evelyn told me that when they were pups, they had striking blue eyes. Over the years they turned that lovely amber colour."

"They really are a handsome pair." Samson went over to their basket and fussed over them. I didn't know he was such a dog lover! What was he up to now? He was inspecting the male dog's collar. "Wow these collars are neat. I love the mosaic of a dog's head with the initial underneath. I've never seen anything like that before."

"Oh, Evelyn had those specially made for them. Some engraver in Swansea market did them. When it came to her dogs there was no expense spared. She designed those tags herself. The mosaic is based on one found in Pompeii apparently."

"Cool," said Samson.

I was a bit bemused by Samson's enthusiasm. Maybe it was partly to do with the fact that this woman was rather attractive. She had a bohemian, hippy crossed with a pre- Raphaelite look. It was an appealing combination of street wise with vulnerability. I could see Samson giving her the once over. I glanced around. Most of the space was set up as a workshop but there was a small kitchen area with a stripped pine table off to one side. We took seats around it. Emily had some coffee brewing. We gladly accepted a cup each.

"I was just about to have some lunch." Emily insisted we join her in a bite to eat. She fetched plates and cutlery for us and laid out a platter of sourdough bread with goat's cheese and salad fresh from the garden. Samson and I sat down and started attacking the food gustily. Emily must have wondered when we had last eaten. Samson reached out for another cherry tomato. They were small but delicious and still warm from the greenhouse.

Once we were sipping our coffees, I asked "Could you run us through once again what you can remember of the morning Evelyn was killed. No matter how insignificant it might seem, just start from when you woke up. I know you've given a statement to the local police already but sometimes we recall more details days after the event. We'd like to hear in your own words exactly how things played out that morning."

She told us that, unusually, Evelyn had been up before her that day. She had let the dogs out into the garden and Emily had awoken to the sounds of them barking at the seagulls perched on the drystone wall that surrounded the garden. "Or at least that's what I assumed they were barking at. In hindsight, there may have been someone hanging around. If there was, I didn't notice them. I got up and prepared breakfast. We ate breakfast together. Nothing unusual, she seemed her normal self. It was a glorious sunny day. She said she would wear her sun hat and splash on a bit of sunscreen to her ears and neck. About 9.30 she picked up the dog's leads and her house keys and they set off as usual for their walk. For a year or so she had been driving her Land Rover to the top of the track, to save herself the steep uphill trudge. It had got a bit much for her. She left the Land Rover parked at the top of the track. I heard her shut off the engine. That's the last time I saw her."

Emily's lips quivered and a single tear dribbled down her smooth cheek. Samson waited a few seconds for her to regain her composure then asked, "Once Evelyn went out with the dogs, what did you do then?"

"I washed up the breakfast things and tidied the kitchen - wiping down the surfaces. After that I went to sit out on the patio for a few minutes. There was a light haze just lifting off the sea. All seemed well in the world. I was getting the kiln warmed up to fire my latest batch of pots when Alan came running down the hill. He was on his own and clearly in some distress."

"Who is Alan?"

"Oh, the dog! He was frantically barking and running around me in agitation. I knew straight away that something was wrong. Both dogs were like Evelyn's shadows. They rarely left her side. I quickly shut off the power to the kiln, grabbed my mobile phone and then I ran with him up the hill and along the clifftops towards Southgate. As we approached Fox Cove, I could see three people crouched over Evelyn who was slumped on the ground. I felt sick. I had a terrible feeling of dread. I called 999 and asked for an ambulance before I even got to her. I was thinking, she'd had a heart attack or seizure or just a bad fall. I could never in a million years have guessed what had happened."

I said, "Okay now think very carefully about the next few minutes. What exactly did the two hikers - Mr and Mrs Jackson say to you. What did you say to them? Did you notice anything or anyone unusual in the surrounding area? How about the bird watcher guy - Dave Roberts? What was he doing? What did he say?"

Emily closed her eyes as if to relive the moment more clearly.

"The dogs were frantic, circling around and around Evelyn. Mr Jackson had tried to administer CPR. By the time I got there he was sitting on the ground next to Evelyn, he had blood all over him. He had put her in the recovery position, but he said it was futile. She was dead and could not be revived. When I got closer, I saw the bullet holes and I started to scream. I was so shocked. I wasn't prepared for that. Mrs Jackson tried to calm me down. She herself was in shock and shaking visibly. They had already called for an ambulance and the police. The local police arrived first and the ambulance a few minutes later. A second ambulance showed up at some point, but I don't remember it arriving. The police were making frantic calls on their phones and arranging a police cordon. They went into what I expect is their set procedure as soon as they saw it wasn't a fall or a heart attack. When the paramedics arrived, they did a few checks and asked Mr Jackson how long it had been since he found her. They didn't attempt CPR or anything. They took me and Mrs Jackson into the back of the ambulance and tried to calm us down. She started to cry, and I was a bit hysterical to tell you the truth. I remember shouting 'help her help her, do something to save her!' But I could see she was beyond help. The rest is a bit of a blur to be honest. I think the paramedics gave us sedatives."

"What about the two men?"

"They were telling the police what they could. I thought the bird twitcher was going to throw up, but he steadied himself. He had binoculars with him, and he kept saying he'd seen a metallic flash out of the corner of his eye before Evelyn went down. I'm sure he told the police officer all he knew. Mr Jackson just kept reiterating 'there was nothing I could do for her' over and over. They were both ashen faced and clearly in shock. I don't remember who gathered the dogs up or how we got back to the house. In one of the police cars, I guess."

Samson grabbed a few more tomatoes and popped them in his mouth, then asked her how she had come to be working for Evelyn and what she had done before working here. She confirmed what he had already found out. She said that the experience of property ownership had been a rude awakening for her. She had worked hard to pay her monthly mortgage. When her home was repossessed, she was gutted when she realised that she still owed the bank money. She went back home for a short time, but she couldn't stand the noise and chaos. Friends let her stay in their spare rooms or sofa surfing. It was embarrassing and she hated being homeless. She was at a very low ebb when Evelyn's daughter, Sian suggested she go to work for her mother. She was looking for a companion housekeeper and cook. I noticed that she hadn't mentioned her drugs conviction. I guess she didn't think it was relevant to Evelyn's case.

Samson asked had she liked working for Evelyn.

"I loved it! My friends thought it must be boring, but I found I thrived on the routine that Evelyn had in her life." Once she got up a head of steam, Emily seemed happy enough to elaborate. Samson and I listened and observed...

She told us; she'd felt at peace at Valland House. She told us that in the three years she'd worked for Evelyn, she had come to love waking up to the sound of the sea and the wet nose of the dogs cajoling her to get their breakfasts. She had her own room and the work studio and could come and go as she pleased as long as she completed her agreed tasks. Evelyn turned out to be an easy-going person to live with. Funnily enough, she had never thought of Evelyn as an old person. She had an agelessness about her - she was still so engaged with life and all its new technologies. The routine and rhythm of each day was soothing and calming. Evelyn had encouraged her to set up a small kiln and studio/workshop in one of the unused outhouses. Evelyn had even paid to get the roof repaired. Emily had done the internal fit out and decorating herself.

I glanced around and thought that she'd done a pretty good job of it.

"Evelyn was so encouraging and empowering."

She went on to relate how two years ago she had sold her first Celtic in-spired mugs and bowls and plates at a stall in Swansea market and now sup-plied some of the more up market gift shops around the Gower Peninsular. Her new venture was her website, and she currently had a big order from a Welsh society in New Jersey and a commission for a large-scale ceramic dragon as a centre piece for an Eisteddfod to be held in Australia! We both made encouraging noises and she launched in again...

With the sudden death of Evelyn, she felt her life had been turned upside down in an instant. So much was uncertain again - her future precarious. What would happen to the house? Evelyn had given her a sense of security and a feeling of safety that was now shattered. Evelyn and Moira had both been so supportive of her art.

"Hang on a minute, who is Moira?" asked Samson

"Oh, Moira was Evelyn's companion. That's what women of that age call each other but I thought they were life partners. Moira was lovely too. She'd got a progressive form of M.S and died nearly two years ago. Moira's loss hit Evelyn hard, but she was a stoic sort and believed in the here and now and enjoying every day. Her grandchildren kept her going and her dogs, of course."

Emily told us tearfully that she had been doing a lot of thinking the last few days and she realised that the last three years had been the most optimistic time in her life. Evelyn had been such a quietly charismatic woman and Emily realised that to a great degree she had given up responsibility for her everyday existence to someone who seemed to have all the answers in life. Ironic really, given that she had been employed to care for Evelyn! To her Evelyn had been the embodiment of an intelligent and totally independent woman. A great role model. She would miss her terribly. Now what would happen? Where would she go? She confessed that she was having nightmares about the horrific manner of Evelyn's death. Suddenly it all overwhelmed her, and she sat on the edge of a small window seat looking out to sea and just wept. The two dogs crept to her and laid their heads on her feet. I felt tears springing to my own eyes at that. And I could see Samson swallowing hard too. She seemed to be very genuinely upset. We let her have a few minutes to compose herself.

I said," When you are ready Emily, tell us what a normal day would be like. You said Evelyn liked routine. How set a routine did she have?"

"Well, you could almost set your watch by it! Almost every day at 9.30 am Evelyn would take the dogs for a walk to nearby Brandy Cove or if she chose to head west towards Oxwich Bay, they would often end up at Foxhole Cove and then stop to pick up her mail in Southgate and have a chat with Gwen, the post mistress. Gwen's daughter kept chickens, grew organic vegetables and baked sour dough bread. Evelyn would buy basic provisions here on a daily basis. Once a month I would drive her into Swansea to do her supermarket shop in Waitrose. We didn't see much of each other in the morning as I would do some cleaning and tidying then come into my studio to get on with my own projects. After lunch though, we spent most afternoons in each other's company."

Samson was jotting down everything on his tablet. He was much faster at typing than me. I was recording everything plus making my own mental notes.

"You say almost every day. What did she do on the days she didn't walk the dogs?"

"Two days a week Evelyn played bridge at a club in Mumbles. Near Langland Bay, I think. She would be gone for the best part of the day. On those days, I would take the dogs for their walk. If I was feeling energetic, I'd sometimes go as far as Pobble sands. Even though they are old those dogs can keep going for hours. They walk slowly but they've still got plenty of stamina."

"Did Evelyn go to the club with a friend?"

"No, but I know she had a regular playing partner - Edward. I don't know his surname. Apparently, they were quite the dynamic duo, winning a lot of games."

"We are trying to build a picture of Evelyn. You spent a lot of time with her these last few years, so we'd like to get your impression and insights into her personality, physical and emotional state."

"Okay, well, she took very little trouble with her appearance. She wasn't one for vanity. Even so, I thought she was naturally a striking woman. She still had a lot going for her. I've seen photos of her when she was younger, and her hair had once been almost blue black. Some would think her beautiful in a non- classical way. Her hair was still thick but had morphed into a shimmering, silver grey. It was cut into a short bob. I know some people felt challenged by her quick wit and playful sarcasm. Some men, and women for that matter, found her intimidating as she was a very un-conventional thinker and obviously an extremely intelligent woman. She liked to speak her mind directly and with no ambiguity. She loved animals and the dogs were her soulmates. She had loved and cherished them for thirteen years.

Raising them from puppies to the slightly arthritic pair they are today. She told me she moved to her beloved Gower when she was in her 50's. Her father was born in Barry, I think. She had a flare for languages - she could speak fluent German, Danish and Welsh. And later she taught herself Russian and French. Apparently, her uncle had also been a great linguist. I think he'd been to Cambridge University too. I'm rambling on. Is this stuff helpful?"

"Oh, yes. Please keep going."

"As you know, Sian her daughter put me in touch with her. Moira was still alive and her M.S was progressing, so they needed some live-in help. I'm a decent cook and no slouch when it comes to a good game of Scrabble! Evelyn thought that was a great combo and took me on."

She recalled Evelyn's words 'We can try it for three months. If we don't suit each other, we can part without acrimony' she had said. That had been three years ago, and they were still together. She considered for a moment then carried on "Moira wasn't such a stickler for routine, but Evelyn was -every afternoon at three o'clock sharp we shared a large pot of Darjeeling tea with a piece of homemade cake or scones. Evelyn relished its subtle Muscatel taste. As one of her few indulgences, she received an order of Bannockburn first flush Darjeeling tea from Fortnum and Mason's, every month. Contrary to Fortnum and Mason's recommendation to drink it black, Evelyn took hers with fresh milk from the farm at Three Cliffs Bay. Lemon meringue pie and Delia smith's lemon curd cake were her favourite accompaniments. Moira used to make the cakes when she was alive. I've become a dab hand at lemon curd this last year!"

Emily spoke lovingly of other precise habits that Evelyn had. She said, "She was a one off. She introduced me to some of the finer things in life. Like the tea - until I came to work for Evelyn, I'd only had P.G Tips or Tesco's own brand! Once I tried the Darjeeling, I really could appreciate what Evelyn was talking about. She also introduced me to classical music and art. I'd always been quite good at art in school, and I loved pottery. She gave me some books and got my interest going. I enjoyed all the hours we spent talking about art and music. She was a great conversationalist, if you got her onto topics that she was interested in. She wasn't one for gossip or small talk. She's probably been one of the best influences on my life."

Tears sprang to her eyes again and made their slow progress down her cheek. "I'm so sorry that her life had to end like this. I'll miss her so much."

She topped up our coffees and we took a couple of sips....

I carried on "What would she do of an evening?"

"Weather permitting, we would sit on the patio overlooking the sea for a game of Scrabble. For the first year I had no chance of beating Evelyn or Moira, but in the last six months I won a few sessions. Evelyn tried to persuade me to learn bridge but after a couple of lessons I had to admit I had neither the guile nor intellect to ever become a good player. So, I threw in the towel."

Emily went on, "By 6pm we would be ensconced in the lounge room enjoying a glass or two of Gin and Tonic. A woman of particular tastes, Evelyn insisted on Hendricks Gin. It is infused with rose petal and cucumber. She told me that! Fentiman's was her tonic of choice, served with plenty of ice and topped off with a fresh sprig of Rosemary picked from the garden. Evelyn told me that she remembered Fearless, Thomas Fentiman's faithful dog, was the winner of Crufts obedience class of 1933 and 1934. The dog's portrait is on every bottle! I loved it whenever Evelyn came up with these fascinating pieces of trivia. I was amazed that she could retain so much information from decades past. She knew how to tell a good story, did Evelyn. Before going to bed at around 10.30 she'd usually watch the late-night news on TV or put on a DVD. She loved 'Inspector Morse' and 'Lewis' and documentaries about history or science."

"Thanks Emily, this is all helping us to form a composite picture of Evelyn. From what you have told us, it would have been easy for somebody who wanted to harm her to get to know her dog walking schedule."

"Yes, I suppose so, but what I can't fathom is who would want to harm her and why?"

"That's the million-dollar question. So far, we can't fathom that out, either. We'll probably come back to see you again in a few days' time. We'll just go over to the main house now and take a look around. Thanks again for your time. If you think of anything else, that you may have forgotten today, please give me or Samson a call."

I wanted to contemplate all that Emily had told us. I went to sit on the steps leading from the garden to the cliffs. It was a lovely suntrap. The stones felt warm on the back of my legs. I closed my eyes and lifted my face to the sun relishing the smell of lavender and rosemary. It must feel surreal to Emily. Everything had changed for her in the blink of an eye and just when her life was coming together so well. I couldn't see her as the murderer. No way. I felt sorry for her.

What fleetingly crossed my mind was that she could have been the target instead of Evelyn. If she walked the dogs a couple of times a week it was just possible that the wrong woman was shot. But that wasn't really a viable scenario. Even from a distance the two women were physically so different the shooter would have to be half blind to mistake one for the other!

The soft hiss of the waves on the shingle below was somehow soothing. I watched a sleek yacht plying its way southwards, its long wake feathering the paler blue of the channel. My solace was pierced by the cry of a gull and Samson making his way down the steps towards me...

"Time's cracking on. We'd better inspect this place then get over to Sian's if we are going to interview her today."

"Yes, I suppose so. It's such a lovely spot, I could stay here all afternoon."

Reluctantly I pushed myself up to my feet, brushing dust off my backside. Just at that moment Emily emerged from her studio. She had obviously been crying. Her eyes were red rimmed.

She said "Do you know the herb garden was planted to replicate Ophelia's bouquet - fennel, pansies, rosemary, rue, columbines, daisies and violets. The things Evelyn taught me! She was a genius that woman."

Now I looked more closely I could recognise all of the herbs and flowers that Emily had listed. The combination gave a magical fragrance and colour.

•••

The dead woman's house had been sealed and a constable from the local force was standing guard at the front door. We flashed our IDs, and he opened the door for us. According to the county registry, the original part of the house dates back as far as records begin, but Evelyn had obviously had a large extension added to the west side and a glass conservatory and patio facing the sea. The ground floor had underfloor heating which was warming the beautiful flagstones beneath our feet. The generous lounge had a fantastic sea view from the expansive bay windows. A wood burning stove sat alongside an original bread oven in the inglenook fireplace. There was a large kitchen-diner which was rustic and could probably benefit from an upgrade, in my opinion. From the kitchen, patio doors opened out into the pretty garden with more sea views.

Fingerprint powder was in evidence on most of the surfaces. No suspicious prints had been detected; forensics had informed us. Samson and I wandered around taking it all in. Was there anything here that the initial police team had overlooked or not thought significant? Seeing nothing that struck us as important on the ground floor we headed up the stairs.

On the first floor there were three bedrooms; the main bedroom with super king-size bed, ensuite bathroom and a glorious view of the bay and cliffs, had been Evelyn's. My eye was immediately drawn to two watercolours hanging on the wall. I knew the artist well - David Roberts. Here were beautiful depictions of the Temple of Abu Simbel in Egypt and a wonderful rendition of Petra, Jordan. I have a series of David Roberts's prints of The Holy Land up on the wall in my office, but these must be limited editions - they were in a different class to my mass-produced prints. I had to drag myself away, as there was work to be done. Samson was wandering around looking at the general lay out, inspecting photos on the tallboy and scouring the contents of her wardrobe. Nothing struck us as odd or out of place. We moved on to the next room, which was at the end of the landing and had obviously been Emily's. It was of generous proportions with a large window giving a partial view of the sea. It was light and bright. Its furnishings were Spartan with a stripped pine sleigh bed and matching bedside cupboard. There were pieces of Emily's ceramics on display on a large dressing table and shelves above. The wardrobe contained just a few well-chosen dresses, four blouses, two pairs of smart trousers, a black linen jacket and one pair of formal shoes. There were a few pairs of jeans, three t-shirts, a hand knitted sweater on shelves with a pair of trainers tucked underneath. That was it. I wished I could be so minimalist. Nothing much to see, here.

Next door was a family sized bathroom. It appeared to have been recently renovated with limestone tiles around the walls and floor, a deep claw footed bath and a double shower. Handrails had been fitted to the side of the toilet and the shower. It occurred to me that Moira with her M.S and Evelyn in her nineties would never be able to get in and out of the decorative but impractical claw foot bath. Two dormer windows let in ample light. Samson opened the cabinet doors to reveal a plethora of soaps, shower gels, environmentally friendly cleaning products and enough medications to kit out a pharmacy! We inspected a few of the medicines. They were prescribed to Moira Henderson and were all out of date. I guess Evelyn hadn't got around to clearing them out or couldn't bring herself to do so. Tucked inside a ceramic willow pattern box was a stash of marijuana. Emily's, Samson reckoned. It was of no interest to us.

The third bedroom must have been the guest room. A double bed was made up with a tasteful Burn Jones inspired duvet cover and a cashmere throw over the foot of the bed. Matching tiffany type lamps were sitting on the bedside cabinets and there was a built-in wardrobe in an alcove. A comfy looking armchair was placed next to a small table under the window which had a view of the garden. There were no clothes in the wardrobe in here. We had a quick look around then moved on to the final room on this floor.

I was particularly interested in Evelyn's office and library. I lingered whilst Samson checked out the rest of the house. There were a couple of old computers on the expansive desk in her office and an up-to-date laptop. We would take that in for further inspection by the techies. The desk drawers contained well organised files for bills, subscriptions for magazines, papers, stationary, pens, pencils, a stapler and various other bits and pieces. There was a stack of National Geographic magazines under the desk and the walls were covered from floor to ceiling with bookshelves straining under the weight of hundreds of books. I could spend hours in here. I started inspecting the titles to see if anything unusual caught my eye. Was the clue to Evelyn's murder here amongst the books and papers?

There were the mainstream titles:

'The complete works of Shakespeare'

'The complete works of Charles Dickens'

'Canterbury Tales'

'Alice in Wonderland' and 'Alice through the looking glass.'

The whole set of Agatha Christie mysteries.

'Byzantine and medieval Art'

'A World History of Art'

Many Atlases - both modern and antiquarian

Two hefty volumes of 'Hitler' by Ian Kershaw. I owned these myself. Kershaw is an absolute authority on Hitler. I also owned the 'The Diaries of Victor Klemperer' but I noticed that Evelyn's hard back editions were signed by Martin Chalmers who had translated it from German into English. Klemperer's diaries have been hailed as one of the 20th century's most important chronicles - an extraordinary account of the Nazi period written by a Jew from Dresden, one of the few to survive the war. I rejected the urge to read a few pages, as time was marching on, and we had more to do today. I noticed a whole shelf of travel guides: - 'The Blue Guide' to: Denmark, Sweden, Germany, Russia, France, Italy and Australia. To my astonishment Evelyn also owned the very first Blue Guide- 'Blue Guide London and its Environs'. It was published in 1918 and is a rare collectible.

There were masses of clippings from newspaper articles and magazine features. I was inspecting a particular bundle bound with a red ribbon – 'Western Mail' article from November 2009 about the diaries of Gareth Jones going on display in Cambridge University, when Samson wandered in. "Nothing of interest in the rest of the house. Anything in here?"

"Her library speaks volumes about the woman - excuse the pun! There's some unusual stuff here. Whether it will shed any light on the case is another matter, but I'd like to come back and spend more time in here, just in case."

I was looking down at a page from the Welsh 'Western Mail' dated February 1933 written by Gareth Jones. According to the clipping, Jones had flown with Hitler and Goebbels to Frankfurt in the 'Richthofen' the fastest and most powerful aeroplane in Germany at the time. He had reported on an interview with them. Quite a scoop back in his day! Further clippings were in evidence from 'The Manchester Guardian', 'The Evening Standard', 'New York Evening Post' and 'The Financial Times' all dating from 1933. These were fascinating snippets from the past, but did they have any bearing at all on this case? I was aware that I was in danger of losing precious hours or even days here, being lured down a time-wasting rabbit hole. Because of my personal love of books and history, I'd been guilty of that in past cases. I needed to be mindful of it in this context too. "I'm assuming Gareth Jones was a relative. He seems to have been quite a high-profile reporter in his day!"

"Her uncle I think", said Samson.

For the next ten minutes we browsed around in companionable silence looking at Evelyn's book collection, flicking through the odd publication. There was a beautifully bound first edition of 'The White Goddess' signed by Robert Graves and dated 1948 that Samson brought to my attention.

"This would be worth a few bob, wouldn't it?" he said.

"I imagine so. Google it."

He did and let out a whistle. "That book is worth eight thousand pounds! I might just tuck this one up my jumper" he joked. "'What's the book about?"

I cast my mind back to try to remember the storyline." If I remember correctly, it's about goddess worship as the prototypical religion."

Samson gave a snort of derision.

I went on unperturbed "Something about a Celtic Tree Calendar and a hypothetical Gallic tree goddess, Druantia. The name is believed to be derived from the Celtic word for oak trees. She's like the eternal mother - a goddess of fertility for both plants and humans. I think that's the gist of it."

"Jesus! How do you know all this stuff? I've never even heard of this book. I can't believe you know all about it."

"Oh, hardly. I read it a few years back. Robert Graves is better known for 'I Claudius'. Do you remember the TV series with Derek Jacobi?"

"No, that was before my time. You're showing your age now!"

I was flicking through a pile of loose-leaf folders. One was particularly chunky and there was a Latin inscription on the front: 'Succinum'

"How's your Latin, Samson?"

"Non-existent, but don't worry I've got Google translate on my phone."

"Right, well look up Succinum. My Latin's not too bad but that's not a word I recognise."

"It translates to 'juice'"

"What the heck?"

"Hang on." I could see he was scrolling down on his phone.

"It also means 'sap' and later used for 'amber'."

"How interesting." This folder was packed with all sorts of articles on amber and various amber art pieces. Stuffed in the back, was a file within a file. A photocopied scrapbook titled 'Yantarny Komnata'. Not Latin, was it Russian? I made a note to come back to it. Evelyn certainly took an interest in amber judging by the size of this file and there was a whole group of books on amber on the top shelf. I got the feeling that these were all spider web strands of an interest that may have some significance to this case. But they would have to wait.

"We'd better get going. I'm going to come back tomorrow and spend a few hours in here. So far, we've still found no motive for Evelyn's murder. There might be some connection to her past that could explain it. It's worth a try."

•••

We had an appointment to see Evelyn's daughter, Sian at 3.30pm. She was a G.P - a partner in a practice in Newport. Not Newport near the English border, Newport near Fishguard in Pembrokeshire. It's a very busy and successful practice, by all accords. We took the M4 from Swansea and travelled west. After about half an hour we took the A48 turnoff from the roundabout onto the A40. The countryside here was beautiful - rolling hills of lush green with old farms dotted around. Turning off onto the A487, we skirted the northern foothills of the Preseli Mountains, past Castell Henllys Iron Age Village and all the way to Newport which incorporates the ancient port of Parrog. We eventually turned off the main Fishguard road and headed towards the sea. Sian's house was a stunning, double fronted Victorian property. We could see that it had been lovingly restored, maintaining many of its original features such as the Victorian sash bay windows and wrought iron railings. This was an imposing family home. We pulled into the off-road parking area which could accommodate two vehicles. A BMW X5 was already parked in one spot. Surrounding the parking area were gorgeous mature garden beds with many shrubs and flowering borders. We could see to the side of the property that there were steps which led to a terraced seating area with views towards the sea. To the rear we glimpsed the side of a summer house and lawns.

"Not bad. GPs don't do too badly, do they?" was Samson's first impressions.

"Oh, I don't begrudge them their pay. They work hard enough for it."

We knocked on the imposing glossy black front door and a few moments later it opened. Sian's resemblance to her mother was striking - the same high cheek bones, the nose, the lips. But Sian retained the lush dark tresses that had turned to silver in Evelyn. You could see in the daughter just how handsome a woman Evelyn must have been when she was alive. My very first impression of her was that she was a very controlled woman with a reservedness about her, but I tried not to be in any way judgemental. After all this woman had just lost her mother in the most shocking way possible. She was definitely wary and used to keeping her emotions in check. She was immaculately groomed. Not exactly what you imagine an over-worked G.P to look like.

She greeted us with professional courtesy and an oblique politeness. She ushered us through an entrance vestibule into an ample hallway and from there into a tastefully decorated sitting room. As we filed into the room, I glimpsed the expansive kitchen with open French doors leading into a con-servatory at the rear. There was the subtle aroma of Lang Lang essential oil in the air. I could see Samson was taking it all in and that included giving Sian the once over. I could detect that look of pure male interest in Samson's eyes. I couldn't blame him, Sian was a stunning woman, although old enough to be his mother. For that matter, I was old enough to be his mother too. According to our records, Sian was three years older than me.

"Do sit down" she said gesturing to a comfortable looking sofa. "Can I get you tea or coffee?"

We both opted for coffee. She went into the kitchen to get it. Samson whispered, "There's no ashtrays."

"Don't go there. You can't smoke in here." I thought it would be sacri-lege to pollute a room like this with cigarette smoke. The sofa was extremely comfortable and the fabric a rich mixture of reds and grey in what looked like an Islamic floral pattern. I noticed the large bay windows were hung with thick, luxurious, custom-made curtains. This house reflected an educated and cultured personality. I mouthed "Tasteful. Expensive. Classy." He nodded "I suppose so, if you like that sort of thing. Not my style." That I could believe.

She came back moments later with coffee cups of what looked like Limoges porcelain. The coffee was rich and dark. Filter coffee. No Nescafe served here! The room we sat in was a combination of designer minimalist with classy pieces of art and sculptures setting it off. A quick skim over the bookcases showed that her choice of reading material was quite different to her mother's. There were no technology books here or mathematics books. In fact, there were no scientific tomes at all apart for some medical journals and reference books. What she obviously did have in common with her mother was the love of modern and classical art. A large part of her book collection was devoted to arty volumes and lots of poetry books. What caught my eye was a slim display cabinet in one corner which held a collection of artefacts that I recognised from the Roman and Greek periods. A couple of genuine Attic vases and a strap handled amphora. On the bottom shelf and backlit by a concealed LED was an exquisitely crafted amber coffer. It really had the wow factor but was somewhat incongruous amongst the much older pieces. I asked if I might have a closer look.

"By all means, please do." She seemed surprised that I'd taken an interest.

It was a fantastic piece. I mused "Ah, amber! Did you know the ancient Greeks called it Elektron? Substance of the sun. If you rub it against cloth, you get an electric shock."

Sian countered with her own piece of trivia, "When burnt it produces Ethylene. The Egyptians used the vapour of burning amber in their mummification processes."

I was impressed and judging by the look on Samson's face, so was he.

"Do you have an interest in archaeology?" she asked me.

I told her of my excavations in Cyprus and working at the British school in Rome and the dig in Umbria that I'd worked on in the mid 80's. These older artefacts could easily have been dug up on any of those excavations. Her attitude towards me seemed to change instantaneously. For the first time since we had arrived, she smiled, and her face looked abruptly younger. Her demeanour transformed from being closed to open. She looked me full in the face for the first time. Her eyes drew me in. A spirit came through her eyes that for a few seconds held me in their blue gaze. In that instant, she was a woman lit from within. We chatted for a couple of minutes about classical sites she had visited - Mycenae, Troy, Delphi and Pompeii. She said she would have loved to become an archaeologist, but her mother had encouraged and steered her towards the medical profession.

"She wasn't wrong" I volunteered. "At least you can make a decent living from being a G.P."

I could have chatted on with her for ages, but I suddenly remembered Samson was sitting there looking bored to death, so I quickly re-focused back to the business at hand.

"Do you mind if I record our conversation?" I asked

"'No that's fine. "

I used the app on my mobile phone. "We'd like to start with some background information about your mother. Also, is your father still alive? "

"No, he died when I was very young."

"Oh, I see. We've spoken with Emily, and she was very helpful, but she wasn't able to tell us much about your mother's earlier life. Could you give us a potted history? Basically, we are trying to find anything from her past or present that could give us a clue to motive."

"I can't imagine who would possibly want to hurt mum, but I'll do the best I can to give you as clear a picture of her as I can."

"That would be greatly appreciated. We want to hear of anything, even if you think it can have no bearing on the case."

I noticed Samson was scribbling rapid notes on his tablet to record the nuances of expressions that flitted across her face as she talked about finding out about her mother's death. Bewilderment, shock, fear, anger. All perfectly normal in a case of this nature, when there is an unexplained murder. She looked at us rather blankly and asked.

"Who on earth can be responsible for my mother's death? Have you made any progress at all?"

"Yes, there has been a bit of progress, but its early days. "

She took a measured sip of her coffee, then began...

"She was a wonderful mother. Very loving and supportive. I admired her intellect even though you would never have known how brilliant she was. Most people that knew her would say she was humble, reserved, and modest, shy, gracious, self-effacing and understated. She had all these mannerisms, and they weren't faked, but I could tell that there was a quiet determination in mum and whatever she set out to achieve, she always accomplished it no matter how long it took. There was a steely core to her. Her soft demeanour concealed a fierce resolve. She was more interested in listening and gathering information than in asserting her opinion or dominating a conversation. Having said that, when she did speak, people pricked up their ears and listened. My mother was a very private person. Until about five years ago she rarely spoke of her life before I was born. On the odd occasion I would catch her and Moira in deep conversation about their time at Manchester University. They were very close. Real soul mates. I liked Moira a lot. She was good for mum. It was so sad when her M.S started to progress so rapidly. Mum was distraught, watching her decline, like she did."

Sian went on to tell us that she, herself had been divorced for ten years and her ex-husband, Mathew lived in Yeovil. It was not an acrimonious split, so they were apparently still on good terms. He was remarried and had a new young family. They saw each other very rarely and he didn't make much effort to see Rhiannon and Owen very often. Sian added that she hadn't been involved with anyone else since they split up. She was enjoying her own space. She was kept very busy by the G.P practice of which she was the senior partner. Samson asked, "Did Mathew get on well with Evelyn?"

"Yes, they got on because Mathew was also a computer nerd, like Owen. But he probably hadn't seen Evelyn for at least three years or more."

"How often did you see your mother?"

"I would visit a couple of times a month. We liked to have lunch together at a restaurant on Langland Bay. We'd walk with the dogs on the beach afterwards."

"So, you got along well?"

"Oh, yes, we loved each other. Mum would also come here at least once a month. One of her favourite places locally was the old church at Nevern. She loved to look around the old gravestones in the church yard. There are two weeping yews and some ancient standing stones in the church grounds. There are runes of ancient Ogham on those stones. They completely fascinated mum. Languages both ancient and modern were her thing. We'd often walk with the dogs over the little stream and wander up to the Iron Age earth works."

Tears were welling up in her eyes and she said very quietly "I can't believe we'll never do that together again."

Samson looked distinctly uncomfortable with her show of emotion. I felt sorry for our intrusion on her grief. "It must be hard to take in and a terrible shock. But all this is helping us greatly to build up a sense of your mother."

Samson carried on relentlessly "We found the keys to a safe on your mum's bracelet amongst her effects at the morgue. Do you know where it is located? We didn't spot one when we were inspecting her house."

"Oh, it's recessed into the wall, behind one of mum's pictures."

"Do you know what she kept in there and have you opened it since your mum's death?"

"I have no idea what she has in there. Share certificates possibly and legal documents, I suppose. Maybe her personal diaries."

Finally, something that might be worth investigating – the diaries might shed some light on things. I asked, "We'd like to take a look, if that's okay?"

"It needs a combination in addition to the key and I'm afraid we haven't found the combination yet. No doubt it will come to light at some point."

Samson said, "We could get a professional to get it open, I'm sure."

Momentarily her face took on its closed expression again. For a few moments the only sound in the room was the ticking of an old carriage clock on the mantelpiece. It seemed to grow louder as Sian's silence lengthened. We both held our breath and waited for her to answer. Clearly there was huge reticence around the question of the safe. Finally, she took a deep breath and said,

"My mother was a very private woman in her lifetime, I'm not going to have her private things scrutinised by all and sundry, now she's dead. Do you really think those documents could be of relevance to your investigations?"

"I'll be candid with you, Sian. So far, we are really struggling to find any motive. Anything that could possibly shed some light on that would be welcome. It's certainly an angle we'd like to explore."

Sian considered "Let me think it over. I don't feel comfortable with a violation of mum's privacy at this point." We had to accept that - at least for now.

"We've made a time to talk to your daughter, Rhiannon and we'll need to speak to your son, Owen at some point. Can you give us his mobile number and address?"

"Yes, okay but he's not in the country at the moment. He should be back a week on Sunday in time for mum's funeral."

With a curt nod, Samson acknowledged this and made to leave. I stood too.

"Thanks for your time. You've been very helpful. We'll be in touch again soon."

With that we walked down the hallway and to the solid front door. It was a balmy summers evening.

"What do you reckon?" I asked.

Samson mused "Evelyn's home and artworks and furnishings certainly give me the impression that she was a wealthy woman. Relatives have killed for less."

"Too true! But Sian seems pretty comfortably off already. "

"That's what it looks like, but she could be in debt up to her eyeballs, for all we know. Maybe the daughter was jealous about the two women's closeness. Maybe she felt a bit left out after Moira had come to live with her mother?"

"Oh, come on that's a bit lame!'"

"Yeah, I know. I'm clutching at straws. Truth is we're none the wiser after that chat than we were before. We need to find out what was in Evelyn's will? I'll get on the blower to her solicitor and arrange a meeting."

I couldn't really conceive of Sian having any involvement in her mother's death, but I couldn't rule it out completely. There was definitely something that Sian wasn't coming clean about. "It's getting late. Let's call it a day. We've got the bird watcher, the hikers and the other witness scheduled for tomorrow afternoon. You've already booked in Evelyn's bridge partner, haven't you?"

"Yes, we're seeing him at his workplace at 11am. All the others are coming into the station. I doubt they can add much more than they've already said. But it will be good to put faces to their statements anyway."

"Okay, great. Can you drop me at my digs?"

"Sure."

I was nodding off in the car seat by the time Samson dropped me off. I'd ask Mrs Parry, my landlady if she could knock me up a meal. I couldn't be bothered going out again to search around for something other than fish and chips or pizza.

•••

The next morning, I met Samson at police headquarters. He was chatting up one of the WPCs as I came through reception. He raised his eyebrows and quickly ended his conversation.

"Don't worry I'm not interested in her. I was just being sociable."

"Okay, if you say so." I wasn't in the mood for office banter at the moment.

"What's first on our agenda for today?"

"The bridge partner, Phillip Edwards. I've booked the twitcher in at 3.15pm."

"Don't call him that to his face!"

"Why, what's so bad about that?"

"Don't you know the term twitcher has taken on a negative connotation nowadays?"

"No, I had no idea. So, what's the difference between a bird watcher and a twitcher then?"

"A twitcher is a type of birder who seeks to add as many species as possible to their life list, and as quickly as possible. They don't tend to sit around for hours observing the birds. They just want a confirmed identification as quickly as possible, so that they can check it off their life list. Do you know where the origin of the word comes from?"

"No, but I'm sure you're about to tell me, aren't you?"

I knew he was being sarcastic, but I pushed on anyway, "The origin of the term 'twitcher' refers to the nervous, twitchy behaviour of a British birdwatcher called Howard Medhurst. He frequently travelled long distances on short notice to see rare birds. The term came into common use in the 1950s and 1960s as the popularity of birdwatching increased and individuals sought to outdo one another in the numbers of birds they'd seen. As I said nowadays it often has negative connotations with the more traditional birders. We don't know which type Dave Roberts is, so tread carefully."

He shook his head "You never cease to amaze me! The next trivia night we have, you've got to be on my team!"

"Anyway, we'd better get a move on, or we'll be late for our appointment with Phillip Edwards in Swansea. The traffic can be bad in the centre of town."

•••

As it happened the traffic was freely flowing this morning and we'd missed the rush hour. We would arrive at DVLA with plenty of time to spare. I asked Samson to give me the Welsh rendition of the name. I remembered that it was a real tongue twister. It rolled off his tongue as only a true Welsh speaker can manage "Asiantaeth Trwyddedu Gyrwyr a Cherbydau."

I laughed and shook my head. "Tourists would have no chance pronouncing that. I took Welsh in school up to the age of twelve and I couldn't pronounce that right!"

The driver vehicle and licensing authority or DVLA as it is known is housed in a prominent 16-storey building in Clase, Swansea.

"I haven't been here since 2007." said Samson

"What were you doing here then?"

"On 7th February 2007, a letter bomb was sent to the DVLA and four people were injured. I was part of the investigation."

"Oh, yeah, I vaguely remember that. Wasn't another letter bomb sent to Capita in London around the same time?"

"Yes, that's right. They were all linked. A school caretaker was charged with both offences. After that DVLA installed X-Ray machines in all their post opening areas. Most of the employees here are women. The year after our investigation they went on a one-day strike over pay inequality I don't blame them. A friend of my sister works here, and it's still crap pay!"

Phillip Edwards worked on the fifth floor of the huge Driver and vehicle licensing complex. It had to be by far the biggest employer in Swansea. We thought that Phillip might be able to give us some personal insight into the woman who he'd played Bridge with, so often over the last 4 years.

Phillip was a robust chap. Heavyset and of medium height. His face was nothing to write home about, but not ugly. His one redeeming feature were his eyes which were green and had a distinct sparkle to them. With dark brown hair and a stooping posture, he was someone that you wouldn't look twice at. Someone who would melt into a crowd. He was 56 years old and held a senior management job here at the DVLA. Samson did the introductions and reiterated why we had come to see him. He was well spoken and obviously intelligent. I thought he would pay tribute to Evelyn's skills or her personality, but all he said was, "I'm not sure how I'll manage to carry on playing without her. I suppose I'll have to start looking for a new partner as soon as possible." As if Evelyn's death was little more than an inconvenience to him.

"She was what I had been seeking for years - a partner who could perform miracles."

There was a decided lack of emotion to the man, which was a bit disconcerting. That's probably why he was such a good bridge player - he would be very capable of bluffing.

It was like getting blood out of a stone, to try to illicit any sense of Evelyn's character from him, but when asked about their bridge playing, he was effusive. This turned out to be very useful background information about Evelyn.

"Most people are inclined to regard bridge largely as a matter of cards, but it should be viewed, in my opinion as a battle of wits. Psychology plays a large part in the game. Here, Evelyn had it all over most players', he said. She was always alert to any opportunity that presented itself and was able to make swift decisions. She was very deft. The grand coup is one of the most spectacular plays seen at the bridge table and it is a rare occurrence. Evelyn accomplished it on several occasions. Most bridge players never accomplish a Grand Coup, ever! I acknowledge that I was by far the weaker player in our partnership. There must have been times when Evelyn felt inclined to tell me what she thought of me, but she was restrained by her old-fashioned courtesy which is characteristic of that age group. I don't recall her ever raising her voice or getting angry. Her self-control was admirable."

He went on to explain "Bridge is a game in which intuition and deduction combined with good common sense plays an important part. To rank amongst the very top players it is not enough to know what to bid and to play the cards well. In addition, you must be a keen observer, be able to make quick decisions based often on little more than a hunch. Evelyn had every one of these qualities and used them all to devastating effect in every rubber she played. She was quite a phenomenon in Bridge circles. She made some of the chaps furious and made many of them look stupid. She shot many huge egos down in flames!"

"Was there anyone who she particularly shamed? Anyone that may take that further to the degree that they might want to hurt her?"

"Good God no, bridge is a gentleman's game. It is JUST a game and defeat is accepted without question. Evelyn had unshakeable ability to concentrate for long periods of time. She would regularly bamboozle our opponents into giving us tricks we should not have made." He explained "One of the great assets of a successful bridge player is the ability to say, "No Bid". There are times when to 'pass' requires great self-restraint. Evelyn had this quality in spades, excuse the pun." he said, laughing at his own joke.

"There is of course a mathematical aspect too and Evelyn was a great mathematician in her day", he enthused. "Her knowledge of the mathematical odds, her ability to count the hands of her opponents and her familiarity with safety play all gave her a considerable advantage over your average player", he concluded.

Samson interrupted him, "What do you know about her university days?"

"Not a great deal but she referred to her time at Cambridge on the odd occasion. I know she studied Maths there and came out with a first! No mean feat for a woman back in the 1930's."

I asked him if he knew of anybody that took a real dislike to her or had any major grudge against her.

"No absolutely not. She was a popular person in the bridge club and was highly respected as a player. She was by far the best player they'd had in years!' Without her, their club might never be as successful again!" He recalled how, before their important rubbers she loved to quip "Careless talk gives information to the enemy." Phillip couldn't agree more.

Samson pressed on, "Did she ever talk about her life after university, during the war?"

"Oh, she did say 'The Times' was the only newspaper to retain its weekly bridge article throughout the duration of the war. Admirals, Generals to the lowest ranks and civilians sent bridge deals and problems from around the world. By the way she could still do 'The Times' crossword in under ten minutes! I watched her do it one day. It was quite something. It can take me two days off and on, to complete!"

"What about her personal life during the war? "

"I knew she got married after the war and that her husband died young. I've briefly met her daughter on one occasion when she came to pick her up after a tournament. She talked of her grandchildren, often. She was obviously quite devoted to them. She talked about living in Manchester for a few years and she did go to a reunion once a year up north. I assumed that was to do with her old Manchester University pals. I assumed, after she got married, she was just a housewife, all be it a clever one!"

I had to bite my lip. That phrase "just a housewife" infuriates me. Always has done.

Phillip was on a roll now. He reverted to bridge anecdotes to illustrate Evelyn's prowess at the game. The man was obviously a bridge tragic, but it was evident that he had held Evelyn in very high esteem. She had been his bridge guru. He would miss her sharp intelligence very much. He rambled on "Evelyn often coached me. I remember she started by saying "At bridge, as in warfare victory doesn't always go to the strongest force. "

Some of this was obtusely interesting, but I thought I should re-focus on our topic.

"Did she talk to you much about her time at Manchester University?"

"Not really. From what I gather, she was quite high up in the team working on the first Ferranti computer. Her and Moira. I met Moira a few times when she came to pick up Evelyn from tournaments. One time they were off to Cardiff Bay to see 'Cardiff Singer of the World' at the opera house. I remember it because she and Moira were arguing about a Wagnerian lieder singer who Moira thought might win and Evelyn was saying how she couldn't stand Wagner. It was Nazi music, as she put it. Hardly P.C, I thought! I never really spoke to Moira, though apart to say hello and goodbye. Evelyn and Moira did go to reunions in Manchester together. After the last one Evelyn came back quite depressed. She said there were so few of the old crowd left. Every year more of them would die off! That's understandable, after all she was ninety."

"Is there anything else at all you can think of that could shed any light on this case?"

"No, I can't think of anything else to tell you."

Samson wrapped up the interview, "Ok, well thanks for your time. You've given us a few more insights into her personality. It all helps."

We shook hands with him and made our way back to the lift.

"Samson, can you go and have a chat to this friend of your sister's. See if there is any office gossip about Phillip Edwards. Do it discretely. Then check his background for any convictions. He seems above board, but you never know. I need some air and a bit of exercise. Meet me at 'The Hungry Horse' cafe on the main road. You can't miss it. We'll get a bite to eat, and you can report back anything interesting that you've found out."

Samson reminded me that I should call Evelyn's solicitor to reconfirm our appointment for this afternoon. He had the number on his phone.

She confirmed, she could see us as planned. As long as we were finished before 3pm. That shouldn't be a problem.

•••

Samson was already sitting at a corner table with a flat white, when I got to the cafe. He'd taken a short cut, down a few back alleys, he explained. We ordered a large bowl of potato wedges with sweet chilli sauce and sour cream, to share. And I asked for a black filter coffee. Once my coffee had been plonked on the table by the over worked waitress, Samson started filling me in on his findings. He spoke in the truncated shorthand that police officers often use:

"Phillip's background. Brought up in Monmouth, to middle class parents. Well educated at grammar school. Trained for the Civil Service. Married with two grown up sons. Had a relatively successful career. Decided to move to the coast, when he was accepted at DVLA. Lives in a modest house here in The Mumbles. Wife teaches at the local primary school. By all accords she's a lovely woman. The two boys live in London.

One works in the city as an account manager for an insurance company and the other is an Articled Clerk at a legal practice in Lincolns Inn. Both doing well for themselves. Apart from his bridge and a bit of rambling and gardening, he doesn't have any other hobbies or pastimes. All very respectable. Appears he would have absolutely no motive to kill Evelyn. If anything, he basked in the glory when they won so many tournaments. She helped him be someone in the bridge world. His work colleagues couldn't add much insight into the man. Seems he was always very punctual and efficient at his job. Not a big talker and never engaged in any gossip. Overall, their impression of him was fair to work for and as long as you got on with your job, he left you to it without any micro-management. He has no past record with the police. Nothing out of the ordinary. Some talk at DVLA that he had got into debt playing online poker tournaments. I asked the techies to check out his online gambling account to see how much he owes. It's chicken feed. A few hundred pounds. I don't get any feeling of unease about the man, do you? The online poker angle isn't of concern, so I think we can rule him out at this stage."

"Yeah, the bloke's a bit of a bore but I just can't see him as a killer. Plus, what motive would he have? He's lost the best bridge partner he's ever likely to have and all the kudos that brought him."

•••

Evelyn's solicitor was in Swansea city centre. We could almost have walked to her offices, but we were pushed for time as always. We drove. It was obviously a thriving practice. Housed in an imposing Victorian double fronted house which had retained many of its original features. There were gorgeous Victorian tiles at the front door, sweeping dark wood banisters and ample proportions to the rooms.

Edwina Cohen was a larger-than-life character. Nothing like most people's idea of a stuffy solicitor. She was dressed in an outfit that could have been Vivian Westwood. Nothing sober and formal, here. Typical that Evelyn would have chosen someone so unconventional to administer her will! Her personal assistant ushered us into a fabulous office that was more akin to an art gallery than a law firm. After the formalities were over, Edwina retrieved a physical file from on top of her desk. The original will was pulled out and copies were handed to me and Samson.

"Maybe you'd like to quickly look through and then please ask me any questions you think may be of help. I was very fond of Evelyn. You don't meet women like that every day, she said. I was shocked to the core by her murder. I'd like to do whatever I can to aid your investigations."

I started by asking how long-ago Evelyn had made her will.

"Oh, over seven years ago, but she'd altered it about a year ago - to add in Emily Evans."

Samson's eyebrows went up. Could there be anything in this? Well, let's see how much she stood to inherit. I looked down at the last will and testament of Evelyn Mary Jones of Valland House, Crag Cove...

Scanning down I could see there were donations of £50,000 each to:

Macmillan Nurses, Wales

M.S Society

Welsh National Opera

RNLI - Penarth

Ci Defaid Cymreig. I looked to Samson for a translation. "What's that?"

"Oh, the Welsh Sheepdog Preservation Society."

I had to laugh!

He said, "This is a bit unusual - her house is left to her granddaughter, Rhiannon, not her daughter."

Edwina said, "I did ask her about that, at the time. Evelyn said Sian was wealthy in her own right and she'd never loved the house like Rhiannon did. Evelyn assured me that Sian wouldn't mind, and neither would Owen. She was a smart cookie, Evelyn. The house was transferred to Rhiannon as a PET."

"'A what" queried Samson?

"Oh, a potentially exempt transfer."

"How does that work?"

"The house would fall outside of Evelyn's estate for inheritance tax purposes if she lived seven years after the transfer."

"'And did she?"

"No, not quite. Another six months would have done it. As it is I have had to get a valuation report drawn up for probate purposes. The estate won't have to pay much, though as under PETs, the inheritance tax reduces on a sliding scale to zero after seven years."

Samson exclaimed "That's how the rich get richer. They can wrangle their way out of tax with all these little-known loopholes."

Edwina just looked at him and made no comment.

I noticed that Evelyn's Landover that Samson had been so taken with was left to her grandson, Owen. Plus, an envelope marked for his attention. Did Edwina have any idea what was in the envelope?

"None."

"Maybe a cheque from an offshore bank account?" Samson asked. He was obviously already convinced that Evelyn was a tax evader.

Edwina said she doubted it because unless Evelyn used one of the more exotic offshore tax havens, a death certificate and the probate certificate would still be required before they released any money. Owen hadn't asked her for anything relating to that.

A payment of £35,000 was to be made to Emily Evans. Samson exclaimed, "That's not bad after working for her for three years, but hardly a motive for murder, is it?"

Edwina said "Evelyn had come to think of Emily as almost a second daughter. She wanted to give her an amount that could make a real difference in her life."

A payment of £35,000 was to go to Estrid Gustaffson. Who on earth was that we asked?

"Oh, Evelyn's cousin's daughter in Denmark."

A payment of £35,000 was to go to the 'Association de la Memoire de Rose Valland'.

"What the devil is this?" asked Samson. I didn't have a clue. I looked askance of Edwina.

She clarified for us, "I asked the same question of Evelyn when she was making her will and she told me Rose Valland was a heroic French woman that she had come to know and respect, during the war. She told me that this association was set up on Rose's behalf to educate people about The Arts. She didn't elaborate any further than that, so I just accepted it.

My mind made the connection that this woman must have had a considerable impact on Evelyn, if she had gone as far as to name her house after her! I made a note to check this out further.

We carried on down the list of bequests…

A pair of early computers - an Apple Lisa and an Acorn Archimedes were bequeathed to Owen. Apparently, these had been two of Evelyn's especially prized possessions.

Her daughter Sian was to inherit the rest of her estate, which amounted to £78,000 cash at HSBC bank and her two David Robert's paintings.

I was in awe at this revelation. I asked Edwina "Are they really originals. Surely, they're prints?"

"No", she assured me they were original water colours. "Evelyn joked with me about them 'If I fall off my perch suddenly, make sure my daughter gets them. Since she was a toddler, she always loved the camels! Just like Evelyn, Sian isn't concerned about their monetary value. She had a wicked sense of humour at times!"

The two paintings were itemised: -

1) The Front Elevation of the Great Temple of Abu Simbel, Nubia. Valued for insurance purposes at £85,000

2) Original Watercolour of Petra, Jordan. Valued for insurance purposes as £20,000

I was very envious. Both are iconic - Abu Simbel Temple is known to Agatha Christie fans from the film 'Death on the Nile' and the facade of the Treasury at Petra is known to all Indiana Jones fans!

As an ex - archaeologist I would love to own either of these pictures. They depict such iconic archaeological sites. I had never seen a David Robert's original outside of a museum or National gallery. I would look more closely at them next time I was in Evelyn's house.

Sian was to inherit Evelyn's rings - a couple of coloured diamonds - one pink and one yellow from the Argyle mine in Australia. Edwina informed us that the rings were probably quite valuable as coloured diamonds are in short supply. There had been no insurance appraisals for these on file. She had put a nominal value of £5,000 for them both.

Sian was also the sole beneficiary of Evelyn's Personal Pension Plan - currently invested in the Friends Provident Ethical Fund. Today's value £97,343.20

Evelyn's cousin Hilde was bequeathed a couple of jewellery pieces- nothing of real value as far as she could see, mostly semi-precious stones - amber in particular. Also, a smallish mosaic which had hung for years on Evelyn's study wall. A garish looking thing, according to her daughter, Sian! Apparently, Evelyn had always promised that to Hilde. An over-the-top baroque monstrosity - in Sian's words! Still, there's no accounting for taste. I was to find out much later just how prophetic a statement that was but at this stage of the investigation, I was oblivious.

Edwina said "I thought the Scandinavians all liked clean lines and simple designs! I put a guestimate value of £500 on Hilde's pieces for probate purposes."

There were some unusual items listed in Evelyn's will but as far as a motive went, there was nothing here that shone any light on the case. When we got outside, I said, "I think Edwina underestimated the value of the Argyle pink diamonds. I happen to know that they are considered the most concentrated form of wealth in the World, due to their scarcity!"

Samson said, "Maybe she just used a price range for normal clear diamonds of that carat weight."

"Whatever the case it will certainly be in Sian's benefit, the value for those two pink diamonds is probably more like £45K."

"Jesus, that woman was loaded. I did a quick tot up in my head and with her house included she was worth well over a £1.5 million!" I detected a note of envy in Samson's voice.

After leaving Edwina we negotiated heavy traffic on our way back to the M4 but from there on it was plain sailing. We arrived back at headquarters with ample time up our sleeve before the next interviews.

•••

David James Roberts was thirty-five years old. Samson pointed out that we'd just been talking about the artist with the same name! If there is a stereotype of bird watchers, this David, was it. Dressed in a navy-blue anorak with brown corduroy trousers and a boffin appearance, he looked every bit the part! Samson didn't use the word twitcher, but Roberts brought up the subject almost straight away, as if he had overheard us earlier and wanted to dismiss any ideas we had that he was an unethical twitcher.

He was adamant. "I'm not a twitcher" he said with some indignation. "Don't get me wrong competitive birding can be fun and can raise interest in the subject, particularly for younger generations who will then grow to support bird conservation. Twitchers can also help confirm rare bird reports, share sightings with other birders and enhance records about migration patterns and population changes. Some do donate to help support habitat restoration and preservation. But their obsession with increasing their life lists can lead to unscrupulous reports and misinformation in an attempt to appear more successful. A lot of twitchers I've met have been rude and pushy."

"So, what birds were you on the lookout for that day that you witnessed Evelyn Jones's murder?"

"Mainly choughs. They've been absent from Gower for years. They breed in caves or gullies in the cliffs. Quite a few sightings were reported along that stretch of the coastal path."

Samson gave me a wink then asked, "Remind me. What do choughs look like?"

Roberts was oblivious to Samson's sarcasm and answered innocently, "Oh, they have coral red bare parts and distinctively fingered wings. If you listen to their calls, they are plainly of the crow family but in a higher register than the jackdaws with which they are often seen. I was also hoping to see an adult female green woodpecker. They are shy birds, but you can spot them occasionally around here on the cliff tops. As it happens. I didn't spot either that day, but I did spot a kestrel hovering above the cliffs."

"As we understand it from your statement you were squatting behind a bush and saw something just before Ms Jones was shot. Is that right?"

"Yes, he wouldn't have seen me because I was hidden behind a bush so as not to scare the kestrel. A figure - a man, stepped out from behind that rocky outcrop, hidden until then from view. He was tall, a well-built man in hiking boots, khaki shorts, check shirt and hunting jacket - multi pocketed. Like a Barbour or similar. The sort of thing you see Princess Anne wearing!

He had an angular face and light brown hair, which was receding. I don't know what colour eyes. He wore dark rimmed glasses. The type that wraps around. Like the ones you see them wear on a shooting range."

"What age would you say?"

"Hard to say, anywhere between thirty and fifty."

"Obviously you got a pretty good look at him."

"Well, yes because I had my binoculars with me. It was only when I caught a flash of sunlight on metal out of the corner of my eye that I turned the binoculars on him. He took something out of his pocket, bent over for a few moments then straightened up. And then it happened. I could barely detect two muffled pops. I had spotted the elderly woman and her two dogs go past a few moments earlier and I swung my binoculars toward where I had last seen her. She was on the ground and the dogs started barking and jumping around. I couldn't rationalise what I had seen. I ran towards her. Two other people were also running towards her. One of the dogs took off. It was all a bit chaotic then. I did swing the binoculars back to where the man had been standing but by then he was gone. When I got to her and I saw the bullet wound, I knew she'd had it. Mr Jackson did try to do CPR, but it was obviously hopeless. She was already dead. There was blood all over him. His wife was in shock. I thought she was going to go hysterical."

"You're sure it wasn't Mr Jackson you had seen behind the rock?"

"Absolutely not. He and his wife came from the opposite direction. Plus, I'd know that face again if ever I saw it. It's probably etched on my memory for good."

"You'd be able to identify him then?"

"Definitely."

"Do you remember Emily Evans arriving?"

"Yes, maybe five to ten minutes later she showed up with the dog in tow. Shortly afterwards the police and ambulances arrived. Then it was mayhem. Lots of action. I think I went into a sort of delayed shock myself at that point. You don't go out bird watching and expect something like this to happen. I'm still getting flash backs. What a horror story!"

I felt sorry for the guy. "Have you been given details of a counsellor?"

"Yes, the police were helpful with all that sort of stuff."

"Is there anything else you can think of that might have any significance at all?"

'Well, thinking back to that morning, I'm not a hundred percent sure, but as I made my way to my observation spot, I did glimpse a man that might have been him coming in the opposite direction, along the coastal path. He was carrying a black backpack, I think. Look it might not have been him. It's only when something like this happens that you wish you'd paid more attention. Know what I mean?"

I did know what he meant. "No worries. You've been very helpful. I know how traumatic it must have been to witness what you did. Make sure you keep up with the counselling for a while. It really can help. We'll be in touch. I'll get an officer to drive you home. Thanks again."

"Well, what did you make of him?" Samson enquired

"I liked him. He'll make a good witness, if we have an opportunity to bring this bloke to justice."

"Yeah, he was okay for a twitcher!" he joked

"How long have we got before the Jacksons arrive?"

"About ten minutes. Enough time to get a coffee and a doughnut."

"Great. I'm in need of a caffeine and sugar hit."

•••

I was just wiping the sugar off my lips from the doughnut when we were notified that the Jacksons had arrived. They were punctual. Bang on time. The man and woman that presented themselves at the front desk, Jim and Fiona Jackson, made a disparate couple. He was tall, slightly bowed, serious with greying hair. She was much younger, slim, alert and vibrant. It turned out; she was his second wife. When his first wife died, he said he had not expected another period of happiness in his life. He was solicitous of her. Overbearing, paternal. I found it slightly cringeworthy, but she seemed totally at ease with his behaviour. Whatever rocks your boat, I guess.

They were members of the Rambler's Society they told us. That's how they had met two years earlier. Jim wanted to get back into socialising after his wife's death and Fiona wanted to get fit. They'd been married for ten months. After the introductions and some polite chit chat, Samson opened the dialogue, "We've read through your statements, and we'd like to go through them with you and ask you a few more questions."

"No problem", Jim responded.

I thought I'd try to get Fiona engaged in the meeting, so I asked her what she did for a living.

"I run a yoga studio. I only work two days a week. It's my own business and it's been more successful than I ever dreamed possible! I now employ two other women to do the bulk of the classes. So, I guess I'm semi-retired."

Jim told us; he had taken early retirement when his engineering firm merged with a bigger European company. He'd got a good package and was ready to do some longer haul travelling and indulge in his hobbies.

Samson asked, "Which are?" "Photography and hiking." Came the answer.

Jim let us know that they were in training to do the Pennine way. They were out to do at least ten miles on the day that Evelyn was shot. They had intended to walk through from Caswell Bay to at least Three Cliffs Bay or if they still had the energy to carry on through to Oxwich and catch a bus back from there. They parked at Caswell Bay and had made good progress at quite a brisk pace past Pwllddu Bay and West Cliffs and were almost within sight of Southgate when the horror unfolded.

Fiona heard something and at almost the same time saw a woman with two dogs fall to the ground. She was vaguely aware of some fellow off to the right of them near the rocks. But she hadn't paid him any more attention once she saw the elderly woman keel over. Jim had heard nothing but had noticed the woman fall. They ran towards her. Jim had the St John's Ambulance first aid certificate, so thought he might be able to assist her. He thought she had just taken a tumble. They were not prepared for what they saw. Who would be? Not in his worst nightmare added Jim, could he have imagined the wounds inflicted on Evelyn. Nevertheless, he did attempt CPR for at least five minutes while Fiona tried to calm one of Evelyn's dogs. She was howling and in great distress.

Jim often replied on behalf of them both, I noticed. It irritated me, but I had to accept that this was how some partner's dynamics played out. Jim took up the story again "I did catch sight of him from afar. It all happened so quickly. I wanted to run after him, but he moved surprisingly fast, and he disappeared into the distance."

Samson prompted "In which direction was he going?"

Fiona finally got a word in edgeways – "East, towards Swansea, I think. I was too shocked to be of much use at that point. Jim was calmer than me. He'd called for an ambulance straight away and then the police when we saw her wounds. He did everything he could to save her, but I think she was already dead before she hit the ground! A few minutes later Emily Evans showed up with the other dog. Poor girl, she lost it when she saw the gunshot wounds. From then on, I think the shock kicked in for all of us witnesses. The police were understanding, and the ambulance crew were very kind. I wouldn't wish that experience on my worst enemies." She lapsed into thought.

I vividly remembered the first time I'd seen a murder victim "No I'm sure it's been traumatic for you both. We really appreciate you coming in today. If there's anything else that you recall in the next few days or weeks, please give us a call." We shook hands and Samson escorted them to the front exit. When he got back to the office he said "God, he's old enough to be her father. What do women see in these older men?"

"Who knows, it's beyond me. Maybe a sense of security?" was all I could offer in explanation.

To finish off our very busy day we had Steve Green coming in for a chat in ten minutes time. He had been sitting outside the 'Crumbs' Cafe in Southgate on the morning of the murder and had given a brief witness statement to the local police. Steve arrived a few minutes late and looking rather dishevelled. He explained that he had come on his motorbike, and it was wet and windy along the coast road. He accepted Samson's offer of a cup of tea. He removed his leather biker jacket and gauntlets and gratefully swigged his cuppa.

"Okay, Steve, we won't keep you long. We just wanted to touch base with you and to ask you to go back over what you saw the morning of Evelyn Jones's murder."

"Well, as you know, I was sitting at a table outside the 'Crumbs' Cafe. It was warm and sunny, and I had a day off work, so I was in no hurry.

I was halfway through a bacon and egg roll when this fella walked past. He was dressed in hiking gear - shorts, khaki colour I think and a brown checked shirt, with a multi pocketed vest, like fishermen wear over the top. He had a dark baseball cap on. He was walking briskly with a black backpack. He just didn't look like a rambler out for a hike. There was something military about him. No way was he out for a leisurely hike! He had a furtive look about him. Out of the ordinary for this neck of the woods. He didn't hang around. He was walking at pace towards Mumbles. I was just finishing my second cup of tea about quarter of an hour later, when I heard the wail of sirens as the police then a few minutes later an ambulance whizzed past.

Samson asked, "Did you see the guy come back past you at any time?'"

"No, definitely not. I would have noticed him. There was something not right about that bloke!"

"Is there anything else that you can remember to add to your statement?"

"Sorry, that's it, I'm afraid. It was just a fleeting sighting. Obviously, if I'd had any inkling of what the bastard had done, I would have followed him."

"Look we don't know at this stage if the man you saw was the murderer. Don't feel bad. How were you to know what played out on the coastal path? At least you were observant and have helped us with your description of him."

He seemed almost disappointed when we thanked him and indicated that the meeting was over. We watched him through the window as he kicks started his black Norton motorbike in the car park and roared out onto the side road adjoining our building. Samson and I both slumped down at our desks. What a day! We'd packed in a huge day of interviews.

"I don't know about you, but I'm knackered, John."

"Yeah, same here. Well at least Steve's statement corroborated the appearance of the man the other witnesses had seen and the fact that he left the crime scene and headed in the direction of Swansea rather than Oxwich. They all agree on that."

I really couldn't do anymore work. My concentration had simply petered out.

I was already heading out the door as I called back over my shoulder. "See you back here in the morning and we'll review everything then."

The next morning Samson was wolfing down a full English breakfast in the staff canteen when I arrived. I opted for porridge and berries and sat down opposite him. "I'd like to spend some time looking through Evelyn's library and office today. I've got a strong sense that there's something amongst all that clutter that will shed some light on this case. Would you mind conducting the interview with Evelyn's granddaughter on your own?"

"No problem. If she looks anything like her mother, it will be a pleasure!"

I had to laugh. "You cad! Make sure you keep your mind on your work!"

I had no real concerns about Samson. He was very professional when it came to his job. I knew from experience that there was no way he would as much as flirt with a witness.

"I'll see you back here later. "

I had to admit, I was looking forward to browsing through Evelyn's books and music collection. I do like an eclectic mix of genres. And I did have a gut feeling that it would be worth my while.

• • •

There was no sign of Emily or the dogs when I arrived at Evelyn's house. I allowed myself a few minutes to take in the glorious view again and to wander around the marvellous garden before entering the house. I headed straight for Evelyn's study and library. I didn't want any distractions this morning as I had to focus on the task at hand - finding a motive for her murder.

My home library is a jumbled mass of books. I love it but anyone else would find it hard to spot any theme or organisation by title or genre. I know it drives my brother, who is a Virgo to distraction. Thankfully, I could see that Evelyn had at least a rudimentary system to her collection of books and music. They weren't arranged alphabetically but her groupings were logical. I sat at her desk and took in the overall scheme of things. Amongst the many foreign language titles were a selection of diaries and memoirs some by obscure authors others by well-known characters:

The Diaries of Roza Shanina - 1965

The Diaries of Gareth Jones

Le Front de l'Art published in 1961 and inscribed "To my dear friend Evelyn" and signed by the author Rose Valland. Here was that name popping up again! I did a quick flick through. It was written in French, so I put the volume aside. I'd start a pile of books and magazines to pay special attention to. Evelyn must have thought very highly of this woman to name her house after her and to bequeath £35k to her charitable association!

There were other noteworthy editions:

'Information Processing' by Cicely Popplewell published as a textbook in 1962.

'Das Kapital' by Karl Marx.

'Collected Works of Karl Marx and Frederick Engels'.

'School for Barbarians' by Erika Mann. I wasn't familiar with this title. Thumbing through, I could see the book described to the world the true nature of the Nazi educational system. I made a note to myself to procure a copy for my own library.

'Alan.M. Turing' written by Sara Turing and dated 1959. Shelved next to this volume were various publications written by Alan Turing, the acclaimed Enigma code breaker. 'The Science News: Article on Computability.' Evelyn had scribbled on the back of this publication – 'The man was a national asset'. She had numerous such articles written by him. I knew he was a front-runner in the pursuit of machine learning. There was a sizeable collection of works written by other early computing authors – George Boole, Charles Babbage, Ada Lovelace and the Bitcoin inventor, Sato chi Nakamoto.

Evelyn had accumulated a huge collection of Modern Art volumes. There were also many catalogues for Leningrad Museums and Art galleries. I referred to my notes from my first visit and pulled out the loose-leaf folder with the heading 'Suciu'. I had looked up the words 'Yantarny Komnata'. They were Russian for The Amber Room. I flicked through the copy of the old scrapbook bearing this name. Evelyn certainly was obsessed with Amber. There were clippings from magazines over many years mostly about Catherine the Great and her 'Eighth Wonder of the World'- The Amber Room. Articles in Russian were pasted into the book. I had to admit the Russian Cyrillic was beyond me. There were masses of annotations scribbled in pencil on some pages. They looked like some ancient language - a blend of secret code and pictorial symbols. Another puzzle Evelyn had left for us to solve. I remembered Sian's comments about the ancient Ogham script on the gravestones that had so entranced Evelyn. I took a snapshot on my mobile and texted it to Samson to check out. Less than a minute later he called me back.

"Heck that was quick."

He was laughing, "Because it's not an ancient language its plain old shorthand!"

"You're kidding. How come you know shorthand?"

"Mum was a secretary for our local MP when I was a kid. She was always typing up reports from her shorthand notes at the kitchen table."

"Brilliant! So, what does it say?"

"Nothing earth shattering. It's a sort of list she's jotted down. It reads,"

'Alternative investments:'

'The Rapaport Diamond Report - Argyle mine, coloured diamonds.' This tied back to the mention in Evelyn's will and the conversation we had had with her solicitor.

'Hatton Garden' I knew enough about diamonds to know that this was the area of London where all the top-notch diamond dealers were located.

'Pre embargo cigars - Sotheby's, Christies'

'Amber items'

'Lisa 1983 '

What an eclectic mix of subjects! Perplexing. But I knew deep down that there was a connection between them all and that they were somehow significant in this case.

My browsing eye had landed on another obscure book: 'Rembrandt als Erzieher' by Julius Langbehn. My schoolgirl German translated this to 'Rembrandt as Educator'. I knew this guy was writing in the late 1890's and was a rabid anti-Semite. He was notorious at the time for his implausible rantings about Germany governing Europe and the World. It was a best seller in Germany at the end of the 19th Century! Obviously, I could see why he would appeal to Hitler and the Nazis. But this was an interesting title for Evelyn to have on her bookshelf. Adjacent to this tome was 'The Kummel Report' by Otto Kümmel. This report was submitted in three volumes to the Reich's chancellery in January 1941. It contained the ultimate wish-list for repossessing works of art from museums as well as from private collections in the western world. The catalogue part of the report listed every work of art that fell under Hitler's nationalistic definition. I scanned through the list. It was extensive and among the long list of demands and the incredulous cases for repatriation, I could see the mad imbalance and inaccuracy in the findings of this crazy report. A huge number of Dutch and Flemish paintings were targeted. Spurious arguments were used to claim them as "Germanic Art". Interestingly, The Amber Room was near the top of this 'wish list'. Here was a common thread. Evelyn had a lot of material devoted to this topic. Hitler claimed it as an item for repatriation as it had been constructed by Prussian craftsmen. Hitler had convinced himself of its Aryan origin.

Evelyn had an extensive music collection. Not dis-similar to my own, I noted. Mostly classical CDs: Beethoven, Debussy, Puccini, Mozart, Bach… She had quite a lot of war time stuff - Glen Miller, Vera Lynn, Edith Piaf, Charles Trenet and more modern artists - The Beatles, Rolling Stones, The Who, David Bowie, Cat Stevens, Lou Reid, Kate Bush, Annie Lennox, Jimmy Hendrix...

I spotted 'Songs of the Auvergne' sung by Kiri Te Kanawa. One of my absolute favourites. I decided to listen to it whilst I searched through her books and papers. I selected a great compilation CD of Opera featuring Pavarotti, Domingo, Joan Sutherland, Mirella Freni and Renata Tebaldi. I fed CDs into the stacker and pressed the start button. I always find music a great help to concentration.

I was in a state of flow - totally absorbed in Evelyn's library. I had been sitting here for hours. For anyone looking in through the window, I must have cut a solitary figure at the desk in the corner poring over hefty tomes, with a pool of lamplight reflecting off my reading glasses. Time could have stood still for all I was aware of its passing. I was engrossed in Evelyn's books and articles. I stretched my arms towards the ceiling easing the muscles in my shoulders. In that moment I promised myself I would go back to yoga twice a week. I'd let it slip the last few months and my joints were letting me know! As I looked around, I took in all the postcards, pictures and little mementos pinned on the cork board and various items of ephemera on shelves. Evelyn's life made perfect sense of them all. Now they were just junk. Bric-a-brac. Probably destined for the local Oxfam charity shop.

I sat at her chesterfield desk and made a stab at drawing some conclusions from all the clippings, annotations and various other scribblings in books and magazines that I had scoured through in the last few hours. I tried to simplify my notes down to places, years, names and connecting events or ideas then group them logically on to a page of A3 paper. I know people rave on about computer programs for mind maps and flow charts and such, but I still prefer the old-fashioned way of viewing data. Somehow this old-style method triggers better thought processes in me. Mind you, this evening I was struggling to make the connections. The backbone of archaeology is a good trustworthy chronology. That's what I needed here...

By cross checking and re-reading my notes, it became obvious that the initials 'BZ 'appeared in several instances. Who or where was B.Z? Why had Evelyn scrawled all these notes in the margins? The many annotations, the highlighted areas of text, what significance did they have? What did they mean? These words long ago marked by the woman whose ghostly presence now seemed to hover at my shoulder, anxious about sharing her secrets or to whisper her confessions.

I came across a Sotheby's Catalogue for sales in 1965 - Lot 56 was described as 'Pre embargo cigars.' This item was marked with a star and a pencil annotation of £9,000. A Christies' catalogue for sales in 1969 - Lot 80 was described as 'Amber items.' This was also marked with a star and a pencil annotation of £12,000. I wondered, was Evelyn simply monitoring prices or had she bought or sold these items? These were considerable amounts of money in the 1960's. I made a note to check her old bank statements and to ask Sian if she could shed any light on it. Suddenly, I felt a frisson of excitement. I knew there was something of vital significance in what I'd just read. I was certainly in need of a penny - dropping moment. This could be it. It was just on the edge of my consciousness...Try as I might I was unable to quite grasp the elusive clue. The moment had gone, for now. I'd probably wake up at 3 am and it would come to me!

My stomach rumbled and growled, and I had to acknowledge that it was time to pack in for the day. I needed food and a break from this intense concentration. I decided to take a couple of bundles of documents and clippings home with me to browse through during the rest of the evening. I'd try to spot any new connections or patterns. So far, this case was bizarre and quite frankly bewildering. In the back of my mind, I kept reiterating the three cornerstones: Means, motive, opportunity. I was still very much drawing a blank on motive!

I picked up a pizza on the way back to my digs. It was half gone by the time I pulled up to the B&B. My legs were leaden as I climbed the steps. I realised I was bone tired. My dad always says, "fatigue is a bad counsellor - sleep on it". That sounded like good advice to me right now. I made a cup of tea to take to bed with me. I was asleep before I even finished it.

•••

Samson had been interviewing Evelyn's granddaughter, Rhiannon whilst I was trawling through Evelyn's extensive library. He described her to me next morning in great detail and played me the recording of her interview. He set the scene for me by reported that, Rhiannon was a slight woman in her mid-twenties. She had a Pre-Raphaelite look to her - auburn hair, corkscrew ringlets and peachy skin, with freckles over her nose and blue eyes. A high-pitched voice with the same lilting Welsh accent as Emily. He told me it was particular to this part of South Wales. She had a very different look to her mother. She must take after her father, he reckoned.

I listened to Rhiannon on the recording …

"Nana was a very clever woman. She could always answer all my silly childhood questions that no one else could. Some of her answers have stayed with me to this day. I remember asking her one day why my tea got cold after a few minutes. Do you know what her answer was?"

Samson couldn't come up with the answer. "No"

Nana said, 'It's due to the second law of thermodynamics. The heat is dispersed to the other molecules in the room.'

"Wow! How old were you at that time?"

"Oh, about five! So many of these interesting snippets have stayed with me over all these years. She tried to get me interested in coding because she thought it would be a fantastic job for the future. But I couldn't drum up any interest." 'Not to worry,' she said 'examples of codes include musical notation, written languages, mathematical equations and computing languages.

I was amazed to hear nana declare one day "todays search engines, which work with such amazing power and speed, are algorithms. They are descended from the use of sophisticated logic, statistics and parallel processing methods that were used for Enigma code breaking". In the 1940's these were search engines for the keys to Hitler's Reich!"

"Hang on! Replay that sentence, John."

"I thought that might have an impact on you. Not your average ninety-year-old, was she? There's more than meets the eye to this old bird." Samson was positively glowing. He knew he'd hit upon something important. A significant nugget of information that Rhiannon had innocently volunteered.

Rhiannon's disembodied voice went on, "Another one of nana's pet phrases was 'algorithms are opinions embedded in code.' These pronouncements were lost on me, but Owen thought they were brilliant. The pair of them were on the same wavelength."

Samson's eyebrows rose, "I'm not quite sure what she's on about but it sounds impressive! No doubt you've got a handle on it."

"As it happens, I do have a good understanding of algorithms and how they are used in so many ways on the internet – Facebook and Google use them and dating websites use them to match up potential couples. On that score I could attest to the fact that algorithms could have disastrous consequences! But I didn't want to go into that just now, so I just shrugged it off. "I know the fundamentals, but I'm no expert, John. Well done getting Rhiannon to open up and chatter on about all this. The pieces of the puzzle are starting to come together."

Samson had hit the pause button, "The next bit of the interview is Rhiannon just rambling on, do you want me to fast forward it?"

"No, I want to listen to it all. It's good background information."

The recording resumed "Nana loved formulae and betting odds. But also liked to look through orchid catalogues. We would spend hours deciding which new hybrids to buy. She loved orchids and I paint watercolours of the Oncidium species in my collection. Some are rare and have exquisite scents. Did you know, the scent of an orchid can contain up to 200 different chemical components? Each has their own fragrance fingerprint. I'm aiming to produce a large folio book on the entire genus."

Samson's voice sounding bored and underwhelmed came back with, "I remember my mum wearing an orchid corsage to a wedding once." He obviously wanted to stop Rhiannon going off on that particular tangent, so he asked, "What other things did you have in common with your grandmother?"

"Oh, she was very knowledgeable about art. Well versed in the Old Masters, but also kept up with the modern artists. She liked Banksy! The only art piece we had to agree to disagree on, was that hideous mosaic she has on her wall. It's way too fussy for my liking. Ostentatious. Not to my taste at all. Nana said it was exquisite workmanship. I guess you would have to be incredibly skilled to cut such thin slivers of marble and travertine. I can appreciate the workmanship. But thankfully, I don't have to keep it on the wall. Aunt Hilde has been bequeathed it. I'm not sure it will be to her taste either. Apparently, it's valuable, so she could sell it and do something useful with the money.

Samson broke into her reverie, "Do you know where the mosaic came from?"

"I can vaguely remember Nana saying it was made by Danish craftsmen. I guess she thought it should one day go back to Hilde and its country of origin."

"Fair enough" was Samson's response.

"I've always loved nanna's house, from my very first memories as a toddler. The sound of the sea, the gardens, the dogs. It always gave me a sense of overwhelming wellbeing and safety. I'm so grateful to be inheriting it. I'll never leave!"

Rhiannon was in full flow, now, "Owen and nanna would huddle over the computers for hours talking about coding and such. Not really my thing. Science and computing, leaves me cold I'm afraid. But he thought it was great to have a granny that knew more than he did about all of that! When we went on holidays to Demark, Aunt Hilde was another old nerd! She was just as bad as nana. Morse code, cryptology, crypto currencies. They'd talk for hours about the latest developments. There must be something in the genes of that side of the family!"

Samson said he'd asked her how often they went to Denmark. She'd replied,

"Oh, most summers when we were kids. Mum came too. Dad only came twice then he said he'd seen it all. He would laugh at us and say – 'most of the kids at your school are flying off to Tenerife or Ibiza for their holidays and coming back with great tans. You lot are flying off to Copenhagen and coming back paler than when you left!' We did get teased by the kids at school, but we loved going there. Denmark is a small country but there's loads of interesting things to see - Viking long boats, the amber workshops, the Tivoli gardens ...There's even an old Zeppelin Museum just down the road from Hilde's house. She bought one of the hangars for a song just after the war and was going to convert it to an amber workshop, but she never got around to it. I'm not sure if she still owns it or sold it on. Once we went right before Christmas for the markets and ice skating. It was magic! When I was a teenager, I went with Estrid to the music festival near Tonder. It's one of the biggest in Europe, apparently. It was great. There were mostly Germans there. Estrid speaks German fluently and I've got a smattering, enough to get me by. Hilde can't stand them. She really hates them. I must say I was a bit shocked. It's not very PC, is it? Still, I suppose if you've had your husband killed by them and they've occupied your country, I guess it's understandable. I'm so glad our generation hasn't had to go through a war! I brought back some fab pieces of amber and had Emily mount them in silver. This necklace is one of them," she said.

Samson explained that she had showed him a pretty lozenge of amber with a tiny leaf preserved in it. Samson said he had to stop himself from yawning. Rhiannon was a big talker and she rambled on. I acknowledged that the girl could win a talking contest, but I reckoned there might just be something in this connection to Hilde, Denmark and the Evelyn's interest in amber. The three were obviously recurring themes in Evelyn's past life.

Samson's voice broke up Rhiannon's monologue.

"How do you get on with Emily?"

"We get on well. I'd like to support her in promoting and encouraging her art. She's pretty good and her business has just started to take off. Nana would have wanted me to keep her on at the house. She and I exchange ideas. It will be lovely to have a fellow artist around the place. She also enjoys gardening, which is one of my relaxations. She knows about the soil types in this area and what will grow well in this microclimate. I think we can co - exist quite happily at nana's house."

In a complete change of tack, Samson asked, "Do you have a partner?"

"Not as such. I have a long-term boyfriend, David, but he's away a lot with his work. He's employed by a renewable energy company. At the moment they are installing wind farms in India! He's been over there for three months, with nine months to go on his contract."

I could hear a rustle of papers as Samson brought the interview to an end. "'Okay, Rhiannon. Thanks for being so candid with me. You've really helped me flesh out the connection with your Danish side of the family. It seems Evelyn and Hilde were very close."

"Oh, definitely. Closer than most sisters, I would say."

I could hear Samson pushing back a chair and the recording finished.

After conducting interviews with Evelyn's family, with Emily and with everyone else she had dealings with, there was absolutely nothing in Evelyn's present that could account for her murder. But there were a few snippets that Rhiannon had volunteered that made me determined to do a thorough investigation into this woman's past connections to the Baltic. It was becoming clear that to get to the bottom of this case, we would have to delve deep into the past.

Maybe Owen could shed more light on things when he got back on Sunday. We'd make an appointment to see him first thing Monday morning. After all, it was obvious that he had been very close to his grandmother.

•••

We had the Sunday off, at least from interviewing witnesses and family members. I needed some time away from the case, not least to do some washing and catch up with personal emails and phone calls. Today, there were fists of clouds dotted across a blue sky. The air was a little cooler, but it was still about 68 degrees. White caps sprang up irregularly along the line of Oxwich Bay. As I got out of the car at the beachside car park, the day smelt of seaweed, dried grass and the faint waft of suntan lotion. Pictures of my childhood comics came back to me where the sun always shone, beaches were golden sand, and the sea was azure blue. Not for the first time, I thought about moving back to Wales. I was meeting Samson for lunch at the hotel, but I had arrived early so that I could sit on the beach for a while and soak up the sun. There were lots of family groups - the children poking around in the rock pools and in and out of the shallow water. A few brave hearts were on surf boards waiting for the perfect wave. Most of them had wetsuits on! Some of these people would be staying at the camp site but most would be day trippers from Swansea, Cardiff or the Rhondda valleys. I spread out a towel and laid back. My tank top and shorts would give my white skin just enough exposure. I hadn't bothered putting on my bathing suit as I knew the water wasn't warm enough to tempt me in for a swim. After the intensity of the murder investigation this sunny morning on the beach was like another world. I'd brought my latest edition of 'World Archaeology' to read but after a few minutes I felt my eyes closing and I started to doze in the warmth of the sun. Bliss! I woke with a start as a shadow blocked out the sun and I heard Samson's voice,

"I didn't know you had a tattoo, Nia."

I have a tattoo of an Athenian Owl on my upper right arm.

"Yeah, I love owls. I had it done years ago when I got back from a visit to Greece. I was a teenager and thought it was a good idea at the time. It doesn't see the light of day much! My dad refers to it as my epidermal epigram! I think he was shocked when I had it done. So many people have them nowadays. It's more unusual not to have one! Have you got any?"

He rolled up the sleave of his casual shirt to reveal a Celtic knot design spanning his left bicep.

"Oh, that's really nicely done."

"Yes, a tattooist in Narberth did it for me."

"Cool! Did you book for lunch?"

"Yes, for 1pm."

"Is it that time already?"

He glanced at his watch, "We've got five minutes to wander up there."

As we strolled up to the hotel, I noticed my shoulders and knees were a bit pink. I was parched and ravenous too. The hotel was crowded but we were given a great table overlooking the 11th Century church sitting just above the beach. What a charming outlook! They had a good menu on offer and the prices were so much cheaper than London. I ordered calamari salad and a glass of cider. Samson ordered the fish of the day and chips and half a Brains beer. The meals came with a basket of sour dough rolls, which were warm and delicious. By the time we ordered our coffees I was feeling totally revived. Samson was on good form, chatting freely about his latest girlfriend who he had met at the pub last weekend. He reckoned that at long last this could be the one. They shared a lot of interests and she lived near him on a farm just outside Carmarthen. He seemed genuinely smitten.

"How about you Nia? You're bit of a dark horse. You never mention any partners."

"I'm taking a break for a while. I've been single for over three years and to be honest, I'm enjoying my own space. I'm not someone that needs to be in a relationship."

"Fair enough."

He didn't push me for any further details of my last break up. Which was a relief. I didn't want to spoil the good vibes of today! It was gone 3pm when we paid the bill and ambled out of the restaurant. Samson headed west and I headed east, back to my temporary digs. I realised that this was the most relaxed I'd been for yonks. All was well with the world, as I played Amy Winehouse, 'Back to Black' loudly on my drive back to my accommodation. After ironing a few items of clothes for the week ahead, I had a leisurely bath and slapped on plenty of Aloe Vera moisturiser, to the areas that had caught the sun. I was hoping my shoulders wouldn't peel. I resisted the temptation to go through the electronic files of the case, instead watching 'Strictly Ballroom' on T.V. I could see why everybody was hooked on it. It definitely gave you the feel-good factor. I was in bed by ten o'clock and asleep within minutes. I awoke to the sound of cuckoos. It was 7.30 am. I leapt out of bed feeling fantastically alive and energetic. I was confident that the coming week would bring a breakthrough in the case. It had to!

• • •

One of the first calls I got on Monday morning was from the local constabulary. PC Samuel Morgan informed me that last night a call had come in from a group of local teenagers who had a bonfire on the beach at Brandy cove. One of them had gone for a pee close into the cliff face and found an old rifle with notches carved into the wooden stock and Greek writing on it. Evelyn's assassin obviously hadn't known when he threw the rifle over the cliff that at low tide a small sandy beach would appear at Brandy Cove. This was invaluable to our case, not just because we now had the murder weapon but because it also told us that the assassin had been on foot and moving eastbound towards Mumbles and Swansea. We could now check CCTV at the car parks and bus and train stations in these two areas. I knew this must be our murder weapon. The youngsters had probably mistakenly identified the Cyrillic letters as Greek instead of Russian. An easy thing to do if you're not familiar with those languages. Samson punched the air and yelled, "Yes!" We both knew how important a find this was. We could only imagine how delighted Tristram Davies would be! He'd be chomping at the bit to examine and photograph the rifle, looking for identifying marks and modifications. He'd been so emphatic about the make of the weapon that I hoped for his sake, it was indeed a Mosin rifle! "Now they've found the weapon we'll drop in to see Tristram again this afternoon and see what more he can tell us. I'm sure it will be riveting!"

●●●

I decided I would revisit Sian alone. I got the feeling she was holding something back from us and that she might be more forthcoming if Samson wasn't in attendance. I like to interact one-on-one, in a casual manner when I feel it will yield better results than a more formal style of interview. I felt we had established some common ground, some rapport once we had got talking about archaeology and artefacts. All that stuff bored Samson. Sian had initially appeared aloof at least self-contained. But as I well know, appearance is not reality. I had a strong feeling that she might be masking a rich inner landscape, full of drama and secrets.

Nowadays I find so many people impatient to talk. Sian didn't strike me as one of them! Here was someone with an inner quietness, I suspected. I felt strongly that we had to get Sian firmly on board as an ally if we were to get anywhere with this case. It wouldn't be too onerous a task for me to try.

As I approached her front door, I felt unusually nervous. It was disconcerting as I am a self-confident person. I knocked and waited. I heard steps descending the stairs inside. The door swung open, and Sian was beckoning me in. I felt momentarily frozen to the spot. There is a beauty that can only be described as that of the mind's migration to the face, the transfiguring beauty of exceptional intelligence. Sian had it. I wondered if, in life her mother had had it too. I was taken slightly aback by her effect on me. But I regained my professional composure very quickly.

I followed her down the hallway to the kitchen at the back of the house. It was filled with the smell of fresh coffee and warm pastries.

"I'm having a late breakfast. Would you like some coffee? Help yourself to croissants."

I sat on one of the bar stools pulled up to the kitchen counter. Sian busied herself with pouring two steaming mugs of coffee then offered me an oval platter with a selection of almond croissant and Danish pastries. A woman after my own heart! Almond croissant are my absolute favourite! I was tempted to take two but restrained myself to one. For a few minutes we just sat and enjoyed the delicious pastries and the rich, mellow coffee. Sian told me that the local bakery had recently changed hands and was now owned by a French guy. The village bakery had never been so popular. His baguettes, madeleines and lemon tarts were to die for, according to Sian. This was another side of her that Samson and I had not seen on our first meeting. She seemed positively animated this morning, with little trace of the reserve that I had noted at our first meeting. A complex woman indeed.

"Since we spoke to you last, we've had a chat with your mum's bridge partner, so we know how often she played and what a brilliant a player she was. Emily has told us about your mum's daily routine, but could you elaborate on her work before GCHQ any other interests or hobbies she had. I've spent some time in her home library and there seems to be a few common themes that keep surfacing. For example, I spotted a lot of clippings of Gareth Jones's articles. Tell me what you can about him."

"Mum went to Aberystwyth often. Her uncle, Gareth was there in the early 1930's apparently. He was a journalist. Claim to fame is he worked for Lloyd George. 'I can't say that Lloyd George knew my father, but Lloyd

George knew my uncle', mum would joke. Mum admired Gareth. He was a great linguist and encouraged her to go to Cambridge. He was a graduate of Trinity College himself. Mum was invited to Aberystwyth University in May 2006, to attend the unveiling of a plaque dedicated to Gareth's memory. It was an extraordinary thing, written in three languages - English, Welsh and Ukrainian. It's on the wall in the Old College at the University. The Ukrainian Ambassador, Ihor Kharchenko, shook hands with mum and described Gareth as an "unsung hero of Ukraine". It was quite a moving event. Growing up, I had no clue about any of that. There was a lot of interest generated at that time. In November 2008, Jones and fellow Holodomor journalist Malcolm Muggeridge were posthumously awarded the Ukrainian Order of Merit at a ceremony in Westminster Central Hall, for their exceptional service to the country and its people. Mum went up to London for that event. The following year, Gareth's diaries recording the man-made genocide went on display for the first time in the Wren Library of Trinity College, Cambridge."

"Okay, I don't know much about this period of Ukrainian history, but it seems that Gareth Jones was a bit of an expert. Would that be fair to say?"

"Yes, absolutely! On 17th August 1935, The Times reported that the Chinese authorities had found Gareth's body the previous day with three bullet wounds. The authorities believed that he had been killed on 12th August, the day before his 30th birthday. There was a suspicion that his murder had been engineered by the Soviet NKVD, as revenge for the embarrassment he had caused the Soviet regime."

I nearly choked on my croissant! Here at last was something very unusual. Was this history repeating itself? What are the odds of two British citizens from the same family being murdered by the Soviet NKVD? Surely it was too much of a coincidence to totally dismiss it, as far-fetched as it seemed!

My mind was turning over all sorts of scenarios. I needed to know more about Evelyn's extended family. "What can you tell us about the rest of your mother's family?"

"Well, on the Welsh side - her father was David Jones. Grandad and his brother, my great uncle Gareth were brought up in Barry, near Cardiff. Their father was a Major in the army. Grandad and his brother both died young, so

I can't tell you much about them, I'm afraid. On the maternal side, they came from Denmark originally. Grandma Else lived with us until she died in 1965. She was a quiet, placid woman. She always encouraged mum in her career. It was unusual for women to be involved in industry in those days. Mum said that her dad had always prodded her to "come out of her shell" but her mother defended her and said, "she was a deep thinker" and that was valued in the Scandinavian tradition. I remember grandma Else saying mum was a quiet person in what was becoming a loudmouth world. Mum was a widow, and she used her mathematics skills to get a job on the early prototype computers and later went to work for the government as a civil servant at GCHQ. "

"Do you know anything about her work at GCHQ?"

"Not a thing. It was always hush hush, cloak and dagger stuff."

"Okay that's something I need to look at more closely, considering the tenuous Russian connection that we now know about. Your mother has a lot of publications devoted to amber. Whenever I think of amber the Baltic comes to mind. What can you tell me about Hilde and the Danish family connection?"

"Mum was very close to Hilde. The pair of them were fascinated by amber. We visited Denmark regularly when I was a child, and we took my kids on holiday there several times. Hilde taught us how to spot amber on the beaches. Estrid, Hilde's daughter collected amber objects. She had some heirloom pieces that had been handed down from Hilde's side of the family. Hilde is another intellectual. Another mathematician. Her and mum had a lot in common. "

"You said your mum was writing her memoirs. What were her source materials? Her diaries? Recordings? I would like to look through any materials she kept as they might give us some ideas as to a possible motive for her murder. If those diaries are in the safe, they may be able to give us some pointers in the right direction."

I noticed that she was watching me closely as I sipped my coffee, clearly weighing something in her mind. As Sian reached for another Danish pastry the sunlight flickered on her earrings. They flashed with a pink brilliance. I had to admire them, "I like your earrings. They're absolute sparklers!"

"Mum gave me this pair of studs for my 40th birthday. They are real Argyle diamonds. Mum didn't like the clear diamonds. 'They have no soul', she would say. The Argyle mine in Western Australia, is famous for these pink diamonds. Not that I'd ever heard of them until mum gave me these!"

"They really are a vivid pink!

"Yeah, apparently with the Argyle diamonds, unlike the normal diamonds it's the colour saturation, not the clarity, that makes them more valuable."

"Well, in that case yours must be worth a pretty penny."

"I'm not bothered about how much they're worth, I just love them because mum gave them to me. She told me they have this unique colour because of the natural radiation from the surrounding rock layers of the Argyle Ore. Isn't that amazing!"

Amazing indeed. I could fully appreciate their fascination. I have a ring made from yellow Argyle diamonds, myself as coincidence would have it! I thought I'd better get back on topic.

"What else can you tell me about your mum's war time experiences and anything you can tell me about her time in Manchester, before GCHQ? You said when we first interviewed you that you felt you owed it to your mum to get her the respect and dignity that she deserved. Is that because you feel she hadn't received that during her life?"

"Yes, the institutions and the State totally undervalued women's contributions to the war effort and she got virtually no pension from them. Her male colleagues came away with the recognition and the monetary recompense. Even at Manchester, although times were starting to change, she didn't get a mention when the first Ferranti computer was unveiled. It might sound a bit sentimental, but I won't rest until mum and all the other women get their proper place in history recorded for posterity."

"That sounds fair enough to me. It's been hard enough for me, getting acceptance in the police force even today. I can only imagine how bad it was back in your mum's day!" I noticed your mother has a lot of Russian language books and periodically and books by Marx and Engels. Did she have strong political views?"

Sian considered this question whilst she munched on her Danish pastry.

"Well mum spoke Russian, German and French fluently. But as far as having strong political views, I certainly wasn't aware of any. I know mum voted labour in the election of July 1945. She told me on many occasions that she had lost respect for Churchill by then.

"Did she elaborate?"

"She held Churchill personally responsible for my granddad's death."

"How come?"

"I don't know if this is absolutely true, but she told me that using Enigma decrypts, Churchill knew that the bombing of Coventry, by the Luftwaffe was imminent. But in order to keep the Germans in the dark about the breaking of Enigma, Churchill did nothing and let the bombing go on un- announced. The people of Coventry in effect were the price paid to protect the Enigma secret. Her father died in that air raid. She said she could never forgive Churchill for that. Her mother only survived because she had gone down to Wales to help her in-laws on the farm that weekend. Her father had gone to church every Sunday - Church of England. Mum said by the end of the war she had seen too much suffering to believe in God. If people asked her if she had faith, she would say, "I have faith in mathematics, faith in logic, faith in nature and faith in the trajectory of the stars! Religions - forget it!"

Mum had been a huge fan of Churchill early in the war. She had met him in person on a number of occasions, but things had come to light whilst she was at Bletchley that had shocked her and had shown the ruthlessness of the top brass. Hut 6 and Hut 3 were mum's world for months at a time. Hut 6 was where the ciphers of the German Army and Luftwaffe were broken. Hut 3 was where the decrypts were sent for translation and onward dispatch to the next step of the process. At Bletchley, for the first time a cipher made by a machine was being broken by a machine - the huge bombes. This is the secret that the German's never got to discover. The secret that had to be kept at any cost. Even the cost of British civilian lives. Mum could never come to grips with that."

I was gobsmacked. "Hang on a minute are you saying your mum was a code breaker with Alan Turing at Bletchley Park?" This revelation made the hairs on the back of my arms stand up. Here at last was a glimmer of a past that might hold a clue to this frustrating case! But how? It was all so long ago. Surely people don't hold grudges for over 60 years. Suddenly the connection between Cambridge in the 1930s and the famous Soviet spies recruited there flashed through my mind. Could Evelyn have been a British or Soviet spy or even a double agent? I dismissed it as ridiculous. I've read too many John Le Carre books!

Sian said, "I knew nothing about mum's involvement until a recorded delivery package arrived. That was sometime in 2009 or 2010, I can't remember the exact date. I was there when she ripped it open and out fell a certificate and a letter from the Prime Minister - David Cameron. Inside was a blue box which contained a gold brooch. Mum was bemused and tried to make light of it, but she couldn't hide it from me any longer. I was amazed. Then it all came out - about her wartime work. I think she found it cathartic to finally unburden herself. I remember we were up until past midnight. I listened entranced as she told me all about it. How they recruited her from Cambridge University. How she figured out cribs and broke German codes. The eccentric characters she worked with. Only after all those years, did the scale and depth of the wartime cryptanalysis at Bletchley Park begin to leak out. When the film 'The Imitation Game' came out with Benedict Cumberbatch starring as Alan Turing, we all went to see it together. Mum said it was Hollywood's glamourized version of events. Benedict Cumberbatch was much better looking than Alan Turing, she announced! It didn't portray the daily grind and the terrible conditions they worked under. And it only skated over the terrible way the women code breakers were treated, at the time. Mum said that 'Science can absorb and overtake individuals.' She had been happy to be a part of the anonymising culture at the time - never trying to make a name for herself, although at times being frustrated for not being taken seriously by many of the Profs!"

"Wow, you must be so proud of her! "

"Yes, after the shock wore off, I thought it was brilliant, what she had done. I always knew she was very smart and very unconventional, but I'd never dreamed that she had the code breaking in her past. She told me that all of them had signed the Official Secrets Act back in 1940 and every one of the women kept their secret. Apparently, there were thousands of women employed in various capacities at Bletchley and other English country houses involved in code breaking and listening to wartime enemy transmissions. Mum and a few of the other women mathematicians were evidently instrumental in breaking Enigma and a few other lesser-known ciphers. I remember mum getting airmail letters from women in France, Germany, Holland and the USA that she still kept in contact with. At the time, it was an unusual occurrence to get letters from all over the World and as a child, I was fascinated by the stamps on the envelopes. I asked a multitude of questions. But she fobbed me off by saying they were just pen pals! With hindsight they were probably all involved in wartime covert operations."

I was frantically scribbling notes. My mind was working overtime. Evelyn had been one of the code breakers! How had this fact not come out at our first meeting? Could Evelyn's disillusionment with Churchill have pushed her towards the Russians after the war? Stranger things have prompted people to switch sides. With the Alan Turing connection and the Cambridge connection cogs started falling into place in my mind. I calmed my thoughts and carried on, "Can you tell me more about Moira?"

She paused and took a swig of her coffee. "Are you familiar with the Carl Jung quote: 'The meeting of two personalities is like the contact of two chemical substances; if there is any reaction, both are transformed?' Mum would often quote that in relation to Moira. She said that's exactly what happened when they first met. They just clicked."

Sian's words came fast now. It was as if she was feeling a definite relief at being able to pour out her story to a sympathetic listener. It was a reaction that I had witnessed many times before and I encouraged her by being extremely attentive.

"How did your mum and Moira meet?"

"They were introduced by a woman called Cicely Popplewell. Apparently, she was a brilliant woman who worked with Alan Turing at the time. Mum was a mathematics graduate and one of the lead researchers on the first computer - at least that's her claim to fame. Moira was a post graduate student who was recruited to help with the computer programs. If we got a hot summer, I remember both of them saying, ' that's nothing, you should have seen us in the sweltering summer of 1950. We were working on the Ferranti computer prototype in stifling rooms at Manchester University. There were no fans let alone air conditioning in those days! It was weeks of hellish conditions, but we all battled on until we had the project completed.' They shared an office in the Victorian fortress - that's what they called the university! Mum's knowledge of probability and statistics which she had used well to help break the Enigma code, came in handy for early computing - apparently."

"So, Moira wasn't a code breaker?"

"No, she was a fair bit younger than mum. She was only involved in the computer developments after the war. There weren't many women involved in computing back then."

"Was your father a codebreaker too? Is he still alive?"

"No, he died when I was only three - pancreatic cancer. I have only a vague memory of a thin man in bed all the time. I know mum and dad were at GCHQ together but I'm not sure if he was at Bletchley too. About a year ago, mum started writing her memoirs. I introduced her to a ghost writer, who was helping with the structure and editing. But mum insisted that she finish the work herself. She was adamant, that although she was no longer confined by the Official Secrets Act, she did not want her memoirs published until 5 years after her death! She could be stubborn!"

"Do you have the name and address of the ghost writer? We'll need to talk to them."

"Oh yes, Jennifer Barnes, she's a published author and is well known in literary circles. I'd met her a few times at the Hay on Wye book festival. She lives in Lisvane, Cardiff. I'll give you her business card." She opened a roll top desk and produced a business card with Jennifer's details embossed on the front.

"Thanks that's great. I really appreciate you sharing some of this more personal stuff about your mother with me. I've been spending time looking through her office and library and I feel I'm getting to know her a bit more. You've just filled in a few gaps. It really does help me. I'm not exactly conventional in my methods, I know, but I do seem to get results."

"I like non-conventional people. Let's hope your methods find mum's killer."

"Obviously I can't make any guarantees Sian, but I'll do everything in my power to bring your mum's killer to justice."

She seemed content with that. As I walked to the door, I felt a major piece of the puzzle had been put into place. Bletchley Park, Cambridge University, The Ukraine connection… I had to find the interplay of threads that had resulted in Evelyn's murder.

Outside it was a warm sunny afternoon. It seemed that I had emerged into the present after being drawn back into the past for the last two hours. I couldn't wait to tell Samson about the code breaking connection. This had to be a game changer, surely.

• • •

As soon as I got back to the main road, I pulled over and left a message for Samson and made a call to Jennifer Barnes. I asked if there was any way she could see me this afternoon. She could, so I headed for the M4 East, towards Cardiff. Once I got to the outskirts of the Welsh capital, I left the M4 and crossed over the motorway bridge and past the Ty Mawr Inn, continuing along the length of Graig Road. I was now in the heart of the leafy north Cardiff suburb of Lisvane. When I came to the address scribbled on my note pad, there was an intercom set into the main entrance gates. I announced who I was, and I was buzzed through. The gates swung open to reveal a sloping driveway through gardens and grounds, I estimated to be a couple of acres. As I drove up the winding driveway I took in the landscaped formal gardens with a wealth of evergreen shrubs and plants, leading the eye to the adjoining paddocks beyond. I stopped in front of a double garage. Jennifer Barnes's house was a handsome, beautifully presented double fronted, executive detached residence. She must have had some success as a writer! These houses didn't come cheap!

As I turned the engine off a woman dressing in jeans and muddy wellington boots came to greet me. She was nothing like how I had imagined her. She was younger than I expected and had a friendly attitude. After briefly speaking with her on the phone, I had imagined an older and much more formal woman. There you go, you can't rely on preconceived ideas about people!

"Hi, you must be Nia. Please excuse my grotty clothes, I've been doing some pruning."

"You've got a beautiful garden. Do you manage all this yourself?"

"No, I must admit I have a gardener that comes in once a month to do the more strenuous tasks. Anyway, come in."

She pulled off her boots and left them at the front door. We entered through a spacious and welcoming hallway. There was a central oak staircase and banister with a galleried landing. Off to the right was the main lounge room. It was a vast room featuring a huge contemporary stone fireplace with a mantle and matching hearth. She ushered me to a couple of two-seater sofas placed in front of expansive windows that perfectly showed off superb far-reaching views over southern Glamorgan - from the Severn Bridge to the East and to St Hilary, near Cowbridge to the West.

"What a fantastic view!" I was quite envious.

She looked pleased with my reaction. "Yes, as soon as I got my first successful book deal, I started looking for property around here. I'm glad I got in when I did. They've gone up through the roof, recently! Can I get you a tea? I don't drink coffee, but I have all sorts of herbal teas. I'm going to have a Fennel and Turmeric. What do you fancy?"

I'm not a lover of herbal teas but I could cope with mint tea, so that's what I requested.

"Okay, I'll just be a minute" and off she went to prepare the teas. I could hear cabinet doors opening and shutting. No doubt her kitchen would resemble a set from MasterChef, judging by the rest of the house. She handed me what looked like a Clarice Cliff art deco cup filled to the brim with my mint tea. "Cheers!" It was surprisingly refreshing. Once she was seated, I made a start,

"As I told you on the phone, I'm investigating Evelyn's death. I'm trying to find out about her past and Sian told me that you were collaborating with Evelyn to write her biography or her memoirs. Is that right?"

"Yes, Evelyn told me she wanted to write her memoirs because as she said 'as I get closer to being something of the past, the past feels closer to me! Recently my war time past has been very vivid in my memory. I'd like it written down honestly for posterity. It may be very interesting indeed in certain circles!' Well that pitch got me hooked straight away. She made it sound as if she had some real revelations involving prominent figures of the time. War time memoirs always sell well in the UK. It was all going swimmingly well, then suddenly Evelyn decided she wanted to put it on ice."

"When was that?"

"It was a few months before her death. She just said she had decided to shelve it for a while. She didn't say why. Maybe the memories it was bringing up were too painful. As I said, I was very frustrated by the delay. I was looking forward to writing with her. But you couldn't be mad at someone like Evelyn, she was a real dear. I was horrified to read about her murder in the' Western Mail'. I also saw the latest article about the Russian rifle. Wow that's sensational stuff!"

"That's all in the public domain, so we can talk about that quite freely. Is there anything you can remember from your interviews with Evelyn that could point to a Russian connection? As I'm still struggling to find a clear motive for her murder."

"I suppose it's possible that some of her escapades from the war time ruffled some feathers, but I can't see how it would lead to murder! She was one of a kind. They don't make them like that anymore! To be a strongly original person takes a great deal of self-confidence and Evelyn was certainly an original. I had lined up a publisher. The women code breakers are very topical and highly sellable right now. Some of the people she rubbed shoulders within the war were amazing – Winston Churchill, Alan Turing, Violette Szabo, Cicely Popplewell, Dilly Knox and the likes. And then her stint on the first computer project. Her story could be made into a compelling book."

"I'd like to look at the material you have."

"Sure. I recorded sessions. By all means, you can listen to them all. Most are on CD Rom."

This was a stroke of luck that I hadn't anticipated. "That's great. It will be helpful to hear the woman herself, speaking about her experiences and for me to get an idea of her philosophy and ideologies."

"I haven't got any other appointments today, so if you want to, we can get started now."

"Brilliant. No time like the present as they say."

"The recordings are a mixture between question-and-answer sessions and readings from her diaries. Come through to my office and we'll get cracking."

I followed her to the back of the house, and she opened the door onto a room I would have given my high teeth for. It was a library in the style of an exclusive man's club - wooden bookshelves from floor to ceiling on three side, leather arm-chairs in the chesterfield style, a huge open fireplace and banker's lamps dotted around on antique side tables. Her computer was sat on a fantastic desk with a leather top that could have been a prop straight from an episode of Sherlock Holmes. My mouth must have dropped open whilst I scanned the room.

"Wow, I love this room" I blurted out.

"I do too. This is where I spend the majority of my time. The atmosphere in here is conducive to productive working."

"I can imagine. It's like being cosseted away from the outside world."

She laughed. "Yeah, I suppose it is. You should see it when the fire's blaz-ing. It's my secret hideaway." We moved across to the imposing desk. She pulled over one of the leather armchairs for me. We could both sit comfort-ably at her desk without being cramped. She turned on her laptop and fed in the first CD. I sat back in my comfy armchair to listen to Evelyn Jones.

•••

The title came up on the screen. 'Evelyn Jones in a question and answers session with Jennifer Barnes.' Jennifer opened the session by asking Evelyn why she wanted to write her memoirs after so many years.

"I'd like some resolution of the past and a lasting memorial to all the women who did such diligent work in order to speed up the end of the war. So often, loose ends are only ever tied up in books. It's no use sitting down to relate one's memoirs and then trying to fudge them or making so many omissions that they become worthless. I am prepared to be utterly truth-ful. At my age, it's important that the record be set straight. Obviously, there are people that would prefer these memoirs not be written and some who would be anxious to prevent their publication. The half-truths I have lived with over the decades. I just want to put the record straight at last."

An intriguing statement. Now I just wanted to get to fast forward to see what she revealed!

Jennifer continued by asking Evelyn to start with her upbringing and teenage years prior to the war.

Evelyn's voice was not how I had imagined it. For some reason I had expected it to be light and higher. In fact, it was husky and magnetic with no trace of a Welsh accent. I sat enthralled as she started to recite her life story:

"I was born on 22nd August 1923 in Hull, England. My parents were Else and Alfred Jones. I was an only child. I attended Sherbrook Private Girls School at Greaves Hall in Lancashire. The mansion was surrounded by sculptured lawns, gardens with ornamental trees and flowering shrubs. Sadly, the school was closed in 1938. I was very happy there. I was a top student and went on to study the Mathematical Tripos at the University of Cambridge. Maths wasn't considered a very ladylike subject at the time! Luckily my parents didn't object. I worked with statistics in the form of punched cards, and I also took summer classes in Sanskrit, Russian, Greek, and German. I became an expert in the Brunsviga desk calculator. That was high tech back then! I graduated from Girton College. Girton was established in 1869 by Emily Davies and Barbara Bodichon as the first women's college in Cambridge. In 1948, it was granted full college status by the university."

Evelyn went on to proudly announce that "Among Girton's notable alumni are Queen Margrethe II of Denmark, the comedian Sandi Toksvig and the economist Joan Robinson."

Jennifer's voice interjected at this point. "Tell me more about your university years. Were you friends with any of the famous spies – Kim Philby, Anthony Blunt or Guy Burgess?

"I can't say I was friends with any of them. I knew of them. I was quite taken with the writings of Karl Marx and Engels at University and many of the young men there were big supporters of Socialism. Like a lot of students, I had been seduced and moved by the lofty ideas of "from each according to his ability, to each according to his need" that Marx and Engels had written about. But my uncle Gareth had warned me about Stalin. He wrote articles for 'The Times' about the shocking conditions and the mass deaths caused by 'the Holodor' - a massive famine in the Ukraine in 1932. It was hushed up by Stalin and my uncle died in very suspicious circumstances in China. My dad believed it was Soviet agents that murdered him. He was sure it was members of the Cheka - in later incarnations the NKVD or as we know it the KGB."

Jennifer raised her eyebrows, "Its intriguing material, isn't it?" I nodded waiting for Evelyn to say more.

"After six years of war and having seen the very worst of human behaviours played out, I realized that sadly, to put Marx's theory into practice was in contradiction with human nature. From 1945 onwards I saw Joseph Stalin working rapidly to transform the Soviet Union into a depraved deformation of utopia. A monster was emerging who was just as bad as Hitler! The Russian and the East German States were travesties."

Any vague idea I had had about Evelyn being a spy for the Soviets was no longer looking plausible. She could feasibly have been a double agent, though. What was it she knew that could have got her murdered? This was all very interesting. I couldn't wait for the next instalment.

Jennifer said "I'd forgotten what a good storyteller Evelyn was. I still can't believe I won't see her again." Jennifer prompted Evelyn "What happened once you left Cambridge?"

"In 1937, when the tensions in Europe and Asia were becoming apparent, the Chief of MI6, Admiral Hugh Sinclair wanted to expand his staff numbers. The recruits were to be 'men of the professor type', primarily drawn from Oxford and Cambridge universities. It soon became apparent that many more staff were needed. So, the heads of Bletchley Park next looked for women who were linguists, mathematicians and even crossword experts. I was all of these," said Evelyn.

I detected a slightly ironic note to her voice.

"They recruited me straight from university in 1940. I was just seventeen! When I was a teenager, I felt trapped in a maze of strict expectations. Women at the time were expected to display a passivity and this was often paired with a persistent underestimating of our own talents. I saw this reflected in so many other young women in the cryptography huts. Such a feminine trait and so undermining to our own self-worth! I found Bletchley liberating. I felt I was making a valuable contribution to the war effort. For the first time I felt I had purpose in life. It was empowering!"

Evelyn took a short pause and I heard her take a sip of a drink. She continued, "All ciphers are broken by applying three tools - mathematics, the laws of frequency and trial-and -error. The prime mover, of course is patience! There were a lot of Debs at Bletchley, who mostly did administrative work but there were also some amazingly smart women. Cicely Popplewell was one of them. Joan Clarke another. Do you know that Cicely went on to teach the first ever programming class in Argentina at the University of Buenos Aires in 1961?"

Evelyn then skipped over her time at Bletchley Park and went on to tell of how in 1949 she had joined Alan Turing in the Computer Machine Learning department at the University of Manchester to help with the programming of a prototype for Ferranti. It was here, she recalled, that they resumed their highly successful Bridge playing partnership.

She recalled "32 different combinations of 0's and 1's in five row tele printer tape had become the language of our Manchester machine. I saw the bloody stuff in my dreams! Alan and I were increasingly arguing about convenience of use. He assumed too much of the user. I probably assumed too little. He referred to these as fussy little matters. But I believed a user-friendly machine was absolutely essential if it was ever to become mainstream."

I remarked to Jennifer, "Wow, what a prophetic statement that was! Many decades later, Bill Gates made himself a billionaire off the back of that insight!"

Evelyn carried on, "By October 1949 the machine was ready for Ferranti to manufacture. My job was almost done. My final task was to work with Alan on input/output routines and mathematical functions. In collaboration, we designed the programming language for the Ferranti Mark 1."

It was obvious from her voice, that Evelyn was very proud of her work on this project.

Jennifer coaxed more information about Alan Turing out of her, "You must have been shocked when Alan committed suicide?"

"Secret State purposes are seamlessly woven into scientific institutions. Individuals often pay the price if they don't fit in. Alan definitely paid the ultimate price. Alan's demand for honesty flew in the face of State security, you see. There was a 'don't ask, don't tell' mentality prevalent at the time, but Alan believed he shouldn't have to hide his homosexuality. It was the tectonic forces of State security and politics that got him in the end. By 1950 Alan was being treated as an un-person. The Trotsky of the computer revolution, if you like. The bigots at the top of the security forces at the time thought his homosexuality would compromise security. Alan was the last person that would ever have divulged any State secrets! His treatment was appalling. I firmly believe that the legacy of Alan's work will last forever in quantum cryptography and quantum computing. I visited him at his home in Wilmslow in early 1954. He was a broken man, but I had no idea that he would take his own life in June of that year."

Evelyn's voice tailed off and I could imagine her thinking back to when she heard the news of Alan's suicide on 7th June 1954.

In an obvious attempt to draw Evelyn out of her sombre mood and to re-engage with her war time work, Jennifer commented, "You must have witnessed so many historic events playing out during your time at Bletchley."

"Oh yes indeed, many of the women and the events we witnessed, shaped me into the person I became. A very different one to the innocent, naive girl I was before going to work at BP. She chuckled, "and I don't mean the oil company! The terrible events of that war are smoothed and blurred by time. Many of my friends at BP were convinced that our lives were part of God's plan - all fate. I never thought that. I lost any religious belief I had during the war. By mid May 1940, messages were coming through that the Germans had broken through the Ardennes. There were reports of columns of German tanks heading N.W towards the English Channel. By June the Boche had taken Paris. We really thought we would be invaded next. But we were too busy decoding German transmissions to have time to get scared! I'll never forget the 27th of May 1941- The Bismarck was attacked and sunk! We had been following its position for days thanks to a nifty bit of deciphering by Joan Clarke. The Royal Navy would never have found Bismarck, without her work at BP. It was a significant victory made possible by us women. It made all the hard work and everyday hardships worthwhile.

Jennifer encouraged her to share more of her wartime experiences, "Didn't you tell me that you met Violette Szabo?"

Evelyn's tone sounded wistful, "Oh, Violette, what a live wire, she was. In November that year, I was attending a course at Beaulieu, Hampshire, to brush up my skills in cryptography. I met her there. Of course, I only knew her then as Violette from London. She was cheeky and had a strong, cockney accent. We had great fun together. Lots of laughs. On our weekend off we went into London to visit her mother and her little daughter. We went out for a night on the town. On the way back we were caught in an air raid. Violette led me down into Aldwych Tube Station, which was partly fitted out as an air raid shelter. She told me in confidence that the tunnels between Aldwych and Holborn were being used to store precious items from the British Museum, including the Elgin Marbles! She knew so many fascinating snippets of information. Her job was very hush hush. At the time I had no idea what she was really doing. I figured out that she worked for SOE. It was a standing joke in the war that "SOE" stood for "Stately 'Omes of England", after the large number of country houses and estates it requisitioned and used. Violette and I had arranged to meet up at Christmas. I never saw her again!"

Her voice caught and she took a few gulps before resuming, "It was years later when I discovered what a heroine she was. She was one of the women the Nazi's executed as a British spy." She virtually spat out her next words, "The Nazis were a contagion of violent, dangerous ultra-nationalism. How anybody could have been taken in by that ranting psychopath, I don't know!" She carried on in an exasperated tone "Violette had smuggled out a little black book from the death camp - the entry for April 20th, 1942, lists 300 names, people recorded as having died at precise two-minute intervals. They were all shot in honour of Hitler's 53rd birthday! The lunatic, horror of it all! Senseless deaths all to pander to an egotistical madman! It's a poignant thing to see a woman's name written in a black exercise book - possibly her only epitaph. The top brass in the Nazi regime were a group of despicable figures. They are etched into my memory and the very mention of their names brings the senseless suffering of the war back to me as if it were yesterday. Goebbels, Goering, Heydrich, Himmler, Hess and Bormann. All of them had their specific remit of horrors. All of them were fanatics of the regime with its anti-Semitic, racist, xenophobic and totalitarian values."

She wasn't mincing her words here. I picked up a deep-seated hatred coming through.

Jennifer's voice again, "It must have been hard for you to cope with death at such a young age."

"Looking back on it, yes. But, at the time we were all caught up in the war effort and you didn't get time to grieve. My father was killed in the bombing of Coventry. I wasn't even able to go to his funeral. Life had been so debased by the glorification of death in war. It's easy to see that with hindsight. At the time, you just had to carry on, regardless. That was the only way to survive."

Evelyn's voice tailed off. Jennifer filled the silence, "I think it might be a good time to stop for today."

I shook my head, "Our generation has no idea what hardships people went through in the war. Can you imagine being bombed, having your father killed and friends disappear never to be seen again?"

"Quite frankly no, I can't imagine it. Thank God we've never had to live through a war."

Jennifer loaded a new CD into the player. When the recording resumed it was Jennifer's voice that kicked off the session, "Okay, Evelyn can you pick up the threads from where we left off."

"Well after my father's death, I just lost myself in my work. We were cracking virtually all the German communications. Reason and scientific methods were the heroes of the hour. After a while we really started to make a huge difference in the course of the war, so it was easy to put all my efforts into something so worthwhile. Each day had a pattern. We worked damned hard and in freezing, damp conditions a lot of the time. One big breakthrough came in December 1941. My friend Mavis deciphered a message between Belgrade and Berlin. This enabled Dilly Knox and his team to work out the wiring of the Abwehr Enigma machine. The Germans thought it unbreakable - ha-ha! An American woman that I corresponded with after the war, Genevieve Grotjan deciphered KGB cables in 1944. Her work uncloaked a host of KGB activities and espionage aimed at the U.S. atomic program. So many women did amazing things back then. Virtually none of them are famous. We just did our duty and carried on."

Did I pick up resentment in Evelyn's voice? She was now in full flow,

"Of course, I recall very vividly that late on the 1st of May 1945 we picked up an announcement on the German wireless that Hitler had died at his command post in Berlin and that he had appointed Admiral Doenitz to succeed him. The place went wild! There were a few stinking hangovers the next morning! It was a tense time for my cousin in Denmark. Montgomery and the 21st Army, with the Rhine crossing behind them, were pushing hard towards the Baltic. As they moved Eastward, Churchill and Eisenhower were anxious that Monty might not beat the Russians from getting into Schleswig - Holstein and then occupying Denmark. Hilde was convinced that they would end up behind Russian lines. Thank goodness we received a message on the evening of May 4th at 18.30 hrs that Monty had signed the instrument of surrender of all German armed forces in Holland, NW Germany and in Denmark. Once the declaration came into force, a virtual stampede by German soldiers and civilians ensued. They tried desperately to get to the American or British Zones, where they believed they would be treated decently. They were terrified of falling into the hands of the Ivan's." Suddenly Evelyn changed the subject, "That summer we had a general election. I voted labour. "

Jennifer's voice broke in, "How come you didn't vote for Churchill?"

"There were several reasons. But, in the main, I didn't want to see a return to the huge inequalities in society that we'd seen before the war. With Hitler out of the picture, the games of Red and White commenced! Atlee replaced Churchill at Potsdam after the election results were announced. The late 1940's and 50's were a time of numbing conformity for most women and I wanted to break out of that. In Germany, Nazi ideology had restricted women to the spheres of children, kitchen and church. But the sad truth is that many women in Britain passively acquiesced and allowed themselves to be restricted to these spheres of society too! Nearly all histories of the war work at Bletchley left out half of those who worked on the codebreaking, as if those women's histories happened somewhere else!"

She was on a roll now, "Today, the Kremlin has the sheen of respectability about it. It's all expensive suits and ties, press secretaries, respectable summit meetings and the like but all the old timers know that nothing much has changed since Stalin's time. It's all clever marketing to peddle the legitimacy of the regime. The 'Rodina' the myth of the motherland - the soil, the hymns, killing Nazis on the Steppes in the great patriotic war. Just as bad as Hitler and his 'fatherland' nonsense! The Soviets were just as bad as the Nazis with their Gulags, The Red Terror and The Great Terror - all horrific acts of a totalitarian state with a monster at its head."

Jennifer could be heard gently steering Evelyn back on track, "So the war ended. Then what did you do?"

In July 1945, I was lucky enough to be invited to visit France and Germany. Ten of us including Alan and a few Americans were sent on a fact-finding expedition to report on the progress of communications. During that trip I got to meet Rose Valland, in Paris. She was an absolute heroine of mine. She saved thousands of pieces of French art by secretly listing and photographing all the items that the German's looted from French galleries. She knew where the German's had hidden them. At the end of the war, she worked with the monuments men to retrieve them. To meet her, you would never have imagined she had that amount of courage in her. She was shy and shunned attention."

Jennifer exclaimed, "I've never heard of her. She sounds fascinating. And is that Alan Turing you are referring to?

"Oh, yes. Did you know he was an accomplished cross-country runner? He was hoping to get in the British Olympic team, but he got injured in training. Of course, everyone thinks of him in regard to breaking The Enigma code. He was a brilliant mind, and he should get the credit, but there were so many women that contributed to that project, who never get a mention."

I could see some strong themes emerging - Evelyn's resentment at the treatment of women and her absolute contempt for the Nazis and the Soviets.

Jennifer moved on to another topic, "How and when did you meet your husband?"

"Ah, Edward Gresham. He came to Bletchley very late in the war. I was only vaguely aware of him. It was later at GCHQ that our paths crossed. When I first met him, I knew he was not long for this world. He was painfully thin, and his fine patrician face was prematurely lined and haggard. We got on at once, Edward and me. In some ways we were birds of a feather. He was gentle, shy and very modest. He was a true boffin - a brilliant mind but not arrogant. He was six years older than me. We decided marriage would be beneficial to us both. I wanted a child at that point in time and Edward was happy to be the father. He had his special friends and I had mine. "

To my mind, this implied that a deal had been done between the two of them. Was Edward a homosexual? Were they both gay?

Evelyn carried on the story, "He didn't deserve the disease he had. He turned into a pitiful waif of a man, as thin as an inmate of Belsen! Unable at the end to be able to keep down the blandest of food. Moira and I comforted him as best we could. She was marvellous in those weeks before his death. He was a thoroughly decent and gentlemanly type. He wanted to make provision for Sian. I received his pension, what there was of it. He had some war bonds and a hundred pounds in the bank. That was it. But I got the jewel, which was my daughter, Sian. She has many of his lovely traits and a fair few of mine of course."

Evelyn's voice sounded full of pride when she was talking about her daughter. Suddenly she veered off into a different realm altogether,

"There were many people, after the war, with aspects of their past to conceal. We all had to abide by the official secrets act and not divulge any information about BP. But I also had other secrets to hide... By the time our ban on talking about it was lifted, even if anyone had been aware of what I'd done, it was a very cold case. Most of the people involved at the time were dead and any associated paperwork had been destroyed. The Russians themselves did me the biggest favour by churning out mass misinformation."

Ha, I thought, now we are getting into interesting territory.

Jennifer's voice was coaxing more information out of Evelyn,

"How do you mean? What misinformation?

"When the Second World War was over, there were still plenty of malevolent minions in Russia and the German Democratic Republic to do Stalin's bidding. West Germany was fascist, imperialist, capitalist - the successor state to the Nazi regime. The GDR pretended it had rid itself of all ex-Nazis into the West. This meant that they shrugged off any national responsibility for the Holocaust. This was the most extraordinary historical sleight of hand. East Germany set about completely changing history by pumping out fiction, propaganda and PR. The GDR was a regime structured as a pyramid of fear. Built on the back of serial betrayal. Not so different to Stalin's Russia or Hitler's Third Reich!"

Evelyn was almost ranting by now, "The regimes may be gone, but their foot soldiers and acolytes are all still there, with axes to grind, pasts to conceal, CVs to doctor and people to silence."

I wondered if Evelyn herself was one of those that had been silenced!

She was still not finished on this topic, "The dark reach of these regimes carried on well beyond their apparent fall. East Germany was portrayed as a safe welfare state with high ideals. What a joke!"

It sounded as if Evelyn had worn herself out with her tirade.

Jennifer intervened. "Maybe we should wrap it up for today."

Evelyn had one last comment, "That all played into the success of my deceit."

These were tantalising suggestions. What was Evelyn hinting at? Was she a spy during the war or the cold war? Quite possible given her university background. Cambridge had been a rich seam of gold for spy recruitment for the Soviets. She certainly knew how to build up the suspense. I was on the edge of my seat by now. I couldn't wait to hear the next episode.

But there the tapes stopped! Excruciating!

Jennifer obviously could see my frustration that Evelyn had not completed her story. As a consolation she informed me that Evelyn had also given an interview for the Women's Institute in 2011, after the women code breakers had been given their medals. I rang Samson and asked him to procure a copy of the interview from the Women's' Institute archives, ASAP.

•••

By the time I got back to the office, Samson had watched the interview which was preserved in the archives of the WI website. He was happy to watch it again with me.

Evelyn was speaking to a matronly looking woman from the Women's Institute who was asking her about her time at Cambridge and how this had led on to her work at Bletchley as a codebreaker?

"I graduated from Cambridge with a maths degree. I wasn't sure what profession I would take up, but before I had a chance to apply for any jobs in industry, I was approached and offered a job in what was obliquely termed 'The code section.' "It would be important war work" I was told. Following my successful maths test and an interview by a panel of boffin types and a very difficult crossword to solve within 15 minutes, I was given the job. At that point I had no idea where I would be stationed. I arrived by train at Bletchley. It's halfway between Cambridge and Oxford. I was initially given a place to stay in a shared barracks but after two noisy and virtually sleepless nights, I found an old couple in Fenny Stratford who would give me a room in their house with breakfast and an evening meal included. They were real dears and I stayed with them until the end of the war. I cycled back and forth to Bletchley Park. After long dogged shifts in the codebreaking huts, it was good to get some physical exercise at the end of a shift and retreat to the peace and quiet of my own room."

The interviewer asked lots of questions about wartime rations and cooking and wartime fashions and the like. Evelyn didn't really seem interested in these aspects of life. Her answers were vague and stilted. She re-engaged again when there was a question about how the war had changed her.

She replied, "Having witnessed what I had during the war, I was no longer the idealistic undergraduate. I abandoned my Christian belief. There was now a political consciousness of the importance of science. Britain would have capitulated without it. The war had dealt a huge blow to fixed moral codes. Social change was accelerated, old authorities were questioned, and new talents employed. Like that of women! I was never going to be content with being re-buried in the menial tasks that women were consigned to before the outbreak of war. This genie was definitely out of the bottle, and I wasn't going back into it!" She chuckled. The interviewer was nodding and smiling her agreement. Evelyn went on, "The war had shown that the system could be changed rapidly and expansively when survival made it necessary. Bletchley Park had been like a microcosm of all this change, with female mathematicians, post office engineers who had risen from the bottom of the ladder, all to play crucial parts in a way that would never have been possible in pre-war Britain. Sharing very limited commonwealth, had united people in a Spartan but joyful way. The simplification of life had built a new national spirit. I very much wanted that to continue."

The matronly woman then changed the focus to Evelyn's work after the war, her marriage and her grandchildren. There was no more mention of Bletchley or anything that could be remotely significant to our case.

The Women's Institute material was worth watching and gave a few general hints as to Evelyn's code breaking, but it was light weight stuff. The tapes and material for her book had been much more enlightening. I suspected her personal diaries were where the real gold nuggets lay. I was sure that more bombshell revelations would come to light.

In the meantime, I would get back to Evelyn's office and continue sifting through her abundant paperwork. With rigorous cross checking between old bank statements and annotations on auction catalogues, I started to see a pattern emerging. Evelyn had made a number of sales over a period of four decades. All well-spaced out and of very different alternative assets. In chronological order, according to the auction catalogues, first off, the rank had been a handsome amber tankard, used by Frederick I himself and engraved with the Prussian coat of arms - a crowned eagle in profile. Bonham's had described it as a very important piece. An item displaying the highest degree of craftsmanship and with the Royal provenance it had sold for £2,100 in 1959. That was a royal ransom in those days! You could buy a house for that sum in the late fifties! How had Evelyn come by this object?

Next came the cigars in 1965. They were simply listed by Sotheby's as 'Lot 56: Pre-embargo cigars'. Evelyn bagged £9,000 for this little lot!

After a four-year interval, an exquisite pair of amber candlesticks and other amber items, dated to 1710 went up for auction at Christies. Evelyn pocketed £12,000 from this sale.

I noted that different auction houses had been used each time. This suggested someone trying to hide their tracks and stay below the radar. On her bank statements I spotted that exactly half of the sale proceeds had been withdrawn in cash, each time an item was sold.

My little grey cells were sparking!

I grabbed for my phone and called Sian. She picked up straight away. "Hi Sian, its Nia, have you got a minute to talk?" "Yes, no problem. What can I help you with?"

"I've spent the day in your mum's office and library and a few interesting things have come to light. I wondered if you could give me any additional details about them."

"I'm happy to help if I can. What do you want to know?"

"Evelyn seems to have sold a number of items via auction houses over the years. In particular there were sales of diamonds, amber pieces and cigars.

Do you happen to know anything about these transactions?"

Ah, yes, I remember the cigars. I don't recall diamonds and as far as the amber goes, mum always had an interest in 'the gold of the north" as she called it."

"Okay. What can you tell me about the cigars?"

"As you know, Mum was a fountain of trivia knowledge. She told me Winston Churchill visited Bletchley Park in September 1941 as a morale booster for the staff. She shook hands with him and asked him what type of cigar he was smoking. He said he favoured Romeo y Julieta. Hilde's husband Ulf also liked cigars. He was killed early in the war. Hilde had kept some boxes of Ulf's cigars, but the temperatures weren't suitable for storage in Denmark. I remember mum making a last-minute flight booking to Copenhagen. Estrid and I went to the cinema whilst Hilde and mum went to some old airfield where Hilde had a storage unit. They came back with boxes stamped with Hilde's initials on them. We brought about twenty boxes home with us. We divided them up in our hand luggage. Mum said she would sell some and store some. Appreciating assets, she said! I was only a teenager at the time. It had completely slipped my mind until you asked. Apparently, they can survive for hundreds of years in the right conditions. Who would have known! Some 600-year-old Mayan cigars were auctioned for half a million dollars last year! Come to think of it I still have a few boxes of cigars stored in my cellar at home. Mum told me to stash them away about ten years ago and I forgot all about them."

Here was something tangible I could investigate further. I asked, "Would you mind very much, if I come and take a look at them?"

"No not at all, I should be home by about 5.30pm. Any time after that would be fine."

She was sipping a glass of red wine and preparing a risotto when I arrived at 6.30pm. She offered me a drink, which I gladly accepted - a lovely drop of Pinot Noir! Once she'd stirred the broth into her rice, she set the pan to simmer. Sian said, "Okay, I'll show you the cigars now. When Mum told me to store these away about ten years ago, she said 'Sian, this is a way to unplug your wealth from the financial system'. "She was full of these sorts of pronouncements. To tell the truth, I had forgotten all about them. I could be sitting on a small fortune. Maybe I'll sell them and take early retirement!" she joked. "You'll have to excuse the state of my cellar. I can't remember the last time I went down there."

We descended a narrow flight of stone steps and entered a musty smelling space. We picked our way through the usual out of fashion household furniture, discarded tools and rolls of surplus carpet. Tucked out of the way under an old rug Sian uncovered a cedar wood container. Stamped neatly on the side of this outer box were the initials 'H.G'. She lifted the lid and packed around with cotton wool and acid free tissue paper, were a quantity of sealed boxes of cigars. Half a dozen boxes of La Aroma de Cuba cigars and multiple boxes of Pre-embargo Dunhill's. As she picked up a humidor with twenty or so Romeo y Julieta inside, Sian mused, "These were Churchill's favourites. Mum figured my cellar would provide the ideal conditions for storage - around 70 degrees Fahrenheit and 70% humidity. Funny how that stuck in my memory."

I had no knowledge of cigars whatsoever, so this was all news to me!

We rummaged through and at the very bottom of the stash was a single cigar in its own presentation case marked with the same 'H.G' initials but also bearing a coat of arms and the supplier's name, 'Gildemann Ltd'. I took a couple of pictures of the boxes in situ with my mobile phone. I would get Samson to check them out.

With a nostalgic edge to her voice Sian said, "It was tragic really, Hilde's husband Ulf loved cigars. These were to be a surprise for him on his thirtieth birthday. She secretly had them shipped to her from Sweden, but he didn't survive the war. That's why her initials are on the packing case – H.G for Hilde Gustaffson, you see". But I was starting to formulate an altogether different theory....

I felt that I was finally starting to get Sian's confidence, so I ventured to ask her again

"'Sian, have you thought anymore about letting us have a crack at your mum's safe?"

"Do you really think there's something in there that could have real significance in bringing mum's killer to justice?"

"Yes, I really do."

"Okay. I'll give it some thought. I promise I'll get back to you before the weekend."

I drained my glass, "Thanks, Sian. I appreciate that.'"

My phone started ringing just as I was pulling out of Sian's driveway. It was Samson sounding hyper excited. I pulled over onto a farm track and listened to the results of his inquiries, "Well, apparently Pre - Bay of Pigs, cigars trade almost like antiques and they appreciate in value in a similar fashion. But they differ from antiques in one crucial way: people smoke them, so there is a dwindling supply.

Christies has been auctioning cigars for 100 years, I had no idea! As you asked, I did some research into cigars owned by famous war time characters - Churchill, Goering and Stalin. I seem to remember Hitler didn't smoke." He laughed before gushing, "My online search brought up some very interesting facts".

"Come on Samson, get to the punchline".

Well, I can tell you that Gildemann Ltd were cigar manufacturers based in Berlin and Hamburg. The coat of arms depicted on the case was that of Herman Goering!

"I knew it! That's what I suspected. But, how on earth did Evelyn get hold of it?"

Samson had more to impart, "Goering lived a lavish lifestyle, often entertaining guests at his grand manor house, called Carinhall. He smoked copious amounts of these custom-made cigars. An empty cigar box once owned by him, recently sold for over three grand. That stash in Sian's cellar would net a tidy penny nowadays!"

I was starting to see a pattern emerge - of a very astute woman, who had known exactly how to invest in off the radar alternative investments that had hugely appreciated in value over the years. But, how on earth had Evelyn got her hands on cigars made for Herman Goering? I needed to start joining the dots in this puzzle. Fish is supposed to be good for the brain, so I stopped for fish and chips on my way home! Sadly, I didn't get a brainwave of enlightenment before going to bed.

•••

Our first appointment the next morning was with Owen, Evelyn's grandson.

Owen was the male incarnation of his sister. The same ringlets - more strawberry blond than auburn, faultless unblemished pale skin. His eyes were lively and a little greyer than his sister's vivid blue. A tall, lean frame and I noticed very fine hands with impeccable nails. He was definitely not a farm labourer or a builder! A very smart dresser - dapper would be the description. He wore a modern tweed, three-piece suit with a dazzlingly white tailored shirt. A striped tie with an old-fashioned tie pin and cuff-links, finished off the look. His shoes didn't disappoint. They were hand-made brogues which you could see a reflexion of your face in! Altogether a very attractive young man. Slightly effete, maybe but it suited him. Unlike his sister, Owen's voice was much lower and there was hardly a trace of the lilting Welsh to be heard. He had a very engaging smile and a manner that put you at ease immediately. It soon became obvious that he also had a great intellect. He had gone to Cambridge University - following in the footsteps of his Nan (as he called Evelyn). He was not a mathematician but had got his degree in Quantum Computing!

Before settling down to a career and family life he wanted to travel around the World. He didn't normally dress so formally, he said. But today he was doing a consulting job for a Tech start-up company in Bristol and had to do a presentation to their Venture Capital backers. By the time he returned from his travels, he hoped that the company would be listed on the Aim stock exchange and his shares would be worth a few million! He laughed and shrugged off the encouraging exclamations Samson and I offered. I realised that within minutes we had come under the enchantment of this young fellow! There was something about him that was enthralling. Was he genuine or a brilliant con man?

"Yes, I was very close to my Nan. We had similar interests and got along famously. "

Samson wanted to know, "What sort of interests?"

"Oh, computers, coding, semiotics"

"What on earth is that?" asked Samson

"It's the study of signs and symbols and their interpretation. Nan took us to Nevern when we were kids and that kindled my interest from an early age. There's an old churchyard there with a few ancient Celtic stones with Ogham script. "

I recalled that Sian had mentioned the place.

Owen continued, "That led on to cryptography. Nan said it was almost a natural progression from the ancient runic systems like Ogham to the Irish codes of the Book of Ballymote through to the codes of Hildegard von Bingen to Cardinal Richelieu's grilles right the way down to the mechanically generated Enigma. She relished the history of it all. She could have written a book on it! Frequency analysis, polyphones, homophones all the nerdy vocabulary attached to cryptanalysis was fascinating to me. When Nan told me about cryptocurrencies, I thought at first, she was having me on, but when I checked it out, I was hooked immediately."

I noted the mention of Enigma again. It was too much of a coincidence. But where was the connection?

"Right, I see," said Samson. I knew he was thinking - what an anorak!

Owen took up his description of his grandmother again. "She never seemed like an old woman to me. She had an ageless quality to her. I think it's because she loved to keep up to date with all the latest Technology and she was such an avid reader. You could have a conversation about any current affairs with her. No matter how crazy an idea I would have, she would always back me and offer ideas on how to make it happen."

"Can you give us an example of the sort of thing" asked Samson.

"When I showed interest in Bitcoin and cryptocurrencies, she already knew all about them and showed me how to set up an online and offline wallet. She encouraged me to invest my pocket money into a basket of lesser known cryptos such as Ripple and Litecoin. I could see that this was all gobbledygook to Samson, but I had some knowledge and understanding of the concept. "Yes, they are the future of micro payments for sure", I said. Owen seemed impressed that a policewoman would be versed in such things! "We understand that there was an envelope left to you by your Nan. Can you tell us what it was?"

"Oh, yes, no problem. It was a line of code that she had copied down by hand."

"Do you still have the piece of paper?"

"Yes, it's here in my wallet. It's the very last thing with Nan's writing on that I have, so I'll always keep it. He fished out a carefully folded piece of standard paper. On it was printed the words 'send 20,000 Bitcoins.' Then there was a sting of alphanumeric characters: bc1qar0srrr7xfkvy5l643lydnw9re59gtzzwf5mdq

Owen, I know I can count on you to carry this through. No questions. Don't try to trace.

All my love

Nanna xx

I asked, "Did you know what it was, and did you carry cut the transaction?"

"Oh, yes, it's a bitcoin address. This is what they call a Bech32 type. It's an identifier of alphanumeric characters that represent a destination for a bitcoin payment.

I did a quick calculation in my head and concluded that we were looking at a sizeable amount of money, so I asked Owen, "Did she have a large amount in there?"

"Well as a matter of fact she did. To be honest, I was staggered when I found out just how much."

Samson and I exchanged glances. We were all ears! Samson enquired, "Are we talking thousands?"

"No, millions."

I'd already figured this out, but Samson was utterly amazed at the revelation.

"So, you had no idea of this before her death. She hadn't confided in you?"

"No, as I say, I knew about her account. She had showed me some of her transactions a few times. But the last time we were trading online, she had nowhere near that amount of money in there."

"When was the last time you were trading with her?"

"About two months before her death. "

"She never mentioned that she was going to do a big deal?"

"No, absolutely not."

"Can you tell us when the money came in?"

"About two weeks before her death. 40,000 Bitcoin arrived in her account."

"Where would that have come from?"

"She could have transferred it from another online Crypto platform. But she never mentioned anything about another account. I've tried to follow her transactions and to me it looks like she got paid 40,000 Bitcoin by someone else. I have some very clever mates who are hackers - working for legitimate companies might I add. But of course, the whole point of Bitcoin is that transactions can be made anonymously. The transaction could be traced on the Block chain but that's where the trail ends."

It was obvious that Samson was all at sea now. He didn't have a clue what Owen was on about. I was still following the thread. I knew the fundamentals regarding Bitcoin and the Block chain, and I'd even dabbled in a few cryptocurrencies as long-term investments.

"Do you think that Evelyn might have sold something on the dark web, and this was payment for whatever it was?"

Samson piped up "So what are we talking about here. How much are 40,000 Bitcoins worth?"

I knew and without flinching I said, "At recent prices of $200 per Bitcoin, that makes $8 Million!"

Samson almost choked. "Bloody hell! Excuse my French, but I had no idea!"

Owen was completely unperturbed. I could see we had a cool customer here.

He turned to me and calmly replied, "In answer to your question about the dark web - Yes that's entirely possible. That was the conclusion I had come to myself."

"Any idea what the object she sold could be and who she would pay half the sale proceeds to?"

"No idea. All I know is that the address Nan gave me is for a European Coinbase account. With some more digging we might be able to find out who the recipient of those funds is. As far as the original sender of the 40,000 though, we have hit a brick wall."

I felt a degree of exasperation. "I wish we'd known this from the start. It's a shame we've had to wait for you to come back from overseas. You didn't think to volunteer this information?"

Owen looked somewhat uneasy for the first time in our meeting. "Sorry, I've been in shock, and I didn't think it was relevant."

My frustration bubbled over at that point. "Not relevant! Where there's big money involved and dodgy characters in the background, a motive will be lurking somewhere. This puts a whole different spin on things. Now we are getting somewhere. We could have been investigating this angle. By not coming forward with this information you've set us back by over a week!"

I had full scale goose bumps on my arms. I just knew that here was the key to the case. The motive for Evelyn's murder had to be linked to this transaction.

With a sarcastic edge to his voice, Samson asked, "Is there anything else you can tell us about your mate's investigations?"

"Well, only that they saw tracking from unknown sources in Belarus. Russian hackers are notorious for being active in the dark web space. They are very skilled. But we have no idea what they were able to deduct from their activities."

"Is it possible that they would have been able to identify Evelyn as the recipient of the money? Obviously by the size of the transfer they would figure it was payment for something of significance. Could they have even figured who and where she was and what it was, she had sold?"

"I can't see how they could do that through the crypto blockchain or her Coinbase account. But, if they were hacking into her email or phone, then who knows what's possible. Not my area of expertise I'm afraid."

Samson looked confused but he offered his opinion, "'Jesus! It makes you realise how much info these hackers can get off your phone and the internet. Makes me want to go back to a landline and note pads!"

I agreed with him.

"We can get our experts in London onto this and see if we can dig deeper into Evelyn's' dealings. Send me everything you have and, we'll need the names of your hacker mates."

Owen looked distinctly uncomfortable. "They won't get into any trouble, will they?"

"No, we have no interest in them. You do want to find your Nan's killer, don't you?"

"Oh yes, absolutely. Do you think this is all connected?"

"Well, put it this way, this is the only thing that we've found so far that could in any way be seen as a motive for her murder."

I gave Owen my card. "My email is on there. So please send me all you have. And I mean everything. Don't make any judgements as to what might be relevant. Just send us the lot."

He looked abashed. "I'll get it to you today. Whatever it takes to get Nan's murderer, I'll do my utmost to help you. I miss her every day. He glanced at his watch. I must dash, or I'll be late for my presentation in Bristol."

"Thanks, Owen. We'll be in touch, and I look forward to receiving all that information, later today."

We watched him gather his leather holdall, his laptop, mobile phone and car keys and stride out with purpose to his incongruous old mud splattered Land Rover parked out the front. He climbed in and revved up the engine before setting off in the direction of the M4 - a man on a mission in Bristol!

As he disappeared into the distance, Samson shook his head, "I can't believe he held back that information. He must have known it was significant. He's too clever by half, for my liking. Maybe he and his hacker friends are up to something they don't want us to know about."

"It's possible. Anyway, whatever the case, get onto the nerds in London. See if we can have a skype meeting with them tomorrow morning. Tell them it's urgent. We should have all the details from Owen by then. Finally, I think this is the breakthrough we've been praying for."

• • •

The top guy in the IT department, Benjamin Klein was booked in for a skype call at 11am the next day. He would be able to answer all the technical questions I had, and I was hopeful he would be available to do some more digging into Evelyn's transactions on the dark web and the block chain.

Next morning, after a quick gossip about a couple of mutual colleagues, we got down to business. I asked Ben to give us a quick overview of Cryptocurrencies in layman's terms. This was really for Samson's benefit, but it wouldn't do me any harm to get a refresher on the subject.

Ben was good at making a dry and very technical topic understandable. Samson took copious notes as Ben brought us up to speed on the fundamentals of crypto currencies and, he homed in on Bitcoin, as in this case it was Evelyn's crypto of choice. He emphasised that, to trade in digital currencies, you need a platform on which to trade them, and an intermediary to communicate with the network. Evelyn had chosen Coinbase as her global digital asset exchange. Her account provided a means to buy and sell, as well as send information about those transactions out to the blockchain network, which would verify the transactions. He reiterated that Coinbase served as a wallet, where Evelyn's Bitcoins had been stored. She needed a public address and a private key to send and receive the coins. The public address is where the funds are deposited and received. The user can't withdraw them without the unique private key. The public key is created from the private key through a complicated mathematical algorithm. However, it is near impossible to reverse the process by generating a private key from a public key.

I thought, algorithms, algorithms. Here they are again! Evelyn was a lover of them back in her day and nowadays they have become central to so many functions we take for granted.

Samson wanted confirmation that he'd got the gist of it. "So, the private key is what allows a user to access his or her cryptocurrency and its security make up helps to protect a user from theft and unauthorized access to his/her funds. Is that right?"

Ben nodded, "Yeah, a private key is usually depicted as a series of alphanumeric characters, which makes it hard for a hacker to crack. Think of a public address as a mailbox, and the private key as the key to the box. Anyone can put letters or small packages into the mailbox. However, the only person that can retrieve them is the one that has the unique key. If the key is stolen the mailbox can be compromised. If the key is lost, the account can no longer be accessed to spend, withdraw, or transfer coins. Therefore, it's imperative to save the private key in a secure location.

In this particular case we are dealing with Bitcoin. The Bitcoin private key is the "ticket" that allows someone to spend the bitcoins. Private keys can be kept on computer files or on a USB stick, but they are also short enough that they can be printed on paper.

The public key is akin to an account name and helps to identify a destination for coins that are being sent to the wallet. Two people making a transaction with bitcoin, where one is a seller and the other a buyer, will have to share their public keys with each other to complete the transaction. The buyer of the commodity or service sends the required number of bitcoins to the seller's divulged address as payment, and the blockchain verifies the validity of the transaction and confirms that the buyer or sender really has those funds to send. Once the payment has been delivered to the address, the seller or receiver can only access the funds through his or her private key. It is, therefore, imperative for private keys to be kept secure because if stolen, the user's bitcoins or altcoins could be unlocked and accessed from the address without authorization.

Private keys stored on a wallet connected to the internet are vulnerable to theft. These wallets are known as hot wallets and all the functions required to complete a transaction are made from a single online device. The problem is that an attacker crawling the networks may become privy to the private key. Cold storage resolves this issue by signing the transaction with the private keys in an offline environment. Any transaction initiated online is temporarily transferred to an offline wallet kept on a device such as a USB, CD, hard drive, paper, or offline computer, where it is then digitally signed before it is transmitted to the online network.

Samson's eyes had glazed over by now. He joked, "We're not talking about refrigeration, I take it?"

"Very droll! The most basic form of cold storage is a paper wallet. A paper wallet is simply a document that has the public and private keys written on. The drawback is that if the paper is lost, rendered illegible or destroyed, the user will never be able to access his or her address where their funds are."

"We believe that Evelyn used the most basic solution – written out the string of letters and numbers on a piece of paper."

Ben shook his head and smiled, "That was risky. The probability that a mistyped address is accepted as being valid is 1 in 4.29 billion."

I suddenly had a thought. "Wait a minute. So, Owen would have had to have knowledge of Evelyn's private key to send the 20,000 Bitcoin from her account. Is that right, Ben?"

"Yes, absolutely. He couldn't send or receive anything without Evelyn's private key."

"He didn't mention that to us!"

Owen obviously hadn't been totally forthcoming with the information he held.

Samson was getting agitated. I looked askance at him.

"I've just had a light bulb moment."

"Well spit it out. Don't leave us in suspense."

"Remember when I was playing with the dogs at Evelyn's house? Well, on the back of the dog collar there was a huge string of letters and numbers. I had no idea what I was looking at. But, considering what I've just learnt about crypto currency security, I'd bet my hat that Evelyn's private key was kept offline alright. On the dog's collar."

I had to agree with him. "We'll check that out for sure, but I reckon you're right. Good thinking, Batman!"

Ben looked suitably impressed by Samson's deduction.

Samson was excited by his newfound knowledge. "What a genius way to use 'cold storage' -her dog's collar is the perfect offline solution - not connected to the internet, thereby protecting the wallet from unauthorized access by hackers. She was a canny old bird. Wasn't she?"

I detected a clear note of admiration in Samson's voice.

I had one last question for our tame nerd.

"Ben, what are the chances of being able to trace the buyer of this unknown asset? The one that paid Evelyn 40,000 Bitcoins?"

Ben pondered for a moment, "Most Bitcoin wallets have a function to "sign" a message, proving the entity receiving funds with an address has agreed to the message. This can be used for example, to finalise a contract in a cryptographically provable way prior to making payment for it. Because this was such a big transaction, Evelyn and her buyer may have agreed to this. If so, we may be able to trace back to the buyer. It's a long shot but I'll give it my best effort. I'll also have another chat to those hacker friends of Owen to make sure they're not holding anything back from us."

"Excellent! So, can you prioritise this case for us, Ben?"

"Yeah, I'll fit you in to my growing 'to do' list for today."

"We really appreciate that. We'll not take up any more of your precious time. We'll speak soon."

Thus ended our Skype call.

Samson immediately put a call through to Emily Evans. He left a message for her to call him back urgently. I wanted to keep the momentum going. "Let's go over there. She strikes me as the type that would have her phone switched off when she's working on one of her designs."

Emily was not home when we called at Valland House. The dogs were nowhere to be found, so we had to assume that she was out walking them.

"Damn. She's not answering her mobile either." Momentarily I was at a loss. We'd have to try again later. Samson had another idea.

"Do you fancy a bacon and egg roll at Swansea market? Let's have a chat with the engraver, if he's still there. Maybe he can remember something. I want to cover all the bases on this one. Not to mention, I've had no breakfast and the stall in the market used to do the best bacon and egg rolls in the country!"

"Absolutely. Good idea. Oh, for the simple pleasures in life!"

As it happened Mr C. Jenkins was still doing a steady trade on his engraving stall. He was in the middle of etching a gothic script of "Conan" onto a cat's collar when we arrived. We showed our ID and asked if he could answer a few questions for us.

"Give me five and I'll be with you." He seemed like an amiable enough chap.

Samson was already on his way over to the cafe that sold the rolls. Whether it was the local eggs or the Welsh bacon, I don't know but they really were delicious. We both wolfed down our late breakfast and got a couple of mugs of coffee to take back to the engraver's stall. Colin - apparently that's what the 'C' stood for, had finished the cat's collar and was sipping a short expresso. In answer to our questions, he told us he did remember Evelyn Jones because hers was one of his more unusual and demanding jobs. She had brought in a picture of a Roman mosaic of a dog's head and said she wanted him to stylise it on the front of the two dog tags. "I was pretty pleased with how they turned out, if I remember correctly. The lady was happy with them". I asked him about the obverse side of the tags.

"Oh, yes I remember the lady was absolutely adamant that I must copy the letters and numbers exactly as they were printed. I can even remember that each string of letters and numbers had to be precisely 32 on each collar.

The old gal checked them three times before she was willing to pay me."

Samson was looking totally smug. "I knew it. It's the private key, isn't it?"

The engraver looked blankly at Samson.

Samson had a brain wave then. He asked Mr Jenkins, "I don't suppose you still have the printed template that Evelyn Jones brought in for you to copy?"

"Oh, probably. I keep a chronological copy of everything. I'm a Virgo," he laughed.

He brought out a clip file from under the counter. It was bursting to capacity with copies of all sorts of designs that had been brought in by enthusiastic dog and cat owners over the years. He flicked through it at lightning speed and triumphantly produced the original copy of Evelyn's design.

"Brilliant" said Samson. He quickly took photos of the back and front designs on his mobile phone. I did likewise.

Mr Jenkins said, "When I saw the article about her death in the' Western Mail', I was shocked. It must have been a huge shock to her daughter."

"Oh, do you know her?"

"No, but she accompanied her mother when she came to pick up the finished articles. There's nothing else I can tell you about it I'm afraid. She seemed like a nice lady and the daughter was a real looker. I remember that!"

The minute Colin was out of hearing range Samson said,

"She's even cleverer than I at first thought. By splitting the characters up, anyone wanting to access her bitcoins would need to look at both collars, simultaneously. Now we have the strings of numbers and letters from both, it's just a matter of figuring out which sequence they go in."

E9873D79C6D87DC0FB6A5778633389F4 was engraved on Alan's collar.

443213303DA61F20BD67FC233AA33262 was engraved on Audrey's collar.

I was inclined to guess that the E would be the start of the private key. In which case the full 64 alphanumeric sequence would be:
E9873D79C6D87DC0FB6A5778633389F44443213303DA61F20BD67F
C233AA33262

I was certain that this indeed, was Evelyn's private key to her Bitcoin fortune!

"Text them through to Ben Klein straight away. He'll be impressed. You've excelled yourself on this one, John."

So, Evelyn's two Welsh sheepdogs had been guarding her crypto password, all along! It really was genius.

"You're having a purple patch with all this private key stuff, aren't you?"

He looked like the cat who'd got the cream, standing there with the biggest grin on his face.

•••

When we got back to police headquarters, we could see Tristram was highly excited. He had the rifle on the desk in front of him and he had already completed most of the tests he needed to confirm his original assumptions. The rifle stock was polished wood and carved with an inscription. As he held it up to show us, he said, "The teenagers thought it was Greek but it's actually Russian and translated it reads – 'Lyudmila Pavlichenko'.

I could see he could hardly contain his excitement. "I can't believe I have such an iconic rifle in my laboratory. Do you know who Pavlichenko was?"

"I'm guessing a Russian sniper?"

"One of the most famous of all! Lyudmila Pavlichenko killed at least 300 Germans in fighting around Sevastopol, in June 1942. Her rifle of choice during the war was the M1891/30 Mosin-Nagant 7.62 mm rifle with a PE 4x telescope. And here it is sitting on my table! I just can't believe it!"

He pointed out to us that the rifle held 5 rounds and had an average effective range of about 1,800 feet, although good snipers were still accurate as far as 2,600 feet away - that's about half a mile!

Samson joked, "I can't even hit the plastic ducks at the local fairground stall and that's about 10 feet away!"

Tristram laughed, "The Soviets had some of the best snipers in the war. Jeremy would have talked to you about the terminal ballistics. Now I have the actual weapon, I can report my findings regarding the internal and external ballistics. He grinned broadly and I knew we were in for a barrage of technical details! In his rapid-fire style of speech he explained, "Internal Ballistics is the study of the propulsion of a projectile within a weapon from the propellant's ignition until the projectile exits the barrel. The type of propellant, the chamber where the cartridge rests before its fired, the barrel rifling and length of the weapon are all significant. Rifling or the groove carved inside the barrel determines the amount of spin imparted to the exiting bullet, which stabilizes flight. Even before the rifle was found I had been able to make a good guess at the weapon, but these are 100% consistent with the bullets we retrieved."

He had such pride in his job, it was contagious. I couldn't help but join in his enthusiasm. "Brilliant!"

He enthused, "Factors like the type and size of both bullet and weapon along with extrinsic factors such as wind and gravity are key components of external ballistics. Gravity and bullet drag caused by friction are the main forces acting on the projectile during its path through the air. They cause the projectile to lose energy during flight. Which results in bullet drop. A bullet commonly travels in a parabolic shaped trajectory whose vertex and distance are determined by the energy of the bullet."

Samson had to pull him up, "Tristram, you've lost me. What does that mean for Ballistics dummies, like me and Nia?"

Tristram realised he'd been getting too technical, "Oh, sorry. I'll try to simplify things. It means, bullets fired at a longer distance need to be fired at a positive angle of elevation to the line of the target.

Samson and I were suppressing yawns at this point, but I didn't have the heart to cut him off in full flow. Thankfully, he showed signs of slowing down and made the point that, "Shooters routinely use the knowledge of bullet drop trajectory to accurately hit an intended target at distance. The bullet in flight also experiences yaw, roll, and pitch. In conclusion, I would say that whoever fired at Evelyn Jones was a very skilled marksman or woman. They were firing from quite a distance and there is always some breeze on the clifftops. All those factors were taken into account by the assassin in order to achieve that degree of pinpoint accuracy. "

Samson summed up, "We're dealing with an absolute pro. So, Evelyn Jones didn't stand a chance once that rifle was pointed at her. Would that be a fair conclusion?"

"Yes, that's about the gist of it."

Tristram was bubbling over with enthusiasm," Pavlichenko was awarded the Gold Star of the Hero of the Soviet Union in 1943 as well as the Order of

Lenin twice. The next best female sniper after Pavlichenko, was Yekaterina Zuranova with 155 confirmed kills."

"Blimey you should go on Mastermind, with Soviet snipers as your specialist subject," laughed Samson.

Tristram was absolutely relishing his time in the spotlight. He was off again with a potted history of the woman sniper, "Pavlichenko went to America in 1942. She met President Roosevelt and Eleanor. In speeches across America often before thousands, she made the case for a U.S. commitment to fighting the Nazis in Europe. And in doing so, she drove home the point that women were not only capable, but essential to the fight. After the war, she finished her master's degree in History at Kiev University. She rose to the rank of Major and was presented with an engraved Colt 1911 pistol while visiting the U.S, an engraved Winchester model 70 rifle while in Canada and after the war she was featured on two commemorative postage stamps in the Soviet Union. You know in the war her nickname was "Lady Death!" He stopped at this point to draw breath!

"Wow, impressive" was Samson's response.

I was impressed too. She sounds like an inspiring woman. I had a thought, "She's not still alive, is she?"

"No, she died back in 1974. But her grandson is, and he works for the Russian State. He's also known as a crack shot. So, he's following in his grandmother's footsteps."

"What's his name?" asked Samson

"Boris Ustinov."

"Wasn't there an actor called that?"

"No, that was Peter Ustinov!"

"Was Roza Shanina by any chance one of the famous women snipers?"

"Absolutely. A very glamorous young woman. Sadly, she didn't survive the war. Why do you ask?"

In Evelyn's library I noticed 'The diaries of Roza Shanina.'

He looked shocked, "Intriguing. There's some connection here, for sure. Wow this is shaping up to be one of the most interesting cases, ever! He enthused.

He told us he had done the tool mark comparison and as he'd suspected it all tied in with the weapon on the table. Various other scientific tests all supported his initial thoughts. This was without doubt the rifle that the killer bullets had been fired from. No DNA, fibres or fingerprints could be obtained from the weapon. The scope hadn't been found with the rifle, but he could assure us it was almost certainly a 3.5×21 PU scope. Because this type of scope was mounted above the chamber, the rifle had been loaded manually.

I thought we had more than enough information. "Well, thanks so much, Tristram. You've been incredibly thorough. We really appreciate your expert input."

He looked pleased as punch.

"It was a real pleasure. I'll obviously prepare the weapon for storage as an exhibit and I'll produce an expert witness statement, in line with current legislation. I'm happy to attend court and present evidence as required, if you need me to."

With that we shook hands with him and left him tending lovingly to his treasure!

●●●

I heard my mobile ping. I had a text message from my boss Brian Smythe to give him a call urgently. What was this about, I wondered?

Brian was old school in much of his thinking and our working relationship was at times strained. He has his ingrained views on women's careers and their place in society. Having said that, he had always been courteous and fair to me. He was smart, intuitive, and absolutely indefatigable. He just kept going, no matter what. He seemed to know everyone in the London police force and a fair few in the regional forces too! I admit I have a grudging admiration for the man. I respect his particular skills. I'd recently been a sympathetic ear when his last marriage broke down. I felt this had resulted in a softening of his response to me. There was talk around the station that he was now contemplating marriage for the fourth time! I can work with Brian, but I shudder to think what it must be like to be married to him. I thought I'd better get the call out of the way, so I clicked on his contact icon.

Brian informed me, that Boris Ustinov, an SVR staff officer with the rank of Major assigned to the Executive Action Department, had been spotted on CCTV at Cardiff central station boarding the 11.55 to Paddington on the day that Evelyn was shot. A shiver ran down up my spine. Oh my god! Tristram had just mentioned this name to us. The Russians were making a statement by using him for this assassination. This must be a symbolic gesture.

Smythe was ploughing on, "From there Ustinov proceeded to Heathrow and boarded an Aeroflot flight to Moscow at 5pm. Further investigations revealed that he was what was known as a "chistilshchik", in other words an executioner for the Russian secret service. In the KGB years this department was known as the Thirteenth Department. Ustinov's face and fingerprints were on MI5 files, so his identity is unquestionable." Smythe went on to tell me that his contacts in MI5 believed that although the age of the umbrella pokers had passed, the Russians were still prepared to use nerve agents or an assassin's bullet to take out a target on foreign soil.

"But why was Evelyn a target?" I asked.

He couldn't answer that. So far MI5 had drawn a blank on that front. Or they were keeping that to themselves, more likely. I thought back to Tristram Davies' words -"A sniper's bullet is personal."

I felt the icy hand of the past taking a grip on this case. Boris had used one of his grandmother's vintage rifles to eliminate Evelyn. I crawled into bed that night, totally exhausted. But, for a while I lay awake, rummaging through the drawers of the filing cabinet in my head, hoping that the files would slot into place. I was sure that most of the files were there, they just weren't in order yet.

The next morning the Welsh papers and the national newspapers had got hold of the story. There were some wild rumours and suggestions being bandied about. They proclaimed that evidence about the case had been suppressed. Rumour had it that MI5 was involved! All the old material about Polonium and poisoned umbrella tips was reiterated. There were all sorts of theories about Evelyn being recruited as a spy whilst she was at Cambridge. All the old spies - Kim Philby, Guy Burgess, Donald Maclean, and Anthony Blunt were mentioned in order to support this theory. Of course, it was all a load of mumbo jumbo, but it sold newspapers!

Mid-morning Sian rang to tell me that she would consent to us opening Evelyn's safe.

Excellent. I called the force's specialist safe breaker to open it. I arranged to meet him at Valland house in an hour.

In the 1950s Chubb made some technical breakthroughs - the rapid increase in oxygen cutting had created a demand for safes with a high degree of protection. Evelyn had such a Chubb safe installed behind a painting of an orchid that her granddaughter Rhiannon had painted. As the technician was working to break the safe open, he gave us a running diatribe.

"Both the outer and inner body is constructed from high grade steel, electrically welded to form one unit. The outer steel door plate is reinforced, and thermal insulation is included, giving excellent protection against high temperatures. The whole unit is secured by a seven-lever anti-drill key lock. A combination lock has also been fitted as an optional extra."

Samson voiced the obvious, "Well, Evelyn made sure that whatever was inside, was thief proof and fireproof!"

It only took the technician a matter of minutes to crack the safe. With a triumphant "Bingo!" he stood back from it, and I looked at the contents that Evelyn had deposited inside. There was a bundle of her diaries and a couple of notebooks. A stash of £50 notes in bundles of £5,000 each. In total there was £50,000 in cash. Apart from the cash, there was a certificate wrapped around a small, blue box, a bundle of letters tied with a satin ribbon and a number of black and white photos of some cobwebbed wooden boxes.

I turned my attention to the letters. I tentatively untied the bundle. There was half a dozen addressed to Evelyn in a bold upright hand. I gently opened one envelope and inside was a folded sheet of cream Basildon Bond paper. I read the first and last lines, then refolded the sheet and returned it to its envelope. These were obviously personal letters from Evelyn's husband and should remain private. They would have no relevance to my investigations, I was sure. The rest of the letters - thirty-one in total were written in an altogether different hand - arty looking, rounded characters, in purple ink. Feminine for sure. Again, I slowly unfolded the first sheet. It started with "My dearest, darling Evelyn and ended with" All my love, Moira xxx" It was a long letter of three pages. I can honestly say, I did not read the contents. Again, these were very personal letters from Moira to Evelyn and they would remain just that. They were not for prying police eyes.

I handed them to Samson to be inventoried and bagged. Next, I turned to the photos. They were all of cobwebbed wooden boxes with indistinct contents. The black and white grainy photos looked like they had been taken with a box Brownie camera. The subject matter was hard to define – possibly panels of some sort and a mosaic, framed as in a picture. As I lifted the photos up to scrutinise them in the light, a slip of thin Manila paper fluttered to the floor. I retrieved it. It was a simple pencil sketch of a woman. It looked vaguely familiar. It was executed in an Art Nouveau style. Although it was just a pencil drawing, I could tell that it was no amateur effort. This was the hand of an accomplished artist. I asked Samson to call in an art expert to look at it.

He looked doubtful, "What, this bit of paper? It's just a few squiggles of pencil. It wouldn't take more than a minute to scribble that!"

"Trust me, I bet you a fiver that it's by a famous artist."

Samson laughed, "Okay, if you want to throw your money away, I'm happy to relieve you of it."

Exciting as I suspected the little picture might be, it was Evelyn's diaries that I was most eager to read. But first I turned my attention to the contents of the little blue box. The certificate wrapped around it was embossed with the words 'The Government Code and Cypher School.' Then proceeded:

'Evelyn Mary Jones,

The Government wishes to express to you its deepest gratitude for the vital service you performed during World War Two.

It was signed by 'David Cameron, Prime Minister.'

It was dated May 2010.

I flipped the lid to reveal a blue velvet lining. Nestled in the cloth was a gold plated and blue enamel brooch, set with small garnets. On the reverse was stamped the words 'We also served.'

Samson was looking over my shoulder. He whistled, "Is that the best the government could come up with! What a load of cheapskates! It's not even real gold."

It really was a pathetic gesture. "Yeah, that's what she got for devoting six years of her life to code breaking, which helped speed up the end of the war!"

Samson added the box and certificate to his inventory and dropped it into the evidence bag with the rest of the items from the safe.

"Get those back to headquarters and give them a thorough inspection. I'm going to take the diaries and go through them with a fine tooth comb. I'll sign them out now and bring them in with me tomorrow."

I gathered up the collection of small leather-bound pocket diaries that were the recollections and impressions of Evelyn Jones. There was also an A4 notebook with 'Notes for Jennifer' printed on the front cover. These were my treasure trove. I felt like Gollum with the ring! These must reveal their long-held secrets. Secrets that would solve this case.

•••

Of course, I am aware that a diary is necessarily an impulsive and therefore somewhat unbalanced record of events. Diaries can never show the whole of a person. Even the most revealing of diaries is an incomplete picture of the person that kept it. But I hoped that supplemented by the interviews and the material from Jennifer Barnes I would finally be able to fit the whole complex puzzle together.

Some entries were lengthy and detailed others were short and abbreviated - probably scribbled down between shifts of code breaking. Some were in a magenta ink, others in pencil. They were myriad. All the war years broken down into days of this woman's life. Many of the entries being witness to huge events in twentieth century history.

Flicking through the A4 notepad I could see that Evelyn had unlocked the diaries when she was talking to Jennifer Barnes. She had copied diary extracts and then added many notes of amplification and comment. These which were much fuller than the original entries were obviously written at leisure and with time for reflection rather than in a snatched moment during the War or late at night after a gruelling shift of decoding.

These two documents, the diary and the A4 notes, made decades later constituted a unique historical record.

My fingers were trembling as I opened the miniature clasp on the diary for 1939-1940.

There was a quotation on the front page: 'For 'tis in vain to think to guess at women by appearances'

I looked it up on Google. It was by Samuel Butler written in the 17th Century.

There was an annotation in pencil in Evelyn's hand beside this quote – 'If they only knew! '

Her first diary was a wonderful testimony to a clever young girl who came of age in an era which briefly defied gender norms, in order to staff a giant secret war machine. Evelyn grasped the opportunity that the War presented with both hands. Her war time diary entries were a mishmash of big politics and bits and pieces that floated by her. Picking her way through the debris of World War Two, both material and human. Gritty fare, day after day. They were an intriguing combination of world history, congealing political theology, frivolous moments, and silly asides. They showed an amazingly clear vision of how future world events may play out. These were the writings of a very independent thinker.

It soon became clear to me that what I was reading was a journal that had been an inseparable companion to Evelyn throughout the war years. And a safety- valve for her repressed irritations, frustrations, anxieties. A reflection of a self that few suspected in this most reticent of women.

Her writing is often stilted, pedestrian, marred by mixed metaphors. For all her faults of grammar and syntax she makes some scenes come vividly to life...

January 1940

B.P - On arrival we were marched towards a set of impressive gates and a sentry box manned by a military policeman. What an extraordinary establishment! Signed the Official Secrets Act which binds us never to reveal, in our lifetime, anything that we do, see, or hear here...

April 9th, 1940

The worst possible news from Hilde. Ulf killed by the Nazis. Denmark overrun in 6 hours! I can't believe it!

I spotted a poignant entry from May 1940

Evelyn had written - I came first in a competition sending and receiving Morse code. I received 71 WPM. World record holder - Ted McElroy 75 WPM in 1939! I sent 30 WPM using a hand key! My prize is a lovely Rolex watch!

I thought back to the morgue. She had still been wearing her Rolex watch, when she was shot. It was amongst her effects, sealed in a plastic bag. It was still keeping time accurately.

Her entries for 1940 clearly illustrate the building sense of dread as Evelyn lists the Nazi's swift conquest of large swathes of Northern Europe. She vividly conveys the lack of the preparedness of Britain's European allies, as they fell one after another to the Nazi's Blitzkrieg.

Evelyn recorded that on May 21st, 1940, the Germans had reached the French coast at Abbeville and turned north to seize the channel ports. Boulogne fell on the 23rd. Only Dunkirk was left intact - but the German pincers were closing fast. The Belgium army was disintegrating.

June 14th, 1940

The Nazis have taken Paris!! Will we be next?

Evelyn was working on a secret project with huge responsibilities, but I had to remember she was just a teenager when she was confiding in her diaries. The rapid Nazi advance must have been terrifying for a young woman at the time.

July 1940

Message from Hilde. Arne had broken T52. Amazing!

I made a note to find out what T52 was. Obviously, a code or cypher of some sort. Then, reading on to an entry of September 20th, 1940 - Inspiration from Genevieve in the U.S.A! She has broken "Purple"! I added this to my list. It sounded like yet another code.

Evelyn's writing was riveting. I realised I had spent hours and hours completely lost in the diary pages, only stopping for a cup of tea and a biscuit when my stomach rumbled. My back was starting to ache and no matter how engrossing these diary entries were, I knew I should take a break and stretch my legs. I wandered out into the garden. The gentle, late afternoon sun felt like a massage on my shoulders. I phoned Samson.

"Did you get the guy from Bonham's to take a preliminary look at the sketch?"

He sounded sheepish, "Oh yeah, I forgot to tell you, he was just as excited as Tristram was with the rifle. Said he couldn't believe what he was looking at. He's getting tests done on the paper, but he's convinced it was drawn in 1903."

My stomach was doing a little dance, "Who is the artist?"

I knew Samson was building up the suspense "Apparently it's a preparatory sketch for Klimt's Portrait of Adele Bloch-Bauer."

My heart skipped a beat, "Holy cow!"

"Hang on a minute, don't get too excited. Sebastian, the Bonham's guy, reckons he did over a hundred of these drawings, so it's not rare, is it?"

"Have you any idea of the significance of this?"

Samson was indignant, "I'm not a total ignoramus. I know who Gustav Klimt is."

"I'm not suggesting you're an ignoramus. Think of his most famous work, 'The woman in gold.' That's Adele Bloch - Bauer. That painting is worth tens of millions."

"Yeah, but this is just a little sketch. Pencil on paper. It's a long way from the portrait with its exquisite gold leaf and sensual Byzantine abstract patterns. Personally, I prefer 'The Kiss'."

Samson was being sarcastic and making a point. He knew exactly which Klimt picture we were talking about. He did make me laugh. I suspected he was quite the culture vulture. I always knew he played down his talents. "Even, so this is a huge find. I can't imagine how Evelyn procured such a thing."

"I know, it makes you wonder, doesn't it? She seems to have had her fingers in many unlikely pies. Know what I mean?"

I couldn't contain my curiosity any longer. "Give me the phone number for the Bonham's guy, I want to ask him some more questions about this."

I was put through immediately to Sebastian Weiss, Impressionist and Modern Art specialist for Bonham's. I could hear in his voice that he was elated by our find.

"John Samson told me this sketch emerged from a safe that was broken open today, is that right?"

"I'm no art aficionado, but as soon as I set eyes on it, I knew I was looking at something exceptional. What can you tell me about it?"

"The sketch is graphite and pencil on paper. There is a very faint signature 'GUSTAV KLIMT' in the lower right corner. It looks to be authentic. In mid-1903, Ferdinand Bloch-Bauer commissioned Klimt to create a portrait of his wife, Adele, as an anniversary present for his wife's parents. Klimt made over a hundred preparatory drawings, many of which the Bloch-Bauer's purchased. I believe this to be one of them. Do you have any idea of provenance at this stage?"

"If you mean, where did she originally get it from? I have no idea."

"As you probably know, the Bloch-Bauer's were Jewish. Ferdinand's assets were plundered by the Nazis after the annexation of Austria in 1938. The family fled to Switzerland. Ferdinand died in 1946, but not before willing his confiscated paintings, including five other Klimt works to his nephew and two nieces. Maria Altmann, one of his nieces filed a lawsuit to recover the paintings. The high-profile case came before the United States Supreme Court. She was successful and the paintings were returned to the Bloch-Bauer family in 2006. Christie's auctioned Portrait of Adele Bloch-Bauer II in November 2006 for $88 million. It's probably the most famous example of Nazi art theft, ever."

"Good grief that's quite a backstory! But we're only talking a pencil sketch, in this case."

"Nevertheless, these things don't come on the market very often. They are highly sought after when they do. It could easily sell for in excess of $50,000, if not more. But nowadays secure provenance needs to be demonstrated. If whoever owns this ever wants to sell it, they will need to prove how they came into possession of it. Apparently, Herman Goering's wife Emmy had one in her private collection. Obtained by nefarious means, no doubt. Nobody knows what happened to it. After the war she claimed it had disappeared during the chaos in 1945!

Here was the Goering connection rearing its ugly head yet again! I didn't mention my thoughts to Sebastian. But, I thought, the plot thickens!

●●●

My stomach was fluttering, from excitement and hunger. I grabbed some cheese and crackers to munch on as I returned to Evelyn's diaries. In her work and subsequent family life, Evelyn kept her own counsel. In her diary, she did not. It is here that she showed her unguarded expressions of exasperation and at time anxiety and the tremendous patience and self-control she exercised year after year. Within the pages covering 1941 were fantastically detailed accounts of some of the iconic battles of World War Two. Many of these wartime entries are contemporary, first - hand records of the cryptographers fight against the Axis powers.

25 May 1941 A big flap on today - the search for the German battleship Bismarck. Very urgent work for us girls. Working crazy hours.

27th May 1941 The Bismarck attacked and sunk! Hooray! Without J.C RN would never have found Bismarck. A significant victory made possible by us women. It makes all the hard work and everyday hardships worthwhile. Celebration drinks tonight!

Nov 20th, 1941. Attending a course at Beaulieu, Hampshire, to brush up my skills in cryptography. Met a very special gal - Violette from London. Impish, cockney accent. We had great fun together. Lots of laughs. On our weekend off we went into London to visit her mother and her little daughter.

We went out for a night on the town. On the way back we were caught in an air raid. Violette led me down into Aldwych Tube Station. Partly fitted out as an air raid shelter! Giant swords of light scanning the sky. Enemy plane caught in the cross beams. A red - orange flash. It fell out of the sky. Violette told me in confidence - tunnels between Aldwych and Holborn are being used to store precious items from the British Museum, including the Elgin Marbles! Her job - very hush hush. I think she works for SOE. Returned to BP. Violette off to Ringway Airport - parachute training! Rather her than me! Promised to keep in touch...

Evelyn had also recorded a comprehensive day by day log of the looted treasures from Pushkin and Leningrad and there were perceptive entries like October 1941 'the horizon is dark from end to end with the only hope being the possible entry of America into the war.'

In December 1941, the Japanese attacked Pearl harbour. At the same time Evelyn wrote – 'Hitler has failed to capture Moscow. In the falling snow and with temperatures 40 degrees below zero the Boche have been repelled from the gates of Moscow. For the first time in months, I may be able to sleep peacefully. A ray of hope at last! The resources of America are boundless.'

It looked like she was an enthusiastic fan of all things American at this time in her life! And she was right - America's entry into the war and the Russian's resistance, greatly increased the chances of ultimate victory for the allies.

I wish I could have met this woman. Her insight into the personalities, characters and statesmen of the time is acute and penetrating. This is contrasted by her warm humanitarian outlook. Her diaries are a patchwork, a treasure trove of historic snapshots combined with humour and poignant feelings. I had the appetite for more...

As I scanned down further my eye caught the fact that there were many mentions of the initials 'BZ.'

I recalled all the references to B.Z that I'd noted in books and pamphlets in Evelyn's library. Maybe I would get to find out who or what this was. In the diaries B.Z first appeared in December 1941. It read 'Hilde and Arne decoded a German transmission. BZ traveling to Konigsberg.'

Was this reference to a Danish resistance fighter that they knew? It was possible, I suppose. But what significance would that have to Evelyn? I must try to find out who this was. I had deduced by cross referencing with dates and events of the time that C.P was Cicely Popplewell, AT was Alan Turing, VS was Violette Szabo RV was Rose Valland, GG was Genevieve Grotjan, JC was Joan Clarke and HG Herman Goering. I was stumped by the initials BZ. Was it a Russian name? There are plenty of Russian surnames beginning with a Z – Zhukov, Zaitsev, Zorin, Zubov, Zarhovich to name but a few...

Inserted into the page dated July 20th, 1942, was a postcard of Konigsberg Museum. The sepia-coloured picture looked like an internal room of the museum arranged in the baroque style. Hardly a gripping subject! It had a Danish stamp and postmark, and the sender was Hilde. It was addressed to Evelyn at her digs in Fenny Stratford in English, but the message was cryptic. Probably just one of Evelyn and Hilde's little foibles. They both enjoyed puzzles and codes, it seemed.

The next two years entries were all devoted to everyday work and social events. The next eye-catching note was in October 1944, 'Terrible news via the grape vine – V.S in a punishment camp in Königsberg. She's felling trees in freezing conditions.'

I made myself comfortable with a cup of Darjeeling and a lemon tart. Immediately on picking up the diaries again, I was transported back to 1945. There were extensive entries for that year. They started with a flurry of entries made in late January through to the end of February:

Jan 25th, 1945. Intercept decoded - BZ on train out of Konigsberg. Window of opp. Contacted Hilde

Jan 26th, 1945. Train making slow progress.

Feb 1945 BZ on train and held in a railway siding. Railways disrupted severely by Russians in East and Allies from West. Hilde's friends on board. Sending progress reports by Morse.

Indeed, there were a bundle of transposed Morse code messages clipped to the page. They were in Danish, or at least that's what I guessed. I used Google translate to get a quick overview of what was in them.

One read 'Secured 27 crates with the fat boy's initials on them.'

Another read: 'There is no pulling back from what we have set in motion. We could pay a terrible price, but if we can pull it off, it will set us up for life.'

What on earth were they up to? Who was referred to as the fat boy? I had a light bulb moment when I realised that the photos in the safe could be of the wooden crates, she referred to here. I thought back to my twentieth century history lessons. Luckily, I had excelled at history. The name that came immediately to mind was Herman Goering. Had the women intercepted messages referring to a shipment meant for Goering? It could be a plausible explanation – the cigars, the sketch, they had tentative connections to Hitler's second in command. It was widely recorded in the history books that Goering was a lover of beautiful things. He certainly appreciated the finer things in life and that included plundered art. The Klimt sketch could well have been acquired for his wife.

A deeply touching submission was dated 6th February 1945. It read: 'Devastated to hear V.S executed yesterday at Ravensbrück. She's only 23! Damn, damn, Damn the Nazis! Despicable monsters! Something like this makes this hideous war all so real.'

The ink was smudged. I could imagine a distraught Evelyn writing these few lines with tears flowing down her cheek and onto the page. I researched the date and first name and concluded that the Violette referred to was Violette Szabo - a posthumously decorated British spy, who had become a legend after the war. I cross referenced back to November 1941; I could see that this was the Violette that Evelyn had met whilst at Beaulieu for training! Was Evelyn one of the British spies? Had she carried on spying in the cold war years and been found out by the Russians?

That would certainly provide a motive for her murder - vengeance a dish best served cold, and all that...Somehow it didn't stack up. I couldn't imagine the KGB waiting sixty odd years to get rid of a spy they had unearthed. Still, I must rule out this possibility once and for all. With that aim I would get Samson to check out old spymasters and see if any of them were still alive and would be prepared to talk to us. If Evelyn was a spy back in the day, then there would be a record of her somewhere. No harm could come of divulging the truth 70 years after the event.

Alongside the record of Violette's death, Evelyn had scribbled 'I'm even more committed to our project! Communism and fascism are both deceivers of the working class! Hideous ideologies, both of them! Hilde, beside herself with fear that she will end up behind Russian lines!'

What was the project Evelyn alluded to? Interesting that she viewed both the Russians and Germans with the same contempt. I was still ploughing through the multitude of entries for 1945 when Samson came back to me, twenty minutes later.

"We may be in luck. There's one old spymistress still alive - Dame Marjorie Peters. She retired to Ludlow years ago and she's prepared to see us. On the phone she sounds like she's still got all her marbles although she must be well into her nineties."

"Excellent! Make an appointment with her for tomorrow afternoon if that's convenient for her."

"Will do."

I returned to my emersion into life in 1945

2nd May 1945 'Thank God! Monty reached the Baltic - sealed off the Danish peninsular with about 6 hours to spare, before the Russians arrived.

Prisoners taken by the 2nd army totalled half a million. All German communications breached. All forms of their transport are in chaos.

May 4th, 1945, 18.30 hrs Monty signed the instrument of surrender of all German armed forces in Holland, NW Germany including all islands and in Denmark. Can't believe it. Is the war really over?? Fighting continuing in The Pacific, though.

May 7, 1945 'Herman Göering arrested by US troops southeast of Salzburg, Austria. This could be a problem!'

I wondered, what sort of problem?

15th July 1945 arrive in Paris. Hot & fine. Hotel Regal, near the Madeleine. Day off before meeting up with the Americans. Visit R.V at the Musées Nationaux. Enlightening chat with R.V. She has so much information about stolen art locked up in her head. She knows all the important European art dealers. Overnight train to Frankfurt.

I was scanning through the major dates that many wartime diarists would have recorded ... V.E Day, Atom bomb drops – Hiroshima, Nagasaki…

14th August 1945 Back to Blighty. What now? Back to academia? Can't stomach that. I need something intellectually satisfying. Women being told to go back to the home. No fear!! We are all ready to contribute to the peace, now. Alan talking of working on an automatic computing engine. Sounds interesting!

In the entries for 1946 I start to see the first mention of Manchester and Evelyn's work on the first computer.

May 1946.

Brilliant! A letter of invite from Newman to work for him in Manchester. A breath of fresh Mathematical innocence - I'll be working with a computer development that isn't about weaponry. Feels good. It's nice to work somewhere 'real" without the affectations and traditional rituals that went with Cambridge or BP life. We still pass coded messages between us ex-employees of BP. Old habits die hard!

October 1, 1946 'Military Tribunal at Nuremberg sentenced Göering to death by hanging. Thank goodness. The sooner the better.'

October 15, 1946, Göering - suicide by swallowing cyanide. Cowardly bastard. But good news for us. Another possible pitfall removed.

This couple of entries reinforced my idea that the two women had appropriated treasures looted by Herman Goering.

December 17, 1946, Announcement today in London Gazette. V.S awarded the George Cross, bestowed posthumously. Finally, some recognition for her sacrifice. Her mother and daughter must be very proud.

From 1948 the first mention of Moira appears, and Alan Turing comes back into Evelyn's life.

28th May 1948 'Alan has accepted a post here. Will be good to be working with him again. We can resume our bridge partnership.'

21st June 1948 'Moira engaged as an assistant to help with the programming. Ran our first program on the electronic digital computer. Hooray!

Under this entry there is another cryptic reference to BZ. Whoever this person is, he or she has been kept hidden for several years now. But why? Who is this? An ex-Nazi? Possibly someone wanted for war crimes? A spy who defected from Russia?

27th July 1948 'West Berlin airlifts underway. Serious talk about war with Russia. Messaged H.

B.Z can't return. Stay put for now.'

I'd ruled out B.Z being a place, but at this point, I still wasn't sure if it was a person or an object.

From entries dated August 1950 I could see that the two women were holidaying in The Gower 'Bliss on the Gower coast - Hiking, swimming, bird watching. If I could afford it, I'd buy a house here...Just don't have the funds.'

September 1st 'Back to Manchester. Everything looks grimy and grey after the Welsh coast! My work here is becoming increasingly frustrating and demoralising. Time for a change me thinks!'

Shortly after I see the first mention of GCHQ. 'Even more hush hush than BP, but at least I'm getting better pay.'

Then come a string of entries over the next few months and years that feature Edward Gresham.

July 1952 'Edward has asked me to marry him - I accepted! What have I done? He's a kind man with a good sense of humour. The marriage will suit both our purposes'

In September 1952, their wedding was simply recorded as 'No fuss at registry office.'

August 1953 Sian was born. 'Our beautiful baby girl! All the pain was worth it. Edward is ecstatic and so is Moira.'

Only three years later is the sad record of Edward's death from pancreatic cancer and Evelyn's practical calculations, 'Edward has left me his pension entitlement. Things will be tight, but I think I can make ends meet if I am careful.'

I saw that Evelyn had noted the death of Stalin in 1953. Her comments were 'Good riddance to that monster.' In pencil alongside was scribbled 'Maybe BZ can finally return?'

In 1957 there was an entry attesting to the return of The Dresden pictures and The Pergamon altar to East Germany from Russia. I wasn't familiar with the pictures, but I knew plenty about Heinrich Schliemann, the famous archaeologist who had excavated Troy and unearthed the fabulous Trojan treasures.

I was reading on through a period of less interesting entries. Then I came upon a reference to the cigars in Evelyn's diary for 1964 'Embargoes imposed on Cuba. Now is the time to sell H. G's cigars.'

I knew 1964 was the date of The Bay of Pigs crisis and that Cuba was famous for cigars. Thanks to Samson's research I now had an explanation for what otherwise would have struck me as an obtuse entry. From the cross checking with the auction catalogues, I knew Evelyn had made a sale of cigars in 1965.

Switching back and forth between the diaries, the auction catalogues, and the bank statements, I spotted that, Moira and Evelyn went a couple of times a year on the train from Swansea to Paddington. They took in an opera, visited a few art galleries, and went to Harrods food hall and Fortnum and Masons to stock up on gourmet foods. They also visited Hatton Garden! I know that Hatton Garden is the hub for diamond dealers in London. I could see that Evelyn had booked several appointments in her diaries to see one Sandeep Sharma. According to her diary annotation, she sold on consignment, four perfect clarity, three carat diamonds for an amount of £18,000. She then got Sharma to use the proceeds from the conventional diamond sales to buy fancy pink and yellow Argyle diamonds. I could piece together the fact that it had taken him a period of eighteen months to procure these very specific Argyle gems. What a canny investor this woman had been. Since then, coloured Argyle gems have been the best performing diamond class. It seems, Evelyn had always been first at spotting a trend!

Am I seeing a pattern of money laundering here? Where had the conventional diamonds come from in the first place? I knew that during the Second World War they were the ultimate when it came to portable wealth. As evidenced by her diaries, I could see that Evelyn had taken a trip to Copenhagen shortly after each auction sale. Interesting!

I skipped through some more mundane entries then in the 1980s a couple caught my eye....

September 17th, 1980. Flew to Paris. Train down to Saint-Étienne-de-Saint-Geoirs.

September 18th, 1980 –R. V's - funeral. What an amazing woman she was. Sad that she's gone. A few interesting characters at the memorial ceremony. Had dinner with S.K and discussed art collections. Must let H know S.K is a possible buyer of taste.

I thought that was an interesting turn of phrase! I knew from my research that R.V was Rose Valland who had made a record of every single art piece plundered by the Nazis from Paris. She had managed to discover the coded numbers referring to their hidden art stores. She led the U.S 'Monuments Men' to six art depositories including Neuschwanstein Castle that were packed with Nazi loot.

Then another in 1984: 'Soviets have called off the search.' The search for whom, I wondered?

From 1986: 'Erich Koch, SS commander. Dead. Last witness - chain severed.'

Witness to what exactly? - such a convoluted enigma!

There was a string of every day, workaday entries for the next few years - nothing unusual.

I was now into the 1990's

April 1994

'Moira and I attended the George Ortiz Exhibition at the Royal Academy, London. Amazing collection of antiquities. Absolute works of art. Met S.K at Claridge's, afterwards.'

I remembered this exhibition myself. I had attended it too! Our paths might have crossed. A weird thought. Here and there Evelyn had made some tantalising statements:

'I've never admitted my doubts and fears, over all these years. I've lived with the constant fear of discovery hovering at the back of my mind. I've been cunning and I seem to have got away with it all.'

What had she got away with? I had to figure it out. I had access to so many pieces of information, but I couldn't slot them together. The full picture was still alluding me.

Another intriguing entry sprang off the page dated, May 13th, 1997

'First visit to Germany in 50 years. Very prosperous! Bremen. Meeting with lawyer - Mr Kaiser. S.K agreed a price for Taste. A Jewish buyer. Sublime irony!'

Another mention of 'Taste.' Was this a painting or a sculpture? I sensed that this was an intricate piece of the conundrum.

May 15th

'Thank goodness, I left Bremen yesterday. German officials have arrested Mr Kaiser! I can only pray that the German authorities believe that only one survived! As, Rohde wanted them to believe.'

I made a note to myself to try to follow this trail in the German press for that date. Who was Rohde?

Years pass by with general run of the mill entries for family birthdays, holidays, and concerts etc…

Then in 2003 more connections to Russia appear in the form of a few very brief entries:

May 31st, 2003. '3.30pm Pravda internet broadcast.'

June 7th, 2003. 'Moira and I, off to St Petersburg to see the duplicate.'

June 10th, 2003 'Tonder. Staying with Hilde.'

Evelyn had obviously gone to stay with her cousin in Denmark immediately after visiting St Petersburg. What was the Pravda broadcast about and why had she gone to Russia? There was no further elaboration, unfortunately. I made a note to investigate this cluster of entries.

Flicking through the next few years, nothing of particular interest grabbed my attention.

I clocked a couple of pertinent dates in the diary for 2009

'Major reunion at Bletchley Park.'

In December 'Wren library, Trinity College Cambridge - Uncle Gareth's diaries on display.'

The next year, in May I saw Evelyn's response to the gold-plated brooch received from the Prime Minister: 'What an insult! That's the final straw. Pathetic token gesture!'

After this the entries virtually dried up. There was a long and poignant entry referring to Moira's death.

The very last diary entry started with a quote,

"Some of the splendour of the world

Has melted away through war and time:

She who protects and conserves

Has won the most beautiful fortune"

I was familiar with this quote from Goethe. I was amused to see that Evelyn had changed the 'He' to 'She'! Beneath the quote was scribbled, 'Listed BZ on the DW. Offer accepted. 40,000 Bitcoin. Reparations completed. Respect at last. Exquisite irony.'

So, finally here it was, the reference to the transaction. Now I knew for sure that B.Z was an object, not a person. Whatever it was, it was of great value.

Yet another maddening comment - 'It can't do any harm if the truth is told now. At this late stage of the game, honesty is possible for me and that's a relief. Most of the sketchy truth is in my diaries, the rest is committed to my memory. Of course, there is another living person who knows the whole truth.'

Before my meeting with Jennifer Barnes, I would have presumed this to be Moira. But, having listened to the tapes I was convinced that it had to be Evelyn's cousin, Hilde.

Prophetically, a final quote was scribbled in pencil, at the bottom of the page. It was from Sophocles, Oedipus Rex:

'Time, which sees all things, has found you out.'

A shiver ran up my spine. It was as if Evelyn had known that by selling this object, she would bring the sword of Damocles down on her head.

My whole body had just about seized up by the time I finished reading. I had been doodling whilst making my notes, in the hope that it would make me think more clearly. I knew I was getting somewhere, but I could only worry about where that was once I had arrived there. I could see why Jennifer Barnes believed Evelyn's memoirs would make a great read!

My head was filled with the chronological events of Evelyn's past life as I tried desperately to switch off my brain processes and get a good night's sleep.

•••

I spent the next morning highlighting entries that I needed to investigate further. Samson tapped me on the shoulder just after 1pm to remind me that Dame Marjorie had agreed to see us at 3pm.

"Shall we head off now and stop on the way to get some lunch?"

"Yeah, I know a lovely gastro pub in Monmouth" suggested Samson.

Greatly revived after a delicious lunch, we arrived in Ludlow. Dame Marjorie lived in a cottage that could easily have been a Miss Marple set. The elderly spymistress bore a marked resemblance to Margaret Rutherford. Of course, Samson had never seen a Margaret Rutherford film, so had no idea what I was on about. Her mannerisms were positively Victorian, but I could tell she had lost none of her instincts. She was studying us like a vigilant old hawk. The blinds were pulled down and a small television was playing on mute in the corner. I noticed an ashtray with one cigarette butt in it. Cuttings from 'The Financial Times' were sitting on top of her Jacobean table and a laptop was open next to them. This was a wily old bird. She must have been a formidable opponent in her day. She greeted us pleasantly enough, but she made no offer of a seat or a beverage, so I got straight down to business.

"Thanks for seeing us at such short notice."

She didn't reply. This was a woman at ease with long pauses. She still knew her spy craft.

"We are investigating the death of Evelyn Jones, late of Cambridge University and Bletchley Park. She knew Violette Szabo during the war and a few other women we suspect were spies. A Russian connection has come up and we wondered if you could shed any light on Evelyn's war time work. Was she one of your women spies or do you think she could even have been a Russian spy?"

I passed her a photo of Evelyn taken in the early 1950's. This all sounded ridiculous to me, sitting in a cosy cottage in Ludlow in 2013. But the question had to be asked.

She glanced at the photo then looked off into the middle distance, trying to summon up the details from a distant past. After a few moments she said, "No, she wasn't a British spy and we got to know about most of the Ruskies too. That name was not among them."

Samson pitched in, "It's a long time ago. Are you sure?'"

If looks could kill, he'd have been a goner.

"I may be in my twilight years, young man, but my recall is excellent. When I say this Evelyn Jones wasn't a spy, I mean it. I can say that with all confidence. The names of my operatives and our adversaries are embedded into my conscience and will be until the day I die."

"Oh, sorry I didn't mean to offend you" offered Samson.

"Apology accepted. Now if there's nothing else, I need to get on. I'm expecting company."

Well that told us! As if to soften the blow, she offered us some insight into her current life. She told us she had always had an aptitude for figures and nowadays she took pleasure in decoding the hints and information that was hidden in company accounts and announcements. She had made a surprising amount of money by sitting in her armchair and placing deals in the stock market. She could never have envisaged such a retirement during the war!

What a formidable character. After thanking her again for seeing us, we made a speedy departure.

I had total faith in Dame Marjorie's recollection.

Samson summed it up "Well, I think we can rule the spy connection out, don't you?"

"Yeah, and I'm glad of that. That theory never did sit well with me. From what I've read in Evelyn's diaries she was patriotic and never shirked her duties, no matter how hard things got during the war. She was definitely hiding a secret but I'm now positive it had nothing to do with betraying her country."

Samson gave me a considered look, "How close are you to solving this one? Sounds like you've made a lot of headway since reading the diaries."

"Oh, there's still a lot of unanswered questions, but I'm inching closer."

"Come on then, spill the beans. Give me a potted version."

As he was driving down the M50, I put into words what I'd concluded so far.

"After piecing together entries from the diaries, snippets that Sian has volunteered and the tapes that Jennifer Barnes recorded. I'm pretty sure that Evelyn and her cousin, Hilde used the atmosphere of chaos and confusion just before the war's end to pull off an audacious heist.

"Makes, sense. You mean the diamonds, the Klimt sketch, and the cigars?"

"Yes, they were a minor part of it. I've been going through Evelyn's old bank statements, and I can see a string of sales over the years that netted her considerable windfalls. But we've got to find out what she sold off shortly before she died. I believe Evelyn and Hilde were able to waylay a consignment of looted art and other valuables that were earmarked for Herman Goering. After all, history at times can present opportunities - a matter of a few minutes here and there when no one is paying attention. I reckon these two women grasped some huge opportunity. With mayhem all around, they made a spur of the moment decision. At the time, they would have had no idea how the results of that decision would cascade down through the decades."

Samson nodded in agreement, "Stranger things have happened! Plenty of Nazi looted art is still missing. What do you think the major artwork was that she sold for the $8 million?"

"Ah, that's where I've still got work to do. If I can find out what B.Z is, I think that will slot the final piece of the puzzle into place. I'm getting close. I can feel it in my water!"

"Brilliant! Let's have a blitz on all the evidence we've gathered tomorrow. I'll chase up the techies and see if they've found anything more that could help us wrap it up."

We were both feeling content with our day's work. I allowed myself to simply enjoy the lovely scenery of the Wye valley as we headed home. I put on Radio 4 before going to bed and drifted off to sleep as the shipping forecast warned of gales in Tyne and Dogger.

• • •

I got a devastating phone call the next morning. I was mid-way through my bowl of porridge when my mobile rang. It was Brian Smythe, my boss. He started by saying,

"Don't get mad because you're not going to like this…"

My stomach churned.

"MI5 has taken over the case and the Met and South Wales police will be closing their files. They have a probable murderer, and it will be up to The Secret Service now to push the Russians for extradition orders for Ustinov to face punishment."

I pleaded, "But, Sir, we are so close to solving this case. Another week could do it. You know as well as I do that the Russians will never return Ustinov to the U.K to face trial."

His laconic reply indicated that it was hopeless arguing for an extension. The decision was final.

I was reeling from this news. I was informed that I must write up my report, include all my research and hand it over to Smythe for onward transmission to The Secret Service operative. Samson must do the same.

When I closed the call, I couldn't eat another mouthful. I felt physically sick. I was wholly invested in this case. Evelyn was a fascinating woman. Although she was a different generation to me, we shared many interests and I felt huge empathy for her. I admired her pluck and intelligence. I had to do justice to the memory of this extraordinary woman! I couldn't just walk away from her case. Not to follow through was anathema to me. After all the hours spent pouring over old transcripts and historic documents, my inquisitive mind needed to know not just the facts and the culprits, but the WHY of it all!

PART 2

Once the case was officially handed on to MI5, or The Secret Service as it is called nowadays, The Met and South Wales police saw no reason to continue with any of their investigations. However, I was determined to make inquiries on my own private grapevine, even if it meant ignoring a multitude of the department's rules of procedure. I felt compelled to pick up the spoors of whatever past events had caused such disastrous repercussions for Evelyn. I was hooked. Even if at first it was to be a thankless task, I had to persevere. I could not let it rest. What had infuriated the Russian's so much? The idea that Evelyn was a spy just didn't fit with what I knew about her as a person, although all the good spies were of course masterful at deception. I felt a compulsion to know how this hand played out, to the grim end.

Samson and I had to pack up our temporary office in Bridgend and say our goodbyes to all the people we had worked with. I was incensed that we had to terminate our work. Samson took things much more philosophically. He gave me a big hug and promised to keep in touch, as he packed his car and waved goodbye. I would miss him. We'd grown much closer over the last few weeks.

Driving back to London, I was in a dark, sombre mood. Instead of Mozart, my choice of music was Wagner – Parsifal and Gotterdammerung!

Over the next few weeks, a significant amount of my time was spent on managing the policing for protests and events put on in London. It was all a bit mundane. I returned home exhausted most days. The sheer logistics of this type of policing is mind sapping. Nevertheless, whenever I had some spare mental energy, I followed up my own research into Evelyn's past.

With infinite gradualness over a period of weeks, the archives, tapes, diary entries and annotations in Evelyn's books and pamphlets began to yield up their secrets. One document led to another; one name stood out above all others - Evelyn's cousin Hilde. The amount of correspondence between the two women was immense. Many of their Morse code messages to each other during the war were cryptic and many of the annotated comments that Evelyn had made were baffling. I was only seeing one side of this correspondence, but it was enough to convince me that they shared a big secret. The documents and tape recordings led off on many murky tangents and quite a few dead ends. Some of my internet searches veered off into crazy avenues that had no relevance at all, just some hook of a keyword that had been used to gain web traffic by obtuse internet businesses. Hilde would surely be able to fill in the remaining blanks. I decided to pay Sian another visit and ask if she would arrange a meeting, on the pretext of gathering more material for the eventual publication of Evelyn's memoirs. After all, I was still in touch with Jennifer Barnes the writer, so it was only a little white lie! I was prepared to go to Denmark at my own expense. I was owed some holidays from work and besides, I'd always wanted to visit the Viking ships at Roskilde and the 2,000-year-old bog burials.

•••

I arranged to see Sian one Saturday afternoon in late September. I booked into a hotel in St David's on the Friday night. The next morning, I walked the segment of The Wales Coastal path between Solva and St Justinian's. The weather was glorious. The coastline sublime. Why would you want to be anywhere else? I had serious thoughts of moving back to Wales! I drove through to Newport for our meeting at 4pm.

Sian's house was just as I remembered it, but Sian herself seemed much more relaxed and at ease. I guess the grief was less raw and her mother's estate had all been sorted out. Whatever the case, she was very welcoming and talkative. She showed me her most recent plantings in her garden, and we picked apples from her small orchard. We chatted about current affairs and the general state of the world. Suddenly she asked, "You're not driving all the way back to London tonight, are you?"

"Oh, no I booked into the Red Dragon Hotel in St David's for two nights."

"In that case would you like to stay for dinner? I'm making a vegetarian lasagne and an apple pie. It would be nice to have some intelligent conversation over dinner."

"Okay, that would be terrific. I'm sure your cooking will be much better than the Hotel food."

With that settled she asked if I'd like a glass of wine. She could offer me an organic Pinot Grigio from Italy or a Rioja from Spain. If sparkling was my tipple, she had a bottle of Blanquette de Limoux she could open. I plumped for the white and she settled for the red. We had a thoroughly delightful meal, and our conversation was about archaeological sites in Europe we had yet to visit and what other travels were on our respective bucket lists. Sian was a great conversationalist and we revelled in each other's company. Before I left, she phoned her Aunt Hilde. A meeting was arranged for mid-October. I would fly across for a long weekend. By the time I got back to my hotel in St David's it was close to midnight. I realised it was the best night out I'd had in ages.

Samson and I arranged to meet for brunch in Fishguard on the Sunday morning. When I told him I was following on with my own investigations, his sage opinion was,

"Leave well alone, if I were you."

"But don't you want to know why?"

"Well, yes, I'd be interested but I wouldn't risk my career for it. I'm up to my eyeballs in a new case anyway. A drug gang. We believe their main base is in Milford Haven."

"Oh, right in your own backyard so to speak."

"Yes, it's good to be involved with a local case of such importance. We reckon they've been importing drugs through the port for at least three years and it's a multimillion-pound business. They have networks stretching out as far as Liverpool and Manchester. They're paying teenagers a pittance to pedal the drugs. Scum of the earth, I call them. Ruining the youngster's lives!"

We had a pleasant companionable time. He asked me if we could meet up again, once I was back. He'd love to hear what I'd concluded. I didn't need much persuading to come back to this neck of the woods. With a pang I wondered if I would ever see Sian again once my investigation was wound up. But I didn't admit this to Samson. "Good luck with nabbing the drug ring bosses."

"Make sure you take your thermals," shouted Samson as I got into my car.

●●●

It was a bright but chilly day as I flew into Copenhagen. Visibility was terrific, so I had a magical view of the city as we circled to land. I am staying at a hotel right on the waterfront in Copenhagen. From here it will be a short stroll to the iconic Little Mermaid statue perched on her rock. I was humming the 'Wonderful, Wonderful, Copenhagen' tune before I could stop myself. Despite this clichéd song, there is indeed something wonderful about Copenhagen. Maybe it's due to the Nordic light, the presence of the surrounding sea or the sense of continuity you get from knowing that the Danish Queen, descended from the Vikings still lives in the very heart of the city, guarded by soldiers kitted out in Hans Christian Andersen toy town uniforms. I dropped my luggage at my hotel, grabbed a quick sandwich of 'kryddersild' – pickled herring on rye bread and caught the train heading towards Esbjerg.

"Flat as a pancake" had been Samson's summation of Denmark. But I could see from the train that this was only a partial truth. The highest peak is 'Himmelbjerget' which means 'Sky Mountain' and falls just shy of 600 feet. Denmark is a land of scenic variety and its own brand of beauty. Since leaving the affluent, metropolitan area of Copenhagen I watched a landscape of fields and forests criss - crossed by roads and interspersed with small towns, each with their own white church. The tree leaves were on the change from golden, to yellow to amber. The sun was a cool, pale disc. As the train rolled on, I observed the landscape shifting between open traditional farms to beech forest, from lakes to islands, from rolling hills to level plains, from drifting sand dunes to steep limestone cliffs. Apparently, wherever you are in Denmark you are no more than 32 miles from the coast. Thinking back to my geography and geology lessons in school, I could see this was a classic glacial landscape. While neighbouring Norway and Sweden are formed largely by glacial erosion, Denmark is made up of glacial deposits, left behind when the glaciers retreated northward. My destination - the Jutland Peninsular is the result of meltwater deposits. The western coast is storm lashed and sparsely populated and made up of an almost unbroken belt of sand dunes stretching all the way from Skagen in the far north to Esbjerg in the south. From Tønder to the German border, salt-marsh plains shape the coastline. Here and there, the wind is whipping up the sand dunes and fluttering the red and white Danish flags. It seems that every proud owner of a house, farm, church, government office or restaurant flies the 'Dannebrog' from a pole in their yard. Although it is early Autumn, I am glad I am wearing my thickest puffer jacket. The digital thermometer on the train is showing 9 degrees C! I shouldn't be surprised as Denmark is on about the same latitude as Moscow!

Whilst I am in Jutland, I hope to fit in a visit to the Viking ring fortress of Aggersborg and the oldest town in Denmark - Ribe. Tomorrow I will do the tourist traps of the Capital and go out to Roskilde, Denmark's first capital, to see the Viking boat museum. Their collection of Viking ships is unsurpassed. The largest is 36 metres long and built in 1030! Time permitting I'd also like to visit Silkeborg museum to view "Tollund Man' — the so called bog man. An old university friend of mine told me that he is so well preserved, you can count the wrinkles on his forehead. Mind you, being only thirty years of age when he died in 200BC, he shouldn't have too many wrinkles! Just as I'd finished these musings, I arrived at today's destination.

The train station in Tønder is on the western side of the charming historic town. I figured I could walk to Hilde's house. I got out my mobile to check Google maps. I turned left into a quaint, curving cobblestone street with half - timbered houses. Like something out of a fairy tale! I was soon in the main square looking up at Kristkirken, a sixteenth century church. I carried on walking south for about five minutes before reaching Hilde's house. It was on the very edge of the town - a fine eighteenth-century property with extensive gardens to the side and back. It was well kept and grand. There was no shortage of money here, I reckoned. I knocked on the solid green door. A moment later a striking woman opened it.

"Hello, you must be Nia," she flung the door wide. "Please come in my mother is expecting you"

"You've got a lovely place here"

"Yes, this house was built by one of the wealthy lace merchants in 1785. We've owned it since the late 1960s."

She took my coat and hooked it onto a coat stand just inside the doorway then led me down the expansive hallway to a gorgeous light flooded room at the rear of the house. Her mother was sitting in a winged armchair by a roaring open fire. She got up to shake my hand and gave me a warm welcome. Once she was up on her feet, I could see that Hilde was physically very different to Evelyn. She could be described as the classic Scandinavian type - tall, blond (now turned to silver) hair and striking blue eyes, undulled by age. She had remarkably unwrinkled skin. Probably a reflection of good nutrition and a cool wet climate. Very slim, she had retained an athletic physique. Not at all what I had been led to expect from Sian, who had told me Hilde was too ill to make it over for Evelyn's funeral. Unless this woman had made a miraculous recovery in the last few months, then Sian had told me a porky!

"It's lovely to meet you Nia, Rhiannon told me how supportive and helpful you were to her mother during the police investigation into Evelyn's death. Please make yourself comfortable."

"I need to make clear to you, that I am here today as a private person. I'm not here as a police officer. The police have closed the case and handed the details on to MI5."

"MI5! Good lord why have they got involved?"

"The Security Service are responsible for counterespionage on British soil. They believe a Russian assassin killed Evelyn. The rifle used was a World War Two rifle that had been owned by a Russian sniper called Lyudmila Pavlichenko. Her nickname apparently was lady death!"

Hilde's face lost all its colour, and I could see her hands were gripping the arms of the chair very tightly. I briefly filled her in about Boris Ustinov, the SVR staff officer that we believed was Evelyn's executioner.

"Oh my God, the Russians are behind Evelyn's death?"

"Yes, it appears so. Didn't Sian tell you that MI5 had taken over the case?"

"No, she probably wanted to spare me that detail. Evelyn and I were like sisters and I was heartbroken by her murder. Sian probably thought the less said about it the better. She might have thought it would finish me off!" She gave a wry smile. "But I'm tougher than that".

Even so, I was sure I detected an element of panic in Hilde's demeanour. I felt the atmosphere had changed in the room. I took the initiative, "When did you last speak to Evelyn?"

"She skyped me about two weeks before she died. I still can't bring myself to say before she was murdered. But that's what you believe happened isn't it?"

"Yes, sadly that's the only conclusion we could reach given the nature of her death. What did you talk about? Did you notice anything unusual in Evelyn's demeanour?"

"We started off with the usual catching up with news of our families and some general chit chat about current affairs. What was unusual was, she asked me to write a coded line on a piece of paper and send it by snail mail to a PO Box in Monaco."

"Do you have a copy of that?"

"No, she made me promise to keep no copies whatsoever."

"Didn't you think that was odd?"

"Yes, but Evelyn and I had a close understanding, and I knew there would be a good reason for her request."

"Can you remember anything about the code?"

"No, sorry. I've seen so many snippets of code over the years and we'd been trained to forget them and not memorised any of them."

"You say it was just one line of code, not a set?"

"Definitely just one line. I would guess about 30 characters."

Obviously, this was part of the dark web sales process that had resulted in the sale of an unknown item that netted Evelyn $8 million! I couldn't quite swallow the fact that Hilde hadn't kept a copy. But I had to let it go for now.

I let her know that I had read Evelyn's diaries and studied the material for her memoirs. I wondered if she could contribute any of her own wartime experiences that might bolster the material that Evelyn had given to Jennifer.

She momentarily closed her eyes, rebuilding old landmarks in her mind. "War makes its own laws, you know. How could we ever explain the complexity of life during the war to generations of free people who hopefully, will never experience the war's cruel and exhausting nature? Youngsters today have no idea! World War Two is so often just viewed in simple terms of good against evil. Only the people that lived through it know the personal deprivations we endured and the extremes of barbarity we witnessed at the hands of the Germans and the Russians. What I didn't witness in person, I eaves dropped on by intercepting the myriad messages of The Third Reich and what we called the Fourth Reich - Stalin's Russia!

It was apparent that for most of their adult lives Evelyn and Hilde were incredibly close, even though they didn't live near to each other, they shared very deep bonds built out of similar life experiences. Hilde mused, "The path to future scientific accomplishments have often emerged out of the carnage of combat. This was certainly true of the Second World War. It paved the way for computers and Evelyn was a big part of that with her work at Manchester University. Our family history, on Evelyn's mother's side is littered with acts of betrayal by both the Prussians and the Russians. Both regimes were as bad as the other!"

Whilst Hilde was talking on this subject, she was transformed from a mild-mannered woman to a fierce opponent of these dictatorships which had been on her doorstep. Her contempt was still strong and ardent!

"My husband Ulf was killed by the Nazis within hours of them invading Denmark. He went out on his bicycle with about thirty comrades to try to stop the Panzer tanks. They had no chance and the Germans showed them no mercy. They mowed him down. Denmark fell within 6 hours. Can you believe that! I was pregnant at the time. That was April 9th, 1940. I remember it as if it was yesterday. The worst day of my life! I sent a message to Evelyn by Morse code telling her that Ulf was killed, and that Denmark had fallen. She was so, so shocked and enraged. Of course, the Nazi propaganda said that we were still managing our own affairs, just under their supervision. We Danes were classified as Nordic by the Nazi's, so we were high up in their order of racial acceptability." Hilde gave an outraged snort. "What a load of racist gobbledygook! Detestable creeps! Meanwhile my Jewish friends were seen as 'Untermensch'. The noose for them got ever tighter and by 1943 things were grim. In October that year they were being rounded up. That was the last straw for me, and I joined the Danish resistance. We ran boats at night to smuggle Jews out to Sweden, which remained neutral. That's a laugh! The Swedes were supplying the Nazis with all the steel they needed and laundering money for them!"

This was all useful background information, but I wanted to cut to the chase, so to speak. "Look, Hilde I know from my investigations that Evelyn was able to procure a consignment of items that she systematically sold off over a long period of time, reinvesting the proceeds into let's call them, alternative investments. I suspect the items had been looted by the Nazis and were earmarked for Herman Goering. I've been able to piece together the general scenario and I know you were somehow involved. I don't know what it was that netted Evelyn $8 Million just prior to her death. I believe that it was this that provoked the Russians wrath." I noticed that at the mention of Herman Goering Hilde's eyebrows had shot up, but she made no comment regarding my conclusions.

Here in this medieval Danish town, I could feel that I was close to the truth. I could feel the charge of history in the room.

Estrid brought over a steaming mug of black coffee and a warm cinnamon bun that she said she'd just got out of the oven. I thought she had the look of Agnetha, from Abba about her. She'd always been my favourite member of the band. Both women were very calm and composed. I felt relaxed in their company. There was an inner strength in these two, for sure.

Hilde mused "War makes its own laws. You must remember that in the context of what I am about to tell you." Her pleasant, soft voice nevertheless rang with the force of an inner conviction which no doubt, all the successful years of keeping secrets had given her.

I was on the edge of my seat, waiting for the story.

•••

Hilde retrieved a sheaf of soviet -era paper from her desk drawer. They were pages of flimsy, almost transparent paper. They were filled with meticulous, tiny, Cyrillic script. She then went upstairs and returned with a cardboard box fil ed with newspaper clippings and old scrapbooks. I took a bite of the delicious bun and just knew that I was going to see and hear some extraordinary revelations...

"Where to start?" she mused.

The warmth of the room and the comfortable armchair lulled me into a sense of benevolent calm, and I listened transfixed as for the next two hours Hilde told a story that could have been the script for an episode of Foyle's War!

"In a way, this whole story starts here in Tonder, in the wake of a huge gale that stirred up the seabed, causing a bobbing mass of amber to rise to the surface and was then washed to the shore. 4400 pounds of amber was collected from the beach one cold March morning by my ancestors, and it was a l fe changing event for my family who lived in a fisherman's cottage on the beach. The Tonder town charter goes back to 1243, you know. And although it's surrounded by marshland today, it was once a busy market town with access to the sea. Amber was known in those days as 'The Gold of the North' and it was very valuable."

I started to think, what's this got to do with anything? Then again, I could indulge her going off on a tangent, as long as she got to the pertinent facts eventually. So, I looked attentive and made some encouraging sounds.

"Have you heard of Fennoscandia?" asked Hilde

"No, I've never heard that term."

"It was a vast forest that stretched from the Norwegian coast to the Caspian Sea. For centuries the humid, coniferous jungle teemed with life and exuded hundreds of millions of droplets of resin onto the heavy clay earth, trapping countless frozen moments."

By now I was listening rapt. I thought this woman should make an audio book of this. I'd buy it! Her voice was hypnotic.

"Over millennia, ice sheets formed and thawed, flooding the Baltic and fossilising, and scattering the 'Gold of the north' or amber as we know it. It was later to be fished out of The Baltic by fishermen with nets or it washed up after big storms, as happened with my family.

Amber had a particular resonance with the Teutonic knights and the Prussian kings. They had a monopoly on its supply for hundreds of years and they used it to forge diplomatic ties with Russia in the 17th and 18th centuries. As far back as 1681 Frederick William sent Fedor II in Moscow, a throne made from Baltic Amber. Gottfried Wolfram was a master amber and ivory carver working at the Danish court. He went to Berlin in 1701 with a reference from the King of Denmark. He made three large ornate amber mirrors as samples and showed them to Frederick 1st of Prussia. He was an expert at intricate, artistic designs. He made the samples from part of his family's stash of Amber washed up on the beach."

I glanced up at the impressive mirror hanging above the fireplace. The exquisite frame was made from amber. The cogs were turning in my brain…

Hilde was back in the 18th Century, "Gottfried worked painstakingly for six years perfecting the special process of fashioning palm - sized leaves of amber, gently heating them to a temperature of between 140 degrees centigrade to 200 degrees, using a new technique developed by The Konigsberg Guild. The amber was dipped into heated water infused with honey, linseed, and cognac, to give a subtle tint to the resin. It was then set to harden on cooling racks before being polished. These 5mm thin slivers were slotted into place on wooden panels backed with feather- thin gold leaf. He even invented a special adhesive of pine resin and beeswax to hold it all together. It was highly skilled work. The finished panels resembled stained glass windows and the amber panels came alive in candlelight. Catherine the Great many years later described them with awe."

Hilde's command of the English language was fantastic. Even technical words were no problem for her. This was all fascinating, but where was it taking us? Maybe she detected my querying frown, because she said,

"Please indulge me. I'm not gaga. I haven't lost my marbles yet. You said you wanted to know everything. You'll see that this sets the scene for everything that Evelyn and I did."

"Okay, no worries. I love history, so this is fascinating to me."

She resumed her tale. "Gottfried's team had completed over a quarter of the total project by 1707. They had expertly fitted together tons of amber, like an epic jigsaw puzzle. It was a work of art. But, then the court favourite, Eosander Von Goethe took over the project. He dismissed Wolfram and refused to pay for all the work already done. The guards removed all the panels made in Wolfram's workshop and transported them to Charlottenburg. Gottfried was devastated and financially ruined. He fled back to Copenhagen with no payment.

Work on the amber chamber became a pet project of Catherine the Great's. A Florentine artist Giuseppe Zocchi was commissioned to create mosaics depicting the human senses: Sight, hearing, touch, smell, and taste that would be mounted in Amber frames. Whilst being transported to The Winter Palace, one of the frames was so badly damaged it had to be replaced. Zocchi contracted out the making of the frame for 'taste' to Wolfram's workshop."

The tentative connections in my brain were starting to fuse together. So here it was, 'Taste' was a mosaic made for Catherine the Great! Blooming heck! My stomach fluttered. What other momentous revelations were imminent?

Hilde carried on, "By now Gottfried's son, Olaf oversaw the workshop. He completed the frame for 'Taste' in 1756. Olaf used the remaining cache retrieved from the beach for this job as it was just the right shade of amber. It was the finest piece of work he had ever completed. The family's claim to fame and riches. But, no! Olaf suffered the same treatment from the Russians that his father had from the Prussians. They were cheated out of their rightful payments and left almost bankrupt.

Down through the generations the resentment and hatred for both countries festered within our family. My married name is Gustaffson but my maiden name was Wolfram. Gottfried Wolfram was my great, great grandfather. I have Gottfried's and Olaf's workshop journals. They are a family heirloom, handed down to my mother then to myself. They record how they used the stash of amber that the family had fished out of the Baltic to fashion into the fabulous Amber room or at least its first incarnation. By a fiendishly clever process Gottfried and Olaf spent thousands of hours working to make a magical chamber that came to symbolise The Age of Reason, in which it was conceived. The Amber Room was their life work. It sent them both to penury!"

Hilde was talking in an almost reverential way now...

"For over 150 years the Amber Room took pride of place in the Catherine Palace. Can you believe it even survived the Russian Revolution of 1917? It remained resplendent in St Petersburg until the invasion of three million German troops in June 1941. For the Nazis, the Amber Room was a priority for removal. It was at the top of their wish list of German made artworks to be "repatriated" to German soil."

We both took a sip of our coffees which had gone stone cold. I prayed she wouldn't stop now. I had to know the conclusion to this story.

She took a deep breath and resumed her tale...

"Evelyn and I were mathematicians. I was a student of Arne Beurling until 1938. He was a Swedish professor of mathematics at Uppsala University. Arne had become a firm friend over the years. In the summer of 1940, Arne came to visit me here in Denmark and over a two-week period, using just pen and paper and copious amounts of strong coffee, he single-handedly deciphered and broke T52."

I blurted out, "Yes, T52. Evelyn made mention of that cipher in her diaries."

Hilde explained, "Using transposition, T52 created nearly one quintillion different variations! The T52 cypher was even more complex than the cypher used in the Enigma machines. You know of course that Evelyn was working at Bletchley. I notified her that Arne had broken T52 - one of the 'Fish cyphers. Well, using Beurling's work, Sweden could decipher German tele printer traffic passing through from Norway on a cable. In this way, Swedish authorities knew about Operation Barbarossa before it occurred. They forewarned the Soviets of their imminent invasion by the Nazis. But because the Swedes wouldn't reveal how this knowledge was attained, the Soviets ignored them. Typical of that idiot Stalin! Don't think I'm rambling - there is a point to my telling you all this background information. Because Arne had broken T52, I picked up German transmissions which included the details of the shipment of works of art plundered by the Germans from Pushkin and Leningrad in

1941. The Nazis Second Special Battalion seized works of art which had been targeted by the Kummel Report. A comprehensive list of art pieces that the Germans spuriously claimed had been stolen from them since 1500!"

"Oh, I remember seeing a copy of that report in Evelyn's library. It made ridiculous conclusions and used crazy notions of what they deemed "Germanic.""

Hilde nodded her agreement and continued, "At Pushkin, the Nazi army thugs denuded the Catherine and Alexander palaces, destroying even the parquet floors, furniture, paintings, tapestries, books, and Catherine II's porcelain collection. The troops removed every single piece of the exquisite Amber Room. The houses of Pushkin, Chekov, Rimsky-Korsakov, Tchaikovsky, and Tolstoy were pillaged, and Tolstoy's manuscripts were burned. They went on a rampage of savage destruction of priceless pieces of art. They acted as absolute barbarians!" Hilde was virtually spitting out her words now.

"The Amber Room was last seen by the Germans on January 12th, 1945. Alfred Rohde who was the museum curator recorded that the panels were being crated for transport out of Konigsberg as the city was being crushed between advancing Russians from the East and the Anglo - American forces from the West. Rohde also reported that three of the exquisite Zocchi mosaics had been destroyed in Konigsberg castle during an allied bombing raid. BUT Herman Goering had a yearning for the Amber Room and its mosaics, so this information could not be relied on to be correct. It is rumoured that one of the mosaics had been earmarked for Goering's private collection along with The Eighth Wonder of the World!"

Konigsberg, Herman Goering, amber mosaics…. click, click the cogs were enmeshing in my brain.

I consumed the last delicious crumbs of my bun. Hilde got up from her chair and called for Estrid. She replenished our drinks and vanished again into the interior of the house. Hilde apologetically informed me that she needed to use the loo. After two mugs of coffee, I could understand why. It's a diuretic after all!

As she lowered herself into the armchair again, Hilde scrutinised my face and said, "I have grown old and the time for holding onto secrets is past" I could tell she was going to relate a story she had rehearsed so many times in her mind it had all but worn a groove there! This was her first chance to tell it out loud after all the years of silence.

"Evelyn told me that five years after her death she wanted that ghost writer to be given all her diaries and the material she had squirreled away for her memoirs. Now she's gone, I want the truth to be told too. It's not an easy thing to keep a secret for most of your life, you know. A conflict has been slowly destroying my integrity – the conflict between truth and the concealment of the truth."

"I can imagine," I said and indeed I did know. I had one or two secrets myself!

"Evelyn was subjected to so many instances of the degrading stereotyping that you saw in wartime society. I think she was grappling with all these inequalities when she saw a chance to make a point. There are brief moments of choice in our lives that have enduring consequences. This was one of them. But little did either of us know that things would pan out the way they did and over so many years!"

I was almost holding my breath by this point. All was about to be revealed!

•••

Hilde took up the story in January 1945. She stated that her account was drawn together from her personal experience, coded messages sent to her by Evelyn, her daily communiques with Danish comrades who had helped her and from an article published in the Stockholm based *'Dagens Nyheter'* that had appeared in November 1946. It was a three-page story based on the testimony of Karl Heinz given in evidence against Herman Goering. It proved that Goering was guilty of receiving vast amounts of art looted by the Nazis for his private collection.

"It was on January 12th, 1945, that Evelyn deciphered what appeared to be a mundane transmission of a train transport. The third Belorussian front was closing in on the third Panzer division and as the mottled brown swarm drew closer, the Russian noose was tightening around the City of Konigsberg. We already knew that looted artworks from Pushkin had been on display at the castle museum there. The transmission was confirmation that 35 crates had been loaded onto a train bound for Esbjerg. What was interesting about this communique was that it was addressed to R. Kropp, who was the personal valet to Herman Goering. Obviously, the cargo was of great importance to the Reich Marshall. By this time Goering and Hitler were completely estranged. Goering was in favour of brokering a deal with the Western allies for Germany's surrender. Hitler had seen this as an act of treason. Goering's wife Emmy and daughter Edda were already making plans to dash to safety in the Bavarian mountains, where he planned to join them later. He had just written his will and crate loads of his looted art treasures from Carinhall, his palatial country residence were being shipped south. The first paladin of the Reich was ready to depart Berlin hurriedly and without fanfare. What was not common knowledge was that a further 35 crates were to be sent north, by rail, towards the Baltic. Goering was hedging his bets!

Evelyn informed me via a coded message and we both concluded that the crates probably contained some of the precious art and gold that he had personally acquisitioned from the stash of looted Nazi treasure.

I happened upon this Swedish newspaper article in 1946. It tells the story of a German Army Captain. He gave evidence against Goering for the Nuremberg trials. This gave us the scenario of what happened immediately before Evelyn stumbled upon the transmission. It's well worth a read. Hilde must have read the article so many times that she knew it by heart. She passed me the fragile, yellowed newspaper clipping and told me to read it, while she prepared some vegetables for a soup. I looked at a grainy photo of a smiling Aryan looking family. It told the story of how they escaped Berlin just before the Russian army arrived. Captain Karl Heinz had been offered a small fortune in cash to perform this last 'favour' for Herman Goering. Money was of little worth to Heinz; it was the power and influence yielded by the corpulent Reich Marshal that interested him. So it was that Captain Heinz had agreed to personally supervise the loading of 35 wooden crates marked with the initials H.G, thus signifying these items as the personal property of Herman Goering. Train carriages had miraculously been requisitioned amidst the pyre of flame and rubble that was engulfing Konigsberg. In the turmoil at the central railway terminus Heinz had no problem recruiting a group of fanatical SS soldiers to physically load the train. No bribe had been necessary. Even though it was too late to avoid Germany's total defeat, the name of Herman Goering was enough to spur the SS men into fervent action. Konigsberg was rapidly being transformed into a heap of smouldering ruins as the last crates were loaded onto the train. Captain Heinz had paid bribes to a multitude of local dignitaries and politicians that were to facilitate the safe passage of the train, through the various borders and railway stations on its journey to the Baltic.

In return for this 'favour', the Reich Marshal had guaranteed the safe passage of Captain Heinz's wife and two young sons. He was desperate to get them out of Berlin especially since a ten- ton British bomb, called the Grand Slam had obliterated three apartment blocks close by. American B-17's flying daylight raids were knocking out power and essential services in their suburb. Things were becoming apocalyptic and both boys were becoming increasingly traumatised. What little remained undamaged by the Anglo - American bombers would be pounded into oblivion by Stalin's rockets and heavy-duty guns. Karl was determined to get his family out alive, before the Russians reached Berlin. He would do whatever it took to achieve his goal. As soon as wired confirmation of loading was received by Goering's valet, Robert Kropp, Karl's family would be flown from Tempelhof to a small rural airfield in Sweden. Here, his uncle would be waiting to spirit them away to safety. God willing, Karl would survive the next few months and join them once peace was ushered in.

Karl had told the reporter that he knew in his heart that the crates should have had A.H chalked on the wooden frames but by this stage of the war, he no longer believed in Adolf Hitler's dogma. The rumours from Berlin were that The Fuhrer had lost the last vestiges of sanity and was spiralling into madness, devoured from within by the all-consuming fact of his total defeat. But, instead of trying to make a peace treaty with the Allies, he would rather condemn the civilian population of Germany to blanket bombings, rape and pillage and other unmentionable tortures. It showed Hitler's absolute contempt for the German Volk. So, Heinz had no real feelings of guilt, as haggard and hungry and with shoulders hunched against the crippling cold, he watched the train pull out of the station on its journey to Denmark.

The article was well written, so it was easy to imagine that I was back in that winter of 1945. I could almost feel the cold and the wet wool smell of the Russian soldiers as they closed in on the city of Konigsberg.

Karl told the reporter that he suspected the ultimate destination of the art works concealed within the crates, would be South America via Spain. However, that was no longer his concern. He had played his part. The last action he needed to take was to find the radio operator before the transmitter was packed up and moved further west. In a partially ruined signal box, a harassed radio operator stooped over a makeshift table on which sat the radio and an Enigma coding machine. Heinz had never seen one before and he thought it bore a resemblance to a typewriter with the addition of a set of four metal rotors. He knew that once the message for Goering was typed into the machine, it would be scrambled by a series of electrical circuits, so that each individual letter was separately encrypted. This system allowed for hundreds of thousands of permutations for every message sent! Heinz handed the brief message to the Enigma operator. In plain text it read: 'Top Secret. For the attention of R. Kropp. BZ aboard train. Departed 18.00hrs. Heil Hitler. Captain Karl Heinz.'

He had no idea what this message would look like once it had gone through the Enigma machine. What he did feel certain of was that it was an unbreakable code. Once encrypted the details of his secret pact with Goering would be safe. And if Goering was true to his word, his family would be smuggled out of Germany to safety. Captain Heinz was never to know that the Enigma code had been broken by the Bletchley cryptanalysts years beforehand.

•••

Hilde re-entered the room, "As you can see the information from that article set the scene perfectly for what was to drop into Evelyn's lap." Hilde lowered herself back into her armchair. I was keen to finish the article, but she took up the story, "As Evelyn toiled away in the frigid air of Hut six that January evening, she noticed a communique from a call sign she recognised. She decrypted a momentous few lines that were to change both our lives. As a fluent German speaker, she didn't need to send it on for translation. She looked down at the plain text and time seemed to stand still - the monumental irony of history coming full circle presented itself. Evelyn knew the huge cultural significance of this short transmission. She filed the triplicate copies as per the normal process, having decided as the duty officer, that this was of no importance to the war effort. It didn't refer to any troop movements or have any strategic significance after all. One copy of the intercept, the decode, the translation, the Z-signal would all be pasted into the 'German Book' and probably this message would never be studied again. It would just be stored away for the records. It was 2am when Evelyn finally arrived home at her digs in the little village of Stony Stratford. She was exhausted after twelve straight hours spent decoding messages from all over Germany. But before she went to bed, she sent me a message. I received Evelyn's 'Kew to Tivoli' radio signal on the 15,460 kilocycles wavelength using the powerful 500-watt RCA transmitter that Arnie Beurling brought with him disguised as a gramophone, in 1941. You will see from Captain Heinz's article that whilst Evelyn slept, the train and a supporting vehicle travelling by road with the documentation and the inventory left Konigsberg in the midst of heavy fighting, with the Russians in control of most of the surrounding area."

I picked up the old newspaper clipping to follow the next instalment of this amazing story.

Captain Heinz reported that, 'Thousands of Wehrmacht and SS troops were fleeing west towards Monty's approaching 21st Army. Other SS units were holding out to the last man. As the final day of reckoning for the Nazi regime approached, many local politicians in towns and cities in the region, revived their regional loyalties. Self - interest came to the fore and self- preservation took precedence. Their future wellbeing depended on per-suading the Allies, when they arrived, they had 'never' been Nazis. To add to the chaos thousands of starving and homeless civilians sought refuge in the country villages that had not been destroyed, others were aiming to get to the relative safety of the Scandinavian countries. It was through this chaos that the train had to travel. Its progress was painfully slow, but it made stuttering headway towards its destination. The first stage of the journey between Konigsberg and Danzig was miraculously uneventful. The first mishap happened between Danzig and Szczecin - a city on the Oder

River in northwest Poland. The vast tower of its St. James Cathedral had just come into sight, when a coupling hook sheared, and the train was delayed for several hours before a repair could be made.

The captain, travelling in the support vehicle caught up with the train at this point. He boarded the train to make sure everything was in order. The locomotive that pulled the train had come with a German operator and four German soldiers to guard it. When the train reached Rostock, a city straddling the Warnow River on the north coast of Germany, a bombing raid was taking place and the general disorder grew. It was here that the support vehicle came under attack from enemy fire. It suffered a direct hit and burst into flames. The driver was killed outright and all the documents pertaining to the cargo were incinerated. At this point Captain Heinz and his soldiers decided that enough was enough. The end of the Third Reich was nigh, and they wanted to save their own skins. From their current position they believed they could just about outrun the advancing Russians and make it to the English lines in the West. If they surrendered to Montgomery, they stood a much better chance of being treated leniently, they reckoned. Before Captain Heinz disappeared, he handed the final message to the radio operator on board the train. The operator transcribed his final communique to Göering's valet, Robert Kropp. That last message read, 'All is lost. The train has been abandoned. It is approaching Rostock. Final destination is Esbjerg, as instructed by H.G. Fate of Bernstein Zimmer unknown. German railway men have fled. My men and I are joining a group of Waffen SS. We will continue resistance to the last man. 88'

I was reading, open mouthed by now, "Oh my god, Das Bernstein Zimmer!" The realisation hit me like a sledgehammer. B.Z - all those entries in Evelyn's diaries that had puzzled me. B.Z was never a person. It was the Bernstein Zimmer - German for "The Amber Room". This was a bit surreal. Where could this be leading? Surely these two women hadn't stolen The Amber Room! I tried to keep a neutral expression on my face. I don't know how successful I was. I blurted out "What does the 88 mean at the end of the message?"

Hilde answered with disdain, "Many of the German communiques finished with the number 88. The eighth letter of the alphabet - one of the childishly simple abbreviations they used for H.H - representing Heil Hitler."

I felt silly for asking. Meanwhile, Hilde was still reliving the events of winter 1945, "Just as you did, Evelyn told me she gasped in amazement as she decoded and translated this final message. It was to have far reaching consequences for our lives! We saw that we had a chance in a million. The monumental irony of history coming full circle presented itself to us. It was a once in a lifetime opportunity. We had to give it a go. Quite frankly, what did we have to lose? By this stage of the war the risks of any reprisal from the Nazis was minimal. The Western Allies were too busy with finishing off the Nazis and liberating the concentration camps and the Russians were focussed on getting to Berlin and exacting their revenge once they got there."

I was staggered by the audacity of their plan. I needed confirmation from Hilde that the consignment they were to steal included The Amber Room. "So, how did you intend to pull this off? The logistics involved must have been complicated.

"We made a split-second decision to grasp reparations for all the wrongs that our families had suffered at the hands of the Prussians and the Russians. The Amber Room was to arrive within a few kilometres of where it had all started. It was an ambitious plan that needed to be co-ordinated from Britain and Denmark. We were both very organised and believed we could pull it off. Evelyn decrypted the initial communique but once I was able to get my Danish guys on board the train, at Rostock, they sent me blow by blow reports of progress by Morse code every day. My husband's best friend, Olaf wanted revenge on the Nazis for Ulf's death. He and I agreed a pact. If he and two of his resistance mates, who worked on the railways, could board the train at Rostock and eventually divert it into Tonder on its way to Esbjerg, they could keep all the paper currency and half of the gold bullion that we removed from the cargo. They had no idea they were stealing The Amber Room. They had no interest in amber. They could trade the gold and cash on the black market, and it would help them rebuild their lives in the aftermath of the war. They were delighted to have this opportunity and they didn't ask any awkward questions.

We felt no guilt. After all, this information could have no bearing on the end of the war. No lives were at stake. At that point we believed we would just remove the gold and hide the crates until a reward was offered for the iconic art works. That could set us up for life and alleviate some of our hardships. I had a small child to support. I was desperate for any windfall that came my way. We even justified our actions by reasoning that at least The Amber Room would be secure and safe under our protection. Otherwise, it was at risk of being destroyed in the final desperate fighting and air attacks in The Gotterdammerung of The Third Reich! "

"Weren't you afraid? Where would you hide it?"

"We all knew it was just a matter of weeks until the Germans capitulated, so we were emboldened. We worked as a team. We had all joined the Danish resistance in 1943 and we wanted our revenge on the Germans. Signals were sent by Morse to divert the train onto the branch line through Tonder with the excuse that a train wreck was blocking the main Esbjerg line. The train was reduced to a speed of just over 5 kilometres an hour as it limped across the German border and into Denmark. In return for a dozen boxes of cigarettes, two cases of wine and a couple of silver candle sticks, the Danish railway officials at Tonder turned a blind eye as the three rear carriages were unloaded of their cargo. In total 76 wooden crates with the name 'Schenker & Cowere' stamped on them were on board the train. 35 of them had the initials H.G branded into the wood. Olaf and my husband's surviving comrades from the Danish Cycle Division who had tried to fend off the German invasion in 1940, helped me to unload the carriages containing these crates. Ulf's comrades believed me when I told them the crates belonged to me. After all, my initials were clearly branded into the crates! They used horse drawn carts to carry the boxes to the abandoned Zeppelin hangar at Tonder airfield. As money was tight and food supplies even tighter, they were satisfied with the payment they received for helping with the transfer of the crates. They never gave it a second thought from then on. The unloading took us less than an hour to complete. The train itself, disappeared into the distance, shrouded in a cloud of hissing steam bound for Esbjerg, with its remaining cargo intact. I had pulled off the hijacking. Oh, yes, I'm proud of that!"

"How did you come to use the Zeppelin hangar?"

"I had been renting it from an old farmer since 1943. It was used as a safe refuge for Jewish families that we were smuggling out to Sweden. I bought it outright just after the war, for a bargain basement price.

Listening to all the logistics challenges that the women had overcome was amazing, but I had no doubt that it had happened just as Hilde said. "So, you hid the crates in the Zeppelin hangar, and nobody asked any questions or came looking for them?"

"Over the decades the crates gathered dust and everyone in Tonder forgot about them. Remember, it was chaos in those last days of the war. The Third Reich was in its death throes. All the action, so to speak was taking place in Southern Bavaria and the Tyrol. 'Bonzenflucht' - the flight of the Nazi party favourites who could escape Hitler's Berlin bunker was in full swing with Herman Goering in the lead. He had a motorcade of cars loaded down with carpets, pictures, jewels, all sorts of loot headed for Bavaria. The whole of the Reich bank's gold bullion, bank notes and vast amounts of foreign currency made its way South in two specially commissioned trains, codenamed Adler and Dohle. All sorts of treasures were pouring into Bavaria from the hard-pressed North. They hid loot in mine shafts, in lakes, buried under barns, churches and in the cellars of private villas. The Allies feared that the fanatical Nazis would hold out for years in the so-called Alpine fortress, so all their attention was focussed on the south.

When Germany was split up into allied occupation zones at the end of the war, there was immense administrative confusion and by the time the Americans and the Russians belatedly tried to put two and two together most of the eyewitnesses to these events were either dead or had dispersed to goodness knows where.

When the Americans sent in the monuments men to repatriate stolen art treasures and Nazi loot, we experienced a couple of anxious years. They were relentlessly searching and tracking down ex-Nazis. We thought for sure we would be caught. Evelyn had struck up a friendship with Rose Valland who worked with the monument's men. She was our ear to the ground. Evelyn made discrete enquiries from time to time about The Amber Room. Rose said the trail had grown cold. It had simply disappeared. The only search that got too close for comfort was when the Soviets sent two divers down to the wreck of the 'Wilhelm Gustloff', in the late 1960s. It was a German ocean liner that was sunk in the Baltic on January 30th, 1945, killing nearly 10,000 fleeing Nazis and civilians. Some bright spark had conjectured that

The Amber Room, packed in its crates was in the hold and went down with the ship. Of course, Evelyn and I knew that they would find nothing. Still, the proximity of the search was nerve wracking!

Other than that, all the attention remained in Bavaria, Northern Austria, Poland and even Czechoslovakia. Rumour and counter rumour were rife in the cold war years. Of course, all of this played into our hands. It was as if the Russians and the East Germans were working to keep the scent off our tails! We couldn't believe our luck. And this stuff just kept happening decade after decade. No one ever came sniffing around us. We were never suspected. By this time, we were both JUST old grannies. But of course, we were never that. We could outsmart all these megalomaniacs with their hubris and egos. To keep a big secret for this long you must be devoid of ego. Most men can't achieve that!"

She seemed mighty pleased with herself. Quite frankly, I was speechless. Hilde was on a roll; it was as if she was shedding an albatross that had hung around her neck for seventy years. "Evelyn decided soon after the iron curtain descended on us that she was not going to return to being voiceless or impoverished. She was not afraid of anything. She was a woman who had an inner core of steel, hidden deeply behind a facade of obedience to authority and the state. She was indomitable, fearless. There was no way she was going to return to a menial job. I remember the first time Evelyn visited me after the war. She came by boat from Tilbury to Copenhagen. We entered the Zeppelin hangar with two powerful torches. We prized open three of the crates sitting on top of the pile. The amber panels glowed a beautiful rich hue. The beams of our torches were glancing off prehistoric air bubbles with tiny insects preserved in them for all eternity. We were looking in awe on miraculous flocks of amber parrots and eagles. All those frozen moments of millennia's past trapped in the light of our torch beams. We couldn't believe what we had in our possession! We were staggered to find an exquisite mosaic amongst the panels. By some miracle of fate, the 'Taste' mosaic was the one that Olaf Wolfram had crafted back in the eighteenth century! It was believed to have been incinerated in the destruction of Konigsberg castle, but here it was in all its glory. It was as if it had been returned to its rightful owners. I was never going to give that back to the Russians. Evelyn would always say to me "Collectors don't plunder artefacts, they save them". In our minds, we were saving The Amber Room. "

• • •

I was stunned by Hilde's revelations. I felt a clammy-handed excitement as the missing pieces to the puzzle slotted into place. There were still a few loose ends, I needed clarifying. "There is an entry in Evelyn's diary dated 1997. She went to Bremen. What was that about?"

"Ah yes", murmured Hilde. Evelyn went to Bremen to negotiate the sale of 'Taste' which was the mosaic in our possession. Evelyn and I were by that time struggling financially and we had to raise some serious money. We saw an opportunity to sell 'Taste' to a deserving buyer. The deal wasn't just about profit. It was about honour, righting historic wrongs and to be perfectly frank, getting respect and reparations. The Russians believed that only one of the mosaics had survived. But our game was very nearly up on that occasion. Evelyn had a close call in Bremen when a German tried to sell the other surviving mosaic on the open market. Apparently, his father had stolen it when the Amber Room was being transported from Leningrad to Konigsberg back in 1941. He had bided his time until then. The German police raided his lawyer's office and seized the mosaic. They had been staking out the place for months, apparently. Evelyn was lucky to get away undetected. Thank goodness she was late arriving at the lawyer's office. She took the mosaic in her hand luggage back to Wales. Owen brought it back to me after Evelyn's death. It was in her will, bequeathed to Estrid. It's hanging on the wall in her bedroom."

Ha, I'd had a feeling that Owen had been holding out on us. Hilde had just confirmed it!

Hilde paused to muse for a few moments then carried on, "We had another panic on last year when the art collection of Hildebrand Gurlitt was found in his son, Cornelius's apartment. Do you remember that? It made international news headlines. During the war, Hildebrand Gurlitt was one of the privileged few given a commission to purchase works for the Führermuseum. He was also one of the main procurers of art for Herman Goering. He obviously took the opportunity to expand his own collection too.

The German authorities were investigating the son for tax evasion; what they found instead was a horde of looted art that had not seen the light of day since 1945. Hidden in filing cabinets and suitcases, investigators found more than 1,500 works by artists including Picasso, Matisse, Monet, Chagall and Delacroix. The 'Munich Art Hoard', as it became known.

Evelyn and I didn't know what Cornelius had in documentation. His father was notorious for making meticulous lists of every item procured for the Nazis. It seems that we dodged another bullet, as so far, no German police have come knocking at our door.

Evelyn nourished her resentment over decades. It became stronger as the years went on. The final straw for her was when she received that brooch and a letter from the Prime minister. She was outraged. She was offended. It acted as a catalyst. She was determined to sell The Amber Room from that moment on. I was happy to go along with whatever she ultimately decided to do.

There was a popular quote just after the war "Works of Art are the patrimony of humanity". The big auction houses flout their own self-regulating codes of practice anyway. These were our justifications for our actions. I'm not sure that either of us wholeheartedly believed them, but they gave us some comfort and assuaged some of our guilty conscience. Switzerland was and still is a marketplace for antiquities and works of art, where dealers, acquisitive museums and individual collectors do their business unhindered.

Hitler and Stalin would have loved the internet. 'Alternative' truths online can be spread around the planet almost instantaneously. They are then cemented in the Google search results as if they are facts. Although Stalin didn't have the internet, the Russian State was able to massively scale their misinformation. They pumped out lies for decades. When they announced that a reproduction of The Amber Room was to be built, we knew that we could never return the original. That would fly in the face of every piece of fabrication the Russians and the East Germans had been circulating for 40 years. We knew what consequences telling the truth about events could have. Evelyn's uncle Gareth had been killed for persisting with telling the truth about the massive famine in the Ukraine. Gareth reported on it for the Financial Times in 1933. Stalin, of course denied it all and from that moment on Gareth was a marked man. Just one of the millions that Stalin had eliminated."

I recalled all the newspaper clippings amongst Evelyn's books. I had no reason to doubt what she was saying.

Hilde was virtually spitting the words out by now. She obviously still harboured a deep hatred for Stalin and his Soviet regime. "The long-suffering Russian people have had to live with one dictator after another. Putin is no different. The oligarchs all pander to him, just like the sycophants that swarmed around Stalin. Anyone that tries to speak out is removed from office and most of them disappear. Now it looks like they got Evelyn too." She caught her breath. Her lower lip quivered but she pushed on, unable to stop now that the dam had opened.

When she finished, Hilde seemed like a woman unburdened, relieved and lighter in spirit for sharing the story. As she stood, I could hear her old bones creaking, but her grip on my forearm was like steel, when she asked "What now? What will you do with the information?"

My mind was in a tangle. Quite frankly I was in two minds, but my reassuring reply was "It's a story shared with a private individual. I didn't come here in a professional capacity."

She seemed accepting of my response.

I didn't have concrete, hard evidence, only some revealing diary entries, the material that Jennifer Barnes had recorded with Evelyn and this amazing testimony that Hilde had recited. Her treasure trove of memories had linked up and made sense of all the loose threads that I had tried so hard to connect over the last few months. The 3D puzzle I'd constructed from Evelyn's diary entries, Jennifer Barnes's tapes and all the annotations and scribbles in various books and pamphlets, together with the cryptocurrency material was now elegantly solved. If I was to put it in mathematical speak.

The police had the Bitcoin details, and the scene of crime reports and ballistics. MI5 would do whatever they were going to do. What would it achieve by me reiterating what Hilde had told me? I hadn't recorded anything, and she could deny it all if she wanted to. There were still a couple of loose ends to be tied up.

I was bemused, "It seems impossible to believe that crates of several tons of amber could go missing and nobody would notice."

"I know, but that's exactly what happened. Many historians did try to solve the mystery. The most basic theory was that the crates were destroyed by the bombings of 1944. Others believed that the amber was still in secret bunkers in Konigsberg, now called Kaliningrad. Some hypothesised that it had been loaded onto a ship and sank to the bottom of the Baltic Sea. Every time Evelyn and I heard about a new conspiracy theory we would laugh our socks off. The East Germans and The Soviets kept the deceptions going and that was a ready-made cover screen for us.

It's probably hard for you to believe but Evelyn and I never really considered The Amber Room's monetary value. One last adventure mattered much more to us than a big monetary gain. I was staggered when I received four million dollars into my account!

In 1941 The Germans took the Amber Room but had also wantonly pillaged the houses of Chekov, Pushkin, Rimsky- Korsakov, Tchaikovsky and burned Tolstoy's manuscripts. The Russians looted in their own right. At the end of the war as they moved west, they emptied many museums of their art treasures. The Allies expected these works of art to be repatriated to their rightful owners after the end of the war, but Stalin refused. Stalin was a dictator just as bad as Hitler. The Russian propaganda machine was in full swing putting out misinformation about The Amber Room. They were just as bad as the Germans. To this day Russian galleries and museums still hold onto vast amounts of looted art treasures. We didn't want either regime to get The Amber Room back.

We agreed that it would be poetic justice to sell the 'Taste' mosaic to a Ukrainian Jew. Hitler and Stalin would have turned in their graves! We made all the arrangements but at the last minute had to abort the deal because of the police raid in Bremen."

I couldn't contain my curiosity any longer, "So, is The Amber Room still in the Zeppelin hangar?"

"No, that's the thing. Evelyn sold it to an anonymous art collector. He paid her in Bitcoin, and it was transferred from Tonder to the Freeport in Sweden. I have no idea of its final destination. She made the buyer prove he wasn't German or Russian. That was the only conditions she put on the sale. So, in her own way, Evelyn outwitted the powerful Russian state. She got huge satisfaction out of that. So did I for that matter. Together we got revenge. Or as Evelyn liked to put it, we got reparations for our family. The Russians have their reproduction of The Amber Room, and they believe their state lies have died with Evelyn. As far as I know they have no idea of the part I played in all this. If I turn up dead in the Baltic soon, you'll know who's responsible."

This woman had a dry sense of humour that I liked.

"Although you don't know where the Amber Room is, if you had to hazard a guess, where would you start looking?"

My guess would be to follow the path to the guy that wanted to buy the mosaic from us. The Amber collector's market is made up of a few dozen wealthy individuals. Within that niche is an elite of five men rich enough to buy any piece they want, no matter what the cost. One of them is Shlomo Kramarov. Evelyn did a whole lot of due diligence on him, and it revealed that his family origins were from the Kiev area. They had suffered terribly at the hands of the Russians during the many pogroms of the nineteenth century. Fleeing from the Holodor and starvation and persecution in the Ukraine, they moved west to Berlin. They thrived as prestigious jewellers. By 1936, the Nazis were intent on the eradication of the Jews from the whole of Europe. After the burning of the Synagogue and the Kristallnacht Shlomo's father saw the writing on the wall for the Jews in Germany. Shlomo was just a small boy when his parents bribed the customs officers at the Dutch border and escaped to Britain. From Liverpool they boarded a ship to New York. The remainder of his family that stayed in Germany were sent to concentration camps and were never seen or heard from again. We had a lot of sympathy for him. He also harboured a hatred of the Nazis and the Soviets. Something we had in common."

•••

Sometimes the facts in our possession interlock elegantly. There were still some murky edges to the picture, but all was becoming clearer. I was staggered by the gravity of the secret that Hilde had just shared with me. Seven decades of searching for The Amber Room had come to an end and nobody knew about it but me and Evelyn's cousin Hilde!

The final pieces of this amber puzzle had been slotted back together here in this forgotten, landlocked medieval town in Denmark, just metres away from where it had all started. Poetic justice, indeed.

I could finally see how this incredible deception had been facilitated. A combination of extraordinary historical circumstances - war, chaos, two clever and astute women who had the guts to seize the moment and pit their wits against the two worst dictators of the 20th Century.

A century's old family grudge against the Prussian and Russian states had finally been avenged by two unassuming women mathematicians, who had all the patience in the world! They had outlived every Soviet and German official whose files on The Amber Room were either broken up, lost, stolen, concealed or classified and forgotten about by subsequent generations of administrators.

Hilde told me, "The National Library of Russia houses more than 32 million volumes but during the Soviet era the book spines were turned away from the reader and their maze of corridors were patrolled by armed guards. Who could ever have discovered any accurate information on The Amber Room in that environment?"

Their deception had been unwittingly aided and abetted by the Russian and East German governments who churned out misinformation, who didn't want to admit that they had lost the eighth wonder of the world. Both regimes operated in a labyrinthine world of conspiracies.

The constant red herrings that the Soviets planted in their press releases deflected any suspicion that could have fallen on Evelyn and Hilde. The preconceived ideas of women's roles also played into their hands. They were the most unlikely of culprits.

"What about during the Gorbachev years? Perestroika, Glasnost and all that... Didn't you worry that something might come to light then?"

"At first, we thought, ah now might be the time that we can give it back. We could feign surprise at finding it hidden away and return it to Gorbachev. We had real optimism for the first time in years. Of course, the Nazis were notorious for recording everything in triplicate, so we could never be completely sure what the Russians might have on record that had survived somewhere."

Hilde thought for a few moments. Her next words were profound, "Even after Glasnost and Perestroika, the most important Russian archives that might have contained the evidence of the official searches for The Amber Room are arcane! Russian confidence tricks were too ingrained and the illusion of power passing to reformers who turn out to be equally vindictive, greedy and corrupt.

Every time there was a transfer of power in Russia, Evelyn and I would think, maybe now we will return The Amber room, but they were all as bad as one another! Nothing really changed. As if to prove what she was saying was true, Hilde picked up the sheaf of yellowing pages of Cyrillic script.

"No one can imagine the lengths that the Soviets went to for decades to mislead the outside world. This is one of their more amusing ruses - its headed 'The Choral Society'. Naturally you would think it had to do with a choir of some sort. But no, the writer was a woman called Jelena Storozhenko, she was head of the secret Soviet investigation into the fate of the amber room throughout the 1970's and 80's. She only retired from it in 1984 when the operation was finally shut down. That's how long the Soviets kept up with the lies. Extraordinary. Evelyn and I watched on bemused as decades rolled on and nothing really changed.

The Germans were no better - here is a photocopy of a gift book from the Konigsberg castle museum. Look at page 141 and item 200. Item 200 was received on 5th December 1941 - it is The Amber Room! It is shown as being gifted to the museum by the German authorities. Of course, it had just been plundered by them from the Russians. The Amber Room completely captured the Nazi's ethos. It fell under the "Führervorbehalt".

"What's that?"

"Führervorbehalt means a direct order of Hitler. The Prussian state had controlled the amber trade for centuries and now they were able to display this amber masterpiece in the Teutonic castle of Konigsberg. The Amber Room became a pawn to be passed back and forth between two of the most heinous totalitarian states in history. As far as Evelyn and I were concerned it was not going to be repatriated to either one. We watched as over the years a myriad treasure hunters from around the globe spawned thousands of potential leads as to the whereabouts of The Amber Room. Little did they know that the Russians themselves believed that their own troops had inadvertently destroyed The Amber Room in their orgy of vindictive destruction that engulfed Konigsberg.

All these treasure hunters, some sponsored by the Russian state went off on elaborate wild goose chases. They might as well have been seeking the Holy Grail, for all they would find!

And all the while it sat in its crates gathering dust in the Zeppelin hangar down the road. When I voice all of this, I still can't quite believe that Evelyn and I pulled this off." She shook her head and looked at me with a wry smile on her lips.

I felt a wave of awe and respect for both women. What a coup they had accomplished!

"Do Estrid and Sian know?"

"No, Evelyn and I didn't want either of our girls to know. It was our secret, and we were solely responsible. The only way we could keep them safe was to keep them in the dark, so to speak. Of course, since the money has come in, they know that Evelyn sold something of great value. But even, Owen who carried out Evelyn's last wishes and distributed the Bitcoin money, in accordance with Evelyn's instructions, doesn't know what she sold."

"So, I'm guessing it was you that received the 20,000 Bitcoins that left Evelyn's Coinbase account?"

"Yes, how do you know about that?"

"Owen has had a few of his mates looking into it. They could see the Bitcoins were transferred but as, yet they haven't found out the recipient's name!"

"Oh, I feel bad about keeping things from him, but that was what Evelyn wanted. The less the kids and grandkids knew, the better was her thoughts."

Before I left Tonder there was one thing I really wanted to see. "Could I have a look at the Zeppelin hangar?"

"If you like. Estrid will take you over there."

We walked through the little town then along a narrow country lane for a few hundred metres.

Estrid seemed a bit bemused that I wanted to see the long-abandoned Zeppelin hangar.

"Well, here it is. There's not much of interest left to see I'm afraid. There's no actual Zeppelins on display. Goodness knows what mum's going to do with this place. It's been a white elephant for years. I don't want to inherit it. I've urged her to sell it and use the money to do an around the world cruise or something. But she's stubborn and not easy to persuade."

I marvelled at the mega structure that had once housed the leviathan but stylish Zeppelin airships in the 1920s and 30's. Estrid unlocked the mammoth doors, and we entered a huge aircraft hangar. We wandered around for a few minutes. It was frigidly cold. The place was cavernous and completely empty. Estrid was right, there was nothing to see. As we exited, it took Estrid and I all our combined strength to pull the sliding hangar doors shut. As they clanged together, I trod on something. In the dim light I couldn't make out what it was but in the light outside I saw that it was a single exquisitely carved sliver of amber. On an impulse, I quickly slipped it into my pocket.

When we got back to Hilde's house, I thought I'd just pop my head in to say goodbye. Estrid retreated to the kitchen to finish the dinner preparations and I found Hilde peacefully dozing in her armchair, as if nothing out of the ordinary had taken place!

•••

When I left Hilde's house, night was down and the cobbled streets of Tonder shone with the aftermath of a light sleet. The revelations were burning a hole in my head. When I got back to my hotel in Copenhagen, I took a hot shower, sat down with a malt whisky purchased from my minibar and started to write down everything I had heard. It helps to have an eidetic memory!

I was faced with a mighty dilemma. I was privy to a huge secret. Hilde had made me complicit. If I made the information public, what would be the repercussions for the two families? Evelyn had already paid with her life. The Amber Room had disappeared again and there was very little chance of retrieving it. The Freeports are places that are routinely used by the world's hyper rich to trade in illicit antiquities, art works with dodgy provenance and goodness knows what else. Many of the well-known auction houses participate in this illegal trade too. The player's anonymity is fiercely protected. Throw in the cryptocurrency element and it would be nigh on impossible to track where the "Eighth Wonder of the World" was currently. I couldn't see that any good would come from my revealing the secret that Hilde had shared with me.

MI5 or MI6 would do what they could to push the Russians to extradite Evelyn's assassin, but as usual, they would hit a brick wall of denial. No doubt her killer would never come to justice.

Churchill's famous quotation, made in a radio broadcast in October 1939, came to mind: "I cannot forecast to you the actions of Russia. It is a riddle, wrapped in a mystery, inside an enigma; but perhaps there is a key. That key is Russian national interest".

This quote was very apt. The key to Evelyn and Hilde's success in evading detection for so long was Russian national interest!

I revisited the three cornerstones of crime: Motive, means and opportunity.

I applied them to Evelyn and Hilde's scenario:
Motive was Evelyn's and Hilde's hatred of both the Nazi and Soviet states. The need to get revenge and reparation for their family. Evelyn was also motivated by smouldering resentment at the lack of acknowledgement and respect for her role in the code breaking during World War Two. Indeed, the writing out of history of hundreds of women's sacrifice and contributions. The irony was that the preconceived ideas about elderly women and their "invisibleness" even in modern day society had in a way played into their hands.

The top brass in MI5 didn't bother to dig deeper as to why the Russians would go to such effort to assassinate an elderly British woman. Only half of her story was revealed. She had got the last laugh. She had stolen "The Eighth Wonder of the World" from under the noses of the Soviets, hidden it for nearly 70 years, sold it for millions and cleverly distributed the money amongst her family members. She had paid with her life, but I had a feeling Evelyn would have seen this as a good trade off. She and Hilde had pulled off one of the most audacious heists of the 20th Century. The original Amber Room was still in existence in the hands of a private collector – in all probability a Ukrainian Jew. It would never be returned to the Russian or German States.
Means was the information gathering by decrypting messages for years until a mind-boggling opportunity presented itself - an amazing masterpiece that had been momentarily abandoned during the Gotterdammerung of

the Nazis. The two women seized the opportunity that would never have presented itself in peacetime. The confluence of intellect, cunning, patience over decades and the ability to keep a secret. All these things aligned to facilitate such a crime.

Opportunity was a specific time in history when chaos reigned, and nobody was paying attention. A split-second decision by these two women to waylay part of the cargo on board a train that pulled into a sleepy town just over the German/Danish border.

I looked up the definitions of 'Respect' and 'Reparations.' From the Oxford Dictionary entries, I read

'Reparation: The making of amends for a wrong.'

'Respect: Feeling of admiration for someone or something because of their qualities or achievements.'

Respect was certainly owed to these women.

Reparations had been justly paid, as far as I was concerned.

•••

My mind was too active to get a good night's sleep, so I had breakfast very early and headed out. To me, the atmosphere of Copenhagen retains the feel of a well – heeled merchant city. Much of the neoclassical architecture seems to fit in perfectly with the austere tastes of the Nordic countries. Copenhagen is vibrant and bustling. Trade here has definitely moved on from herrings! I took the train to Roskilde. The archaeological restorations of the Viking long boats are a marvel. I browsed around the various workshops and had a thoroughly enjoyable time. Roskilde was the site of Zealand's first Christian church, built by Harald Blue tooth in 980. In 1026 King Canute 1, in a rage over a chess match, had his brother in law, Ulf Jarl assassinated in this church. Ulf's widow, Estrid had the church torn down and replaced by a stone construction. This is the site of Roskilde cathedral. She and many Danish royals are now buried beneath it. The names- Estrid and Ulf brought me back to Hilde's revelations of yesterday. I realised I wouldn't be able to push the story to the back of my mind for long. Time was ticking by. I made the 30km train journey back to my hotel.

At the airport I felt compelled to look in the windows of the Georg Jensen shop. I've always loved the modernist, curvilineal styles of this Danish silversmith. To the right hand side of the window I spotted a gorgeous silver ring in the form of an elongated open heart. There was no price displayed on the tag but, as I had suspected it was by one of my favourite designers - Henning Koppel. I pushed open the shop doors and walked inside. A very smartly dressed assistant immediately gave me his undivided attention. He pulled out the velvet cushion with the ring on and I was able to inspect it more closely. It really was a beautifully piece of jewellery and I knew just the person to buy it for. The price was almost immaterial, as by this stage I just had to buy it. And it didn't come cheap. I left the shop with a perfectly boxed and packaged ring and a hefty debit on my Barclay card! I just had enough time for a very strong coffee before my flight was called. As my plane banked steeply over the Danish capital, I had to concede that 'Tollund Man' would have to wait until my next visit to Denmark. I was sure I would come back.

EPILOGUE

A week after returning from Denmark, I had secured a meeting with Shlomo Kramarov. Before me sat a rotund man with a long grey beard and side locks, dressed in the black garb of Ultra-orthodox Jews. Shlomo was a learned man who was considered one of the most prominent collectors of Baltic amber. As a member of the Satmar Hasidim, he lived for most of the year in a Brooklyn neighbourhood. His daughter lived in Stamford Hill, so he still travelled regularly to London even though he was now well into his eighties.

Shlomo's fascination for amber came from his mother's side of the family. Her ancestors were from near Danzig. Her grandfather and father had crafted beautiful pieces of jewellery from Baltic amber at their business premises in Warsaw. None of his wife's family had survived the war. All had been gassed at Bergen Belsen. His wife, Naomi had been put on the kinder transport as a toddler and had ended up in London. It was in The Savoy Hotel in London that I was meeting him now.

I'd found out by talking to a few of his competitors, that The Amber Room was at the top of his acquisitions list and that he would occasionally buy a piece with uncertain provenance!

He told me "I only deal in extremely rare pieces - ones with talismanic qualities or pieces that have major historic significance."

Well, The Bernstein Zimmer would tick all those boxes, so I asked him directly had he bought the Amber Room from Evelyn?

He looked completely shocked. He said, "I've read every report the Russians churned out. I've had a network of art and antiquities dealers follow up every possible lead and spurious sighting. They all led to dead ends. I've given up on ever owning The Eighth Wonder of the World."

"Until you met Evelyn Jones! How was it that you two crossed paths?"

He gave it a moment's thought, "We were introduced to each other by Rose Valland, just after the war. Evelyn was on some fact-finding mission with a group of English and American boffins. They came to Paris and Rose hosted a dinner. That's how we met."

That made sense and tallied with Evelyn's diary entries of that time.

"Did you discuss the mosaic at that meeting?"

"Heavens, no. I had no idea at that time that Evelyn possessed it. It wasn't until we bumped into each other again at Rose's funeral that we got talking about art collecting. Even then Evelyn kept her cards close to her chest. She only gave me a vague hint that she had a piece I might be interested in. I was in London many years later. She and Moira had lunch with me at Claridge's and Evelyn indicated that she was in possession of a mosaic that had been part of The Amber Room ensemble. Of course, this immediately piqued my interest. She showed me all the photos that she and Hilde had taken of 'Taste', and she brought me a tiny sliver of exquisitely worked amber to examine. I listened enrapt whilst she related the story of how she had come into possession of such a thing. It all sounded plausible to me.

"So, she did tell you about stealing The Amber Room.?"

"Oh, no. She only ever referred to the mosaic. The only photos I saw were of the mosaic. She did say there was more loot in the crate – some gold bullion, a handful of diamonds, silver candlesticks, a painting and so forth. I had no interest in any of those objects. I could appreciate the long-term nature of her plan. The patience she had shown over all those decades. I could understand her reasoning and how she had developed her intense hatred of the Nazi and Soviet states. I felt a degree of mutual respect. Her sentiments were very much aligned with my own. That mosaic is sublime. I knew I had to have it. Ultimately, the sale of the mosaic fell through, due to that idiot lawyer, Manhard Kaiser. He was caught by the German police. But I am a persistent and patient man. I kept in touch with Evelyn Jones hoping that another opportunity would arise to do a deal. But sadly, that didn't eventuate. I was terribly shocked by the nature of her death."

This guy was good at deception. There were no tell-tale signs that he was lying, but I knew he was. Oddly enough, I realised I didn't care. If he was the new owner of The Amber Room, I was sure it would be lovingly conserved. It was a fitting end for a treasure that had been used as a political pawn by two tyrannical regimes that had both persecuted the Jewish people.

The weather was unseasonably warm at the end of November, so I thought I'd take the camper van down to The Gower for a long weekend. If the weather held out, I wanted to walk a section of the Wales, Coastal path, from Rhossilli Bay to Carmarthen. I could do with some serious physical exertion.

As I still had a few niggling questions going around in my head, I thought, maybe I'd drop in on Evelyn's granddaughter who was now living at her house. As I wound my way down to the house, I could see that builders were working on the east side of the property, constructing a large extension with a glass roof. Evelyn's old Land Rover was parked to the side of the driveway and a swanky new Range Rover was by its side.

I knocked on the door and Rhiannon answered within moments. She did a double take, recognised who I had then invited me in. The banging and noise of the builders was muted inside the house.

I explained I was walking the coastal path and just on impulse I'd dropped in to see how they were all doing. "Would you like to take morning tea with me? I've just boiled the kettle."

"If I'm not imposing, that would be lovely."

We walked through to the kitchen, and I was struck by the fantastic upgrade that Rhiannon had done. This kitchen was fit for a top chef - very high spec. She'd also had sky lights installed, so that the room was flooded with natural light. The overall effect was sensational.

"Wow, this is fab", I said. You've been busy. What are you having done on the side?"

"Oh, that's my piece de resistance, she enthused. A heated swimming pool and gym. I've always wanted one!"

"I'm impressed. Fantastic. Have you won the National lottery?"

She laughed at that. "No, Nanna left us very well off you know."

I let her explain this with, "She apparently invested heavily in cryptocurrencies when they were just getting started. Bitcoin, you know."

Oh yes, I did know.

She continued "In her will she left an envelope for Owen with instructions on how to distribute the money from the Bitcoins. Mum got the bulk of it, but Owen and I also did rather well. He's travelling around the world in style now. There was only one odd condition. Owen had to fly to Copenhagen before embarking on his travels. Apparently, Hilde had some old crates in storage in Tonder that needed to be packed off to some fellow living in Monaco. Owen said there were nearly 30 crates bearing Hilde's initials. Cobwebs everywhere! Goodness knows what all that was about!

Hilde and nanna were never conventional. Eccentric to the end. Once this building work is finished, I must go over and visit Hilde. We used to collect amber on the beach together when I was little. Around the bonfire she would tell us stories of her great, great grandfather who once found 4000 pounds of amber washed up on the beach after a wild storm. Those were happy days!

I spent the next half an hour savouring my cup of Darjeeling tea whilst Rhiannon brought me up to date with Emily's latest achievements and showed me Owen's postcard from Australia. After our little chat, I was satisfied that Rhiannon was completely innocent and had no knowledge whatsoever of Evelyn and Hilde's wartime heist. I wasn't so sure about Owen. Now I had to find out if Sian knew.

I drove from the Gower to St David's, or Tyddewi as the Welsh call it. Even in winter this is a gentle place. It has an air of magic and security about it. As you approach St David's all you see is a pretty village of a few streets, with the ground falling away sharply at the end of the main street. But below you lies one of the great surprises of Wales, a beautiful Cathedral where you might have expected a regular parish church! Next door to it are the remains of the 14th Century Bishop's Palace. For many centuries it has been a place of pilgrimage - two visits to St David's equalling one to Rome!

Since my return from Denmark, I had been plagued by contradictory thoughts about what to do with the information Hilde had divulged.

I am sick of the preconceived ideas about women that still proliferate in society - especially about elderly women. They are ignored, overlooked and generally their opinions on anything other than their grandchildren, are discounted. Women overall have been written out of history. Here were two women who had carried out an audacious and clever heist. They had been involved in ground-breaking advances in mathematics and computers. Yet they had been given scant recognition. It did infuriate me!

To me, Evelyn Jones typified the virtues of an indomitable strain of 20th Century British women: loyal, intelligent and determined to pursue a worthwhile career while maintaining a happy family life. Such women had a strong sense of duty to their country and to the wider community. Devoid of ego, nevertheless these women achieved extraordinary things.

On the one hand I wanted to make sure that Evelyn, Hilde and the cohort of other women from World War Two were written back into the history books. However, I was now faced with a tricky dilemma. If I revealed the conclusion of my investigations, Evelyn would get notoriety not acclaim. She would also be exposed as a criminal. The consequences of my revelations could have a terrible impact on Sian and Hilde too, not to mention Owen, who I was sure knew more than he claimed. He would probably be charged as an accessory to the crime.

What to do? I needed time to think. The benevolent atmosphere of St David's Cathedral was just the place for me to calmly think this through...

I sat in a pew in this ancient place which has seen so many pilgrims come through its doors over so many centuries. I am not a religious person, but I do believe that there is a spiritual energy that lingers in many such places on earth. I felt the embrace of that energy now. I have no idea how long I sat there but when I finally pushed myself up from the pew, I had reached my conclusion and was aware that I needed to see Sian.

I phoned Sian and we arranged to meet the next day.

I went to Newport to have lunch with her. There was an easiness between us now and something else that I couldn't quite put my finger on. We decided that to give us an appetite we would climb up to the Neolithic burial chamber of Pentre Ifan. The true origins and purpose of this megalithic chamber are obscured by antiquity. The Preseli hills truly have an otherworldly air about them. The mists roll in from the sea and you can believe there is only a thin veil between this world and that of the ancients. The blue stones from here were transported the huge distance to Stone Henge, they held such magic! It is a landscape where the unexplained and the inexplicable lie still and close. Wind swept and mist – ridden, you feel there is a blurring of what is revealed and what is hidden. I thought how fitting a parallel to Evelyn's life.

Both of us were breathing heavily by the time we reached the summit of the hill and the ancient site. We looked down on a sparsely populated land-scape - a farmhouse tucked into shelter against the wind, a sunken narrow lane with high hedges and a trickling stream. A backbone of hill running steeply down to the sea covered in cropped gorse and heather with the thrust of rocks here and there, small fields spread like handkerchiefs all the way down to the coast. Nature, both generous and austere.

Standing on the hilltop with Sian, I felt elevated above the mundane life, like being winged, poised above my everyday existence. We stood in silence for a long time just soaking up the atmosphere and appreciating the peace. Eventually Sian grabbed my arm. "It's a very special place, isn't it? I can tell you feel it too."

I did indeed. I felt a strong connection to this woman. I had to ask her if she knew what Evelyn and Hilde had done. I had to know if she had been deceiving me throughout the course of my investigations. It mattered to me.

She closed her eyes and leaned her head back on one of the three 'up-rights' that support the giant 16-foot capstone. It seemed precariously bal-anced on the 'uprights' but then again it has remained in place for over five thousand years, it wasn't going to fall on us in the next five minutes! I waited with bated breath for her to answer.

"Mum said only that she was in possession of something very valuable. She had not stolen it she said, rather she had saved it. I suspect Moira knew and I have an inkling that Owen knows more than he admits. Evelyn and Owen were birds of a feather. He would never betray the secrets of his nana."

When Evelyn's safe was to be opened, Sian admitted she dreaded what we might find. She herself could never find the combination, so the key she was given by her mother was useless. She said "That let me off the hook, so to speak, at least until you showed up. Then I really was torn. I didn't want to breach mum's privacy but on the other hand I wanted to help catch her killer and I knew deep down that her past was the key. The ultimate sad irony is that mum met the same fate as her uncle who was also murdered by the Russians in revenge for writing the truth about the famine and exposing the myth of Stalin's utopian propaganda."

I pondered on the irony of it all. Evelyn, an elderly woman in her nineties with liver spots and bad knees had outwitted the powerful Russian state. But ultimately, their revenge had been brutal.

The wind was starting to whip around the burial chamber and the temperature was dropping as clouds started to obscure the weak sun. As if Sian sensed the chill that had started to creep into my bones, she said, "'Come on let's go down."

When we got back to Sian's house, we sat side by side in front of a roaring fire and sipped on Glenlivet whiskies - just to warm us up. I felt that the time was right to give Sian the Georg Jensen ring. She blushed profusely as I produced the glitzy package and presented it to her. I knew she would fully appreciate the superb silver workmanship of its simple lines. It sat perfectly on her finger as if it had always been there. She gave me a quick peck on the cheek and said " I love it. I'll treasure it always". That was reward enough for me. We sat in companionable silence for quite a while. Sian seemed to be inwardly contemplating. Eventually she went to her roll top desk and came back with Evelyn's diaries. "Would you agree that these are my property, to do with what I like?"

"Yes of course." I had a moment of dread.

"'Good." In one quick movement she approached the blazing fire and flung them into the flames! They smouldered sluggishly at first but within minutes they flared and burnt vigorously. "One of the most improbable stories I ever heard. Without a single scrap of evidence to support it" she said. She stacked the last of the diaries in the fire's centre. The flare from their burning cast flickering lights around the room, lighting up the flecks of gold in the exquisite amber coffer sitting on her shelf.

AUTHOR'S NOTES

One of history's great lost treasures, The Amber Room has fascinated me for a very long time. I started making my notes for a fictional book back in 1999, but everyday life and work got in the way of writing it. An article in 'The Guardian Weekend' magazine in May 2004 re awakened my interest and I experienced a flurry of writing. Since then, it's been on the back burner, but it's never gone away.

Fast forward to April 2020 and the Covid19 restrictions stopped my business in its tracks. The positive side of this was that it bought me the time to finally complete my book...

I was deeply saddened when I noticed an obituary in 'The Guardian' UK.

'Helene Aldwinckle, who has died aged 99, was one of the most senior female codebreakers working to break the German army and air force Enigma ciphers in Hut 6 at Bletchley Park. Born 26 October 1920; died 24 April 2020.

Then another on May 17th, published on the BBC website: 'Tributes as World War Two code breaker Ann Mitchell dies aged 97. Ann Mitchell - one of the last of a World War Two code-breaking team at Bletchley Park - who has died aged 97. She had tested positive for Covid-19 recently.

Nearly a year later, whilst I was still writing the book another obituary grabbed my attention, printed in "The Times" UK –

'Bletchley Park codebreaker who helped to crack the Flora Dora code, fled Egypt during the Suez Crisis and tried pot in her eighties. Patricia Marjorie Brown, codebreaker, born 1 May 1917; died 26 February 2021. Maiden name, Patricia Bartley.'

These women and countless others who played significant roles in the code breaking and radar tracking stations dotted around the UK in the Second World War, need to be remembered.

I have made a plot with characters that have fictional connections to real historical events and people. My story sits in a framework of true events, but it is entirely fictional.

The "Eighth Wonder of the World," - The Amber Room that once symbolized peace between the Russians and the Prussians was stolen by the Nazis in 1941. In 1945 it disappeared for good.

Since the end of World War Two, historians, art lovers, and treasure hunters alike have sought the lost Amber Room, looking in silver mines, lakes, diving on shipwrecks in the Baltic Sea and scouring secret caves in Bavaria. It has never been found.

Against a background of myth and conspiracy theories that still surround The Amber Room, Evelyn and Hilde's audacious theft of The Bernstein Zimmer from a train in 1945 is just as plausible as any of the other claims!

Much attention has been focused on the mystery of The Amber Room, especially since the advent of the internet. I believe that unless water-tight proof is provided, there are plenty of people willing to continue on with the hunt.

.

APPENDIX

When the word Amber is mentioned, many of us associate it with the casing for dinosaur DNA in the film 'Jurassic Park'. In real life, amber has enthralled Europeans, and especially Russians, for centuries because of the golden, jewel-encrusted Amber Room, which was made of several tons of the gemstone. Construction of the Amber Room began in 1701. The room was designed by German baroque sculptor Andreas Schlüter and constructed by the Danish amber craftsman Gottfried Wolfram. It was actually a series of large panels designed to be mounted onto walls within Berlin's Charlottenburg Palace. The original project took 13 years to complete. Once it was finished, Frederick's son, William I, presented the amber panels to Peter the Great of Russia to commemorate a treaty between the two rulers. The panels were installed in the Winter Palace in St. Petersburg and in 1755 moved to the Catherine Palace. Catherine, who came from the amber mining region on the Baltic Sea, ascended the Russian throne in 1767 and eventually became known to history as Catherine The Great. Catherine expanded the original Amber Room, added another 900 pounds of amber to the room, replacing some sections with large windows. She also commissioned four stone mosaics corresponding to the senses of sight, taste, touch, and hearing. Visitors to the completed chamber were awe struck and said it "came alive" in candlelight. There it remained in all its splendour for nearly 200 years. It even survived the Russian Revolution of 1917!

The Amber Room had started out as a gift, celebrating peace between Russia and Prussia. However, the room's fate became anything but peaceful: Nazis looted it during World War Two and in the final months of the war, the amber panels, which had been packed away in crates, disappeared.

THE LOOTING OF THE ROOM

The Amber Room remained resplendent until the summer of 1941, when 99 German divisions, stormed into the Soviet Union along a front from the Baltic to the Black Sea. For a month, the Nazi blitzkrieg was unstoppable. In the north the army group under Field Marshal Wilhelm Ritter von Leeb moved closer to its objective, the Soviet Union's second city of Leningrad. By the end of August, the battle for Leningrad had become a siege.

Soviet officials began evacuating palace treasures east toward Siberia. As the Germans advanced toward Leningrad (St. Petersburg), the curators of The Amber Room attempted to dissemble and evacuate the panels for safe-keeping. But the years had made the amber brittle and the pieces crumbled easily, forcing the curators to abandon the effort. Instead, they covered the room with wallpaper veneer in an attempt to disguise it. Their attempts were futile. The Germans had earmarked The Amber Room for priority removal because it had been included in the Kummel Report, a list of German-made artworks to be "repatriated" to Germany. The German army dismantled the room within 36 hours, packing it in 27 crates. It was sent by rail to Konigsberg, where it was reassembled and displayed in the city's castle. By late 1944 Allied air raids on Konigsberg had begun, though the castle had remained intact. The air raids eventually destroyed most of Konigsberg Castle, leaving only the outer walls and some battlements.

The original Amber Room was last seen by the Germans on January 12th, 1945. Dr Alfred Rohde, the museum curator, wrote that the panels were being crated for transport out of Konigsberg as the city was being surrounded by advancing Russians from the east and the Anglo - American forces from the west. Konigsberg was rapidly being reduced to a heap of ruins and rubble.

In the spring of 1945, Soviet troops advanced into the city and levelled the remainder of the castle.

Immediately following the war, the Soviet government made finding the Amber Room a priority. It seized the territory of East Prussia as a Russian province. Konigsberg was renamed Kaliningrad in 1946. A group of Russian investigators were sent to search the ruins of the castle. They located several items of furniture from the Catherine Palace in an intact tower and the following year, discovered the ruins of three of Giuseppe Zocchi's Florentine mosaics from The Amber Room.

While there have been numerous theories about the fate of the Amber Room, the only certainty is that it disappeared between the time of the German invasion in 1941 and the arrival of the Soviet troops in Konigsberg in 1945. Erich Koch, the SS commander who had ordered the removal of the amber panels from the city, reportedly led a group of Russian officials on a search during the 1950s but failed to find them. He died in 1986 without ever providing additional information. In 1967, the Soviet government formed a commission to systematically search known art repositories in the USSR and Germany for The Amber Room panels. The commission continued the search until 1984, five years after the decision was made to make a replica of the original room.

Most historians believe that the Amber Room was probably destroyed by Allied bombing raids on the castle after January 1945 or the subsequent Russian invasion and shelling of the city.

While the room panels have never been found, some pieces of the original have surfaced over the years, most importantly one of the Zocchi mosaics, 'Touch and Smell'. This piece had been considered lost. It was offered for sale by Meinhardt Kaiser to an antiques dealer in Bremen, Germany, in 1997. The dealer alerted police, and Kaiser led them to a man named Rudi Wurst, whose father had been part of the SS unit that escorted the train carrying the Amber Room components from the Catherine Palace to Konigsberg in 1941. Police believe that this mosaic had been separated from the rest of the room's treasures, at that point.

THE RECONSTRUCTION

The history of the new Amber Room, at least, is known for sure. The reconstruction of an exact replica began in 1979 at Tsarskoye Selo and is housed in the restored Catherine Palace. It took 25 years to complete and cost over $11 million. Ironically the bulk of the funding for the re-construction came in 1999 from the German energy company Ruhrgas!

With the approval of the Soviet government, the reconstruction team was given access to the amber deposits in the Sambia Peninsula, which were then under state control. Just as well, because the completed room used some 100,000 pieces of amber encompassing more than 150 square meters of wall space.

In May 2003, as the city of St. Petersburg celebrated its 300th anniversary, a summit of world leaders—including Russian President Vladimir Putin, German Chancellor Gerhard Schroeder, U.S. President George W. Bush, French President Jacques Chirac, British Prime Minister Tony Blair, Italian Prime Minister Silvio Berlusconi, and Japanese Prime Minister Junichiro Koizumi, formally opened the reconstructed Amber Room to the public.

The room remains on display to the public at the Tsarskoye Selo State Museum Reserve outside of St. Petersburg. According to the website saint-petersburg.com, the tourist attraction receives about 7,000 daily visitors during the peak summer months.

Amber is called a 'living stone' because it reacts to relatively small changes in temperature and humidity. The Tsarskoye Selo Amber Workshop remains on site for ongoing maintenance because the temperature-sensitive adhesives require constant attention. The studio continues to produce amber objects for sale to help offset the high costs of maintaining The Amber Room.

If you love amber as much as Evelyn and Hilde, you can buy your very own piece of The Amber Room and help support the ongoing maintenance of the reconstructed "Eighth Wonder of the World"

ABOUT THE AUTHOR

YVONNE JENKINS

Born in Cardiff, Yvonne spends her time between the "old" South Wales and New South Wales, Australia.

Yvonne has a degree in Archaeology from University College London and has excavated sites in Turkey, Bahrain, Cyprus, Isreal, Spain, Portugal and Germany.

Founder of one of the inaugural ethical financial brokerages in the UK, Yvonne has written a huge body of web content on ethical and alternative investments.

She invested in Cryptocurrencies back in 2013 and has written Kindle books on Bitcoin and Crypto currencies for charities.

Hidden Agenda is her first foray into writing and independently publishing historical fiction.

Yvonne does her best thinking whilst hiking or snorkeling at her local beach.

She's an avid orchid collector and can spend hours in her shadehouse tending to her botanical babies.

She loves traveling and exploring archaeological sites, but when she's at home she turns into a recluse.

She loves Darjeeling tea and cake!

You can contact Yvonne via her website www.yvonnejenkins.co.uk